SPACE JUMPER

2

SPACE JUMPER

2

MARK RANKIN

Library of Congress Control Number:		2020903616
ISBN:	Hardcover	978-1-7960-8967-7
	Softcover	978-1-7960-8966-0
	eBook	978-1-7960-8965-3

Print information available on the last page.

Rev. date: 02/21/2020

To order additional copies of this book, contact:
Xlibris
1-888-795-4274
www.Xlibris.com
Orders@Xlibris.com
809897

Contents

Dedicated to my family and friends.

Preface

After travelling across his home Universe, The Space Jumper explored many different galaxies in his itinerary for tranquility. His journey carries discovery, pain, and triumph in hope of spreading the good name of humanity to the many species around us. On his quest to find the origin of his shoes, Mark is lead to aliens involved in deep conspiracies of tracking and monitoring. On the run from his troublesome and heartbreaking past, the Space Jumper has found the end of his home universe. He dives through a wall of white mist known as the Alter Zone, to discover another universe. Standing in space, he finds a coalition of space police, ready to capture him.

Chapter 1

Jail

On a new planet in an unknown galaxy, the Space Jumper sits with his head down in a cold jail cell, with his hands and legs handcuffed together in front. The outside world appears bright through a small window. The nice day gleams against his rough, orange prison garb, as he stares at the floor, noticing not stars, but small rocks. Focusing on the rocks, he notices his ghostly, bare feet without his special cool shoes, and thinks about what went wrong.

Mark stands in space, beaten and bruised from the exploration and evacuation of his home universe. Fully decked out in his gear, his hands are up, as the police in space aim their weapons at the Space Jumper. He does not move an inch, forward, backward, left, right, north, west, south, or east. "I surrender!" Mark yells, still in space.

The police use their vehicles as cover, breathing naturally through their strange shaped faces. They have large, square foreheads, with pronounced eyebrows, and small mouths. Their skin color varies among their squad. They wear tight, thin clothes, providing warmth and maneuverability. Three of the police officers move towards Mark using special rocket propelled shoes.

The Space Jumper watches uncomfortably as the police close in on him, holding guns and ropes in each of their hands. They hover in the quiet and cold space towards Mark, and catch him in ropes. The ropes expand using zero gravity, and electrify around Mark's wrists. The police officers hold the light blue rope with two hands, and quickly tie them around the Space Jumpers legs. The other two officers tighten another rope around Mark's hands, locking him like an electrified zip-tie.

The police grab the Space Jumper, and slowly push him across the low gravity away from the edge of the Alter Zone. Standing mercilessly in space, Mark calmly aims his body towards their vehicles. Five other officers surround the Space Jumper to help escort him inside a sleek, dark, hovering space vehicle. He slams down on rough, plastic seats like a child's toy, and makes himself uncomfortable. The police slam the door closed, and away from the Space Jumper's grim memory. Mark awakes from his trance to the sound of a banging vibration inside his jailed room.

The large, metallic gate in front of Mark's cell suddenly explodes open, blowing a hole through the door. The force of the explosion whiffs Mark's hair with dust and small rocks, as he sits in his jail cell. After a moment of allowing the dust to move away and settle, Mark looks up with his hand in front of his face, when he notices an ally turn the corner of the busted gate.

Samantha, the rebellious alien girl Mark once met in the Pinwheel galaxy of his home universe, stands in front of him. She wears private military gear, covered in brown leather armor. "Space Jumper, I've come to get you out." She says in her alternate English accent to Mark, who sits on the stiff, wooden bench. "What's going on?" Mark replies, standing up from the seat with interest. "There is no time to explain. We must go." Samantha says, looking around the room.

"Do you know where my shoes are?" The Space Jumper asks, limbering up his joints. "Yes, just follow me." She says hastily. "Alright, let's get out of here." Mark replies as he looks up to Samantha. They carefully walk down the hallway, past the other empty special cells, towards a thick security door. Samantha slides a keycard across a miniature wall computer. The door opens, revealing a bright day outside, with tall, green trees surrounding the jail. A courtyard is ahead, with weights scattered around the area, and a basketball hoop next to a tall, clay fence. Clouds move slowly overhead, weakening the Space Jumper as he looks up without his cool shoes. The air outside is fresh to Mark, on the new planet, on the new day.

The doors at the other end of the courtyard burst open, when a pair of heavily armored security guards from the jail walk through. They carry batons and rope to try to subdue the two escapees. Samantha carries special grenades attached to her belt, along with a mini bat on her bag, as Mark watches from behind. She takes out her metal mini bat and rushes the two guards. She dodges an attack from one of the guards, and bashes him in the side of his head with the dense, brushed space metal. He falls to the ground, stunned from the dense blow. The second guard kicks Samantha away from the first guard with the side of his boot, knocking her back to the metal fence behind.

With his eyebrows raised at the commotion, Mark immediately tries to run at the guard. He finds a deep lack of strength in his legs as he tries to perform his classic double-fisted punch. The attack does very little damage without the immense advantage gained from the cool shoes. The heavy-set guard stands unfazed, and towers high over Mark, and his downplayed attack. The guard takes a deep breath, and slowly looks like he is about to throw a heavy hand in the puny prisoners face. As the guard pulls his arm back, Samantha shoots an electric bolt from her space blaster.

"I don't think I showed you my gun, Space Jumper." She says on the quiet basketball court in the courtyard. Samantha walks with excitement in her breath towards Mark, standing innocently with his prison garb as pants, and a white t-shirt on top. She presents her gun to him, as the guards lay on the floor, alive and shaking in pain. "This is a boa constrictor, from my crew. It shoots non-lethal electric charges that only subdue the enemy." Samantha says, spinning the circular gun away from Mark. "Makes me wish I had my gear." Mark replies, moving towards the new doors ahead.

Since losing his cool shoes, Mark has lost an immense amount of care for the things around him. When the police or government took his shoes, they took a part of his soul, as he recalls flashbacks from a few days ago.

The police have the Space Jumper bound tight in the back of the small space cruiser, and have just touched down on the densely forested planet of the jail. Three aggressive officers pull him out of the car, and force him to stumble inside the jail. They quickly throw him in a small room within the walls of the jail. As he lays on the cold, hard floor, bound in electrical handcuffs, a swarm of police officers, men and women with weird faces, rush inside the room, and hold him down on the ground. Around a dozen officers take hold of Mark's arms, body, and legs, as the massive body count in the room makes it difficult to see out the door.

Several officers tie a wet rag over Mark's face, completely blocking his view. Multiple sets of hands slowly begin to grasp his shoes, and pull them from his legs. The pain is immense, and eerie, causing Mark to scream, as the shoes dislodge from his ghostly and ghastly feet. A cold breeze moves up his legs as he begins to drift in and out of consciousness. "Take them away." A deep voice says near the door. Mark yells out a deep roar, and blacks out from pain.

"Hey, you ready?" Samantha asks Mark, awaking from his brutal daze. "No." He responds honestly and confidently. "Stay behind me." Samantha says as she makes her way to the closed double doors. She slides a keycard across an electronic lock next to the door, buzzing it unlocked. She shoulders through the double doors, and runs inside towards the back of the room. Mark loses sight of her as she runs ahead. She jumps at the jail guard at the end of an office room, kicking him in the throat as he drinks water from a small cup by a watercooler.

He flies back to the wall, and is out of the fight. She takes out her blaster upon recovering from the kick, and shoots a pair of quick shots at the two guards by the outside door. Mark peeks inside of the room to watch them fall to the hard ground.

Samantha aims at a guard going for guns behind a table in the office, and pulls her trigger. The gun clicks, and fails to shoot. A change of momentum sweeps across the room. The guard unlocks the cabinet, and reaches for a gun. Mark runs in with his no feet and punches the guard in the head, knocking him out into the gun rack. The light skin, light-bodied jail guard falls to the ground. The final guard in the room rushes Samantha during her misfire, and attempts to grab her. She jumps up, and spin kicks the jail guard in his face, spinning his body away like a pirouette. His body crashes into the water cooler, spilling water everywhere.

"Grab a gun." Samantha says to Mark, motioning to the rack on the wall. "I don't feel like killing anyone here, I would rather fight." Mark says out of breath, winded from moving around without his shoes and feet. "We have to keep moving." Samantha says as she checks the gear of the downed guards. She pulls a device off one of the guards belt, and rises up to open the security door with her keycard. The doors automatically slide open, revealing the main prison.

Hundreds of jail cells line down the row for at least a mile. Several sets of staircases lead up the three level structure, where the prisoners on the planet do their time. Some of the prisoners do not even care about what is going on, asleep in their cell, while most of the other prisoners are acting crazy. "Let's move up." Samantha says smiling, moving towards the closest staircase. She jogs ahead, across the noisy prison floor, where inmates scream and yell their delusional thoughts. Guards patrol the area, and run their batons through the metal bars. Mark and Samantha move forward across the open floor, where cheering and hate speech from the prisoners begin to give away their position. Samantha runs up the metal staircase to the second floor of the jail, towards a guard by more stairs leading to the third floor.

As Mark slowly begins to move up the stairs, he sees Samantha choking out a guard with her mini bat. Time slows down for the Space Jumper as he looks to his right at the jail cells directly next to him. A pink alien with big eyes, viscous teeth, and a body full of tattoos, lunges forward and tries to grab him. The alien crashes into the bars and slowly moves back. It begins to yell maniacally at the top of its lungs, as Mark looks to his left at a vast array of inmates watching him realize what is going on. He looks forward to Samantha, motioning for him to move up.

She quickly climbs up the stairs to the third floor of the jail, where gunshots begin to ring out. Samantha takes cover behind the top step of the stairs as large projectiles fly over her head. She selects a special grenade from her belt, flicks a pin while holding it aside of the narrow walkway, and rolls the grenade across the metallic floor towards the guards. Smoke begins to fill the air inside the jail. The guards are stunned from the smoke and stand still. Samantha aims her gun over the stairs to where she hears the guards standing, and fires multiple shots down the walkway. She hears one of the guards crumble to the metallic walkway, as the other guard tumbles down the stairs to the second floor.

Mark stands on the steps beneath Samantha, and looks up to her. "We're clear, let's move." She whispers down. Samantha moves up the top step, and runs across the narrow walkway in front of the prison cells. Mark slowly climbs the stairs, finding a large cloud of smoke at the top. He moves forward across the narrow, metallic walkway, through the smoke, to where he sees nothing but white.

Over encumbered by the strange white haze, lost in a fog, the world around the Space Jumper slows down. Nothing appears ahead, nor behind, with noises and flailing arms to his side. Mark walks with the light impression of his phantom feet across the cold, metallic walkway, to what appears to be Samantha, waving him down. The first guard appears unconscious in front of the cells, with prisoners trying to grab the keys from his waistband. As Mark walks by, he nudges the guards body over with some ghostly force from his foot towards the hungry prisoner reaching for loot. Several prisoners in their cells take notice of the minor deed, as Mark looks up, and strolls through the fog.

Samantha watches Mark slowly make his way towards her, when she turns back around to notice the final door to the long jail quarter. A pair of heavily armored guards stand on ground level, and finally figure out the fuss from above. Samantha hops over the guardrail to her left, and takes out her space blaster, the boa constrictor. In mid drop from the third floor to the second, Samantha shoots a pair of shots at a guard at the opposite side of the jail, and drops down a level towards the ground, landing on top of the final guard with her knees. She rises to a stand and looks up to where she jumped.

Mark finally emerges out from the fog above, and looks ahead to the door below, assuming it is the correct way to go. He takes a moment to collect himself after the smoky haze, and sits on the rail. He slides down the handrail to the stairs as Samantha watches him move ahead towards the door. After a fast and smooth slide, the Space Jumper propels vapor to the ground floor with his gassy feet. His legs shake, stopping momentum from his body. "Ahh." He cringes in pain as he rises from a crouch. His shins tremble where his skin transforms to white fire. An ache in his back arches his body down.

"Hang on Space Jumper, we are almost there." Samantha says loud to Mark, struggling to hear and see well without his gear. Mark reaches his hand up to hers, out of breath while hovering over the ground with a hunch. Samantha walks quickly to the final door in the jail, and swipes the keycard. The door buzzes open, where Mark and Samantha shoulder through together to a security checkpoint.

Two lightly armored guards crouch behind their desk and chair, awaiting the runaway prisoner. Mark rolls forward on the ground towards the guard by his chair, and double fist punches him back into the checkpoint. Samantha moves the other way towards the woman guard behind her desk. Samantha maneuvers low, and slides through a thin back cover to sweep the woman guard to her feet. Crashing through wood, Samantha straddles the heavy guard, and punches her in the nose. The guard appears out cold, when Samantha quickly shifts attention to Mark, fighting the guard in the middle of the cold police checkpoint.

Mark is taking punches to his body from the guard, struggling to move quick enough to evade. Mark jumps back with his phantom feet, sliding above the ground. Samantha pushes him forward, and aims her blaster at the guard. She pauses for a delayed effect, before pulling the trigger, firing a blue blob of electricity at the guards chest. He shakes from the electricity, and quickly struggles to stand. He falls down to ground, absorbing the moment when Mark and Samantha walk past his body.

At the opposite end of the checkpoint is a gate, leading to a locker room ahead. Samantha unhinges the gate, and quickly enters the locker room. Another lightly armored guard sits on a stool at the corner of the tall lockers. The medium height guard reads a comic book, paying no attention to his post. Mark crouches low, quietly approaching the unaware guard. He punches the guard through his book, knocking his head into a metal locker behind. The stool tips over, the book falls down, and the guard drops awkwardly to the floor.

"Space Jumper, over here, I think I found something." Samantha says to Mark, who checks back to her looking at a locker. A label over the lock reads Space Jumper. Mark walks to the locker, and peeks through the cracks of the tall metal. His gear is inside, including the space board.

"It's my stuff." He says with an excited smile to Samantha. He walks back to one of the guards, and checks his body for either keys, or a blunt object.

He digs around, but struggles to find anything useful. He takes the dense wooden stool from the ground, and walks back to the heavy metallic lock. He tilts the chair back over his shoulders, and arches the seat with great force at the lock. The tumblers crack from the force, loosening the hinges to break the lock, as it drops violently to the ground, popping open the tall locker.

His backpack sits at the base of the locker, with the space board next to it. A set of plastic bags contain his worn out clothes, stacking up the locker. His face brightens at the recovery of his tools from Earth. Opening the locker, he knew the shoes would not be there, being a longshot. He takes the bags with his clothes, and rips them open to find his shirts and jackets, crumpled into a ball.

"Turn around." Mark says with a smile to Samantha, circling his finger. She sighs a breath, and turns the corner in the locker room to check what is ahead.

Mark throws on his shirts, pants, and jackets for warmth and protection. He ditches the used plastic bags, and reaches back in the locker for his backpack. He pulls it out, testing the weight to see if things may be missing. He unzips the bag, and digs his hand inside, reaching for his tools and notes. His tablet, BB gun, bullets, and hatchet are an immediate joy to hold.

He zips the bag, and throws it over his shoulders. Standing up with most of his gear, he inspects the space board sitting inside the locker. It looks unpowered, and cold. He grabs the dead board, and wraps it around the straps of his bag. Almost completely geared up, remaining barefoot, Mark moves around the corner and out of the locker room to Samantha. An open door leads to the next room, with a long hallway to the final door out of the jail.

Another pair of guards lay unconscious on the floor, as Samantha stands at the entrance, motioning all clear. Mark develops a jog with his phased feet, bouncing his gear across the prison lobby. "Let's go." Samantha says as Mark approaches the door. They give each other a quick look, as she kicks open the door.

A bright sun shines outside, providing heat through Mark's gear. Another pair of guards standing next to a watchtower wait for the escapees. Samantha runs ahead out of the jail, as Mark follows a few paces behind. She notices the guards, and shoots three shots from her blaster, one at each guard, and one at the heavy locked gate in the front. The electric door slowly swings open as the guards fall to the ground. Mark and Samantha run towards the tall trees ahead of the long, isolated road. Shrubbery in the area grows thick, as Mark and Samantha escape the jail.

Walking slowly over a grass terrain with his bare, ghost feet, Mark moves a bush and its leaves aside. Ahead, Samantha walks forward through the plants and trees. Fifty yards of walking through plants, Mark moves a branch from a bush to the side, revealing a silver and green circular spaceship sitting amongst the trees. Samantha moves toward the ship, dropping stairs down from the entrance with a remote. She waits for the ex Space Jumper to move in to the ship, as she quickly follows, climbing up the walkway behind.

The ship smells of musk, rust and metal as Samantha brushes past Mark, and jumps in the cockpit. She starts the engine after a few seconds, when the medium height spaceship lifts off the ground, and rises fast through the atmosphere. Into space, Mark takes his tablet from his bag to find the battery is extremely low. "Samantha, where are we?" He asks the pilot as she angles the ship in space. "We are in Universe Four, on the Melon galaxy. Speitz is behind us, home to one of the most notorious jails in this universe." She explains while flying her ship deeper into space. "Why was I even arrested?" Mark asks, using his fingers to spread his maps on his tablet for reference. "You have one guess, Space Jumper." Samantha replies sarcastically. "I'm guessing it's because of the shoes?" He answers back sarcastically. Samantha smiles, and nods at his answer while flying forward. "Your shoes are banned in this universe. Infinite power is criminal here." Samantha says from the cockpit, focusing on flying, while Mark looks down at his tablet. "Those were my shoes. Who are they to confiscate my shoes?" Mark replies with annoyance in a weakened tone, browsing through outdated maps from the previous universe. "Your shoes come from very high up apparently." Samantha replies.

"We have to get them back. I can't let anyone interrupt my destiny." Mark replies, setting down his tablet to look at Samantha. She looks to him, as he looks at her. He places his bag with his board on the cold floor of the ship as they rise higher and higher.

"I was hoping you would say that, Space Jumper. I can take you where the police who arrested you stay. I acquired their location in the jail while breaking you out. It will not be easy getting your shoes back. The planet is heavily guarded with special galactic security." She says. "Well what are we waiting for?" Mark replies.

As the small spaceship speeds through a silent space, enemy ships from the jail zoom in from behind, and begin to give chase. "We have company, Space Jumper. Take the gun in the back." Samantha says from the cockpit. He slowly hops up from his seat on the floor, and moves gingerly on his knees with no shoes on. He slides on the ground to drop down a hatch at the rear of the ship, landing at a lower level with controls to a gun turret.

Behind the ship, at the corner of the wall and ground, is a small bubble connected to a chair with a window presenting space outside. Mark slowly hops into the chair behind the gun, and checks the dashboard for power. He likes the first button he sees on the right side of the desk, and reaches for it to activate the turret. A heads up display opens around the glass, as Mark aims the gun to wherever the lever moves. He clutches his fingers around the triggers of the aiming stick.

Five ships from the fancy jail fly through space, diving and swooping closer to Samantha's ship. They coordinate, and fire at Samantha as Mark moves the gun using the aiming reticule on the glass. He aims ahead of the ships, and fires the duel cannons back at them. He nails the lead ship with the first shots, sending it spiraling down space. "That's one down." Mark yells up to Samantha. "Buckle up Space Jumper, we're moving!" She yells down. Mark tightens the shoulder straps next to him, and continues to aim ahead at the approaching ships.

Samantha rolls the ship left and right, moving up and down, evading the fiery shots of the enemies. Mark lines up a shot, and unloads a burst of blasts at a lucky grouping of the ships. A few sets of shots take out the circular wing of one of the space ships. It flips up in the air and loses pace of the flight. Three ships remain, and scatter, as Mark tries to aim the gun ahead of them all. He lines up another shot, and holds the aiming stick firmly. He pulls the trigger, sending endless rounds at the enemy. The recoil of the gun being in space alters the aim, but finds benefit, striking all three targets in critical locations. Two of the ships fly in to each other and explode, while the remaining ship dive-bombs away into space.

"Good shooting, Space Jumper." Samantha says back to Mark, looking up the hole in the basement. He turns around to look back to space, when he notices another large spaceship directly behind his bubble shield. The ship is similar looking to the ones he just shot down, but much, much bigger, with several more engines and larger guns.

"Yo, we're not done here, there's one more behind us. I think it's the Warden." Mark says back up to Samantha. He grabs the aiming lever on the mounted gun and aims forward.

Samantha continues to fly through the depths of space, dodging multiple planets within the galaxy, noticing colorful blasts of lasers fly past her ship. She drops the ship down, and rises up quickly to evade some of the blasts. Mark is down below, firing the mounted turret at the large, approaching, silver spaceship's guns.

The large alien ship shoots grenades and missiles from a set of boxes in front, opening and closing. Timing his aim correctly, Mark fires precise rounds into the box, exploding a missile to incapacitate part of the weapon. The enemy ship continues to fire from its four laser machine guns, and one remaining grenade launcher. It opens a hatch from above, and extends a very large laser weapon. The front of the cannon slowly glows bright red, sustaining power.

Mark continues to fire the turret, shooting missiles out of the open gravity. "Make a move Samantha." Mark says up the cabin, as she checks behind the ship. The bright red bulb emerges from its main cannon. She cringes at the sight of the gun, and dives to the right. She twirls the ship vertically down, leveling out beneath the enemy ship, continuing forward. She holds the set of steering and acceleration levers, breaking a fierce sweat.

"Do we have any bigger guns?" Mark asks up the ship. "This is all she's got Space Jumper. Pick your shots." Samantha replies, yelling down the hole. Mark becomes aggravated aiming the gun around the small bubble screen.

Samantha moves her ship upward to follow the enemy. She lines up a shot using a leveling device on her dashboard, and pushes a button on the handles. Six missiles quickly fire out front towards the enemy ship, one at a time, booming in a line from left to right. All six of the shots strike the back of the ship, matching the rhythmic pace of the firing order. Blasting away big parts from the enemy, Samantha moves to pass around the side. "Get ready Space Jumper." She yells back.

Mark browses through the bubble to find the enemy ship severely damaged, now trailing behind. He aims the turret ahead of the ship, and fires a multitude of relentless rounds in its direction. Quickly out of view, an explosion lights up the space behind. The aftershock from the explosion sends a shockwave that quickly hits Samantha's ship. They avoid collateral danger, and maintain speed forward towards their next objective.

Chapter 2

Melon

Samantha slows the speed, and sets her damaged ship to autopilot. Mark climbs out from the lower hatch, popping his head through the hole to the floor. Samantha walks over and gives him a hand. She carefully pulls him up and gives him a tight hug. "I missed you, Space Jumper. I told my group of rebels about you, how you helped me back on your home universe. We would love to have you as an ally." Samantha says in a calm tone. They look closely at each other, glad to be alive, and on the same side.

"Consider me your ally." Mark replies, stepping back towards the passenger seats of her ship. Samantha continues to look at Mark and smiles as he sits. She walks forward to him and slowly climbs on his lap. She begins to kiss his neck like a vampire. The hairs on his arms stand up beneath his jacket, enjoying the electric sensation. She moves from his neck to his mouth, where they lock lips and kiss. He wraps his arms around her body, placing his hands on her green skin above her lower back. Out of jail, Mark continues forward on his mission of space exploration.

Time passes in the vacancy of quiet space, as Samantha and Mark sit in the cockpit of the ship, heading towards a dull colored planet. Stripes of light brown, dark blue, and dark green highlight the height of the land from space. The dark blue looks like water, but as Samantha flies the ship closer to the surface, it is actually sand.

She moves down towards the blue ground through a thick plot of grey clouds. Flying fast above the surface of the planet, Samantha waits for a better opportunity to land.

"There it is." She points out towards a small, fenced in base a few miles down the surface. She slows the silver spaceship, and parks on the blue and green sand. Debris flies in the air and scatters around as the ship lands smoothly down. Samantha kills the power, and quickly walks to her gear after a seductive look at the Space Jumper.

The bottom hatch of the ship slowly opens, unveiling the silhouettes of Mark, wrapping his backpack on, with Samantha walking down the ramp to the dark blue sand. Mark spins his BB gun in his hand while Samantha carries her space blaster on her hip pocket. The air outside of the ship is cold, being in the dark, with the dark colored sand providing little warmth from the lack of suns.

Samantha sneaks towards a rock near the ship, as the hatch door and ramp automatically closes. Mark follows close and low behind, as they peek ahead at the vacant area of sand, noticing a few stray trees amongst a sea of broader sea of sand. "Let's go." Samantha whispers.

Mountainous ranges stand at a very far distance, barely glowing blue and black from the shining of the stars above. The particular part of the planet they are on appears vacant, and eerily quiet. Samantha leads the way forward over the very fine and dark blue sand. Mark creeps awkwardly behind without his cool space shoes, holding his special gun with the telescopic bullet expander. They slowly move forward toward the base that may contain the Space Jumper's cool shoes.

Behind their position, the sand begins to shuffle and trickle across the hills. Mark turns around to watch a strange bug crawl up to the surface. Long and huge, the bug fully emerges, with seven legs surrounding a bulky, three-portioned torso. The brown bug has antennae's on its head that move around the already strange planet, observing smells, vibrations, heat, and movement.

Mark stands still on the sand, petrified, as Samantha looks back to see the bug. She watches Mark slowly aim his gun up at the bug.

"Is that a good idea, Space Jumper?" She whispers to him behind a small sand dune.

Mark peers his peripheral vision slightly towards Samantha, acknowledging her observation. He says nothing to her, looking back at the bug with his gun up. He adjusts his left hand beneath the particle accelerator, and twists the main dial to shrink the size of the BB. Like aiming a shot at pool, Mark pulls the trigger.

The gun pops, launching a quick little projectile towards the front of the alien bug. The bullet smashes into its head, knocking it back and unconscious. The direct hit to the head throws the bug to the sand, where it lies motionless in a daze.

"Nice shot." Samantha says from her hill. Mark takes a final look at the bug, and moves up towards Samantha. At the peak of the dune, vibrations within the shuffling sand shake the ground. Down the dune, two more large bugs pop out of the sand, and sniff the air. A third bug springs out behind Mark to aid their downed friend. Mark and Samantha look at each other, wielding their weapons.

Mark aims at the two bugs ahead, while Samantha turns around to fight the bug in the back. She runs back down the dune with her mini bat in hand, and jumps from the base of the small sand hill towards the similar looking bug, big and gross. She swings the bat down like a sledgehammer towards the top of the leggy insect. A dense cracking noise shakes the air, as Mark fires a shot at one of the two bugs.

A medium sized BB floats through the open air, making contact with the bug to his left. The top part of its body, appearing to be the head, dislodges from the midsection and lower end. The second bug begins to move to the right, slowly over the sand, and up the dune towards Mark. He aims the gun, and pulls the trigger several times towards the front of the bug. The quick set of bullets strike the bug in its head and body, burying it back down to the sand, as Samantha runs up the hill from behind. "Let's keep going." She says with hurry.

Mark and Samantha run forward across the dark blue sand with a bunch of dead bugs behind them. Ahead, a steep cliff creates a problem for the not so space jumper. As Mark slows his pace, Samantha builds hers, and jumps over the seemingly large gap. She catches about a second and a half of airtime before landing safely on the other side of the sand. She turns around out of breath, and looks at Mark. "You can do it Space Jumper." She encourages. The Space Jumper tries to jump in place, but struggles within the fine-grained sand. Mark groans loud in agonizing frustration and demoralizing pain.

He builds some momentum forward across the sand with his remaining body weight, believing he has his feet beneath his legs. Belief can hurt when you know what you want to believe in is not real. He focuses on moving forward fast, being one of his only options left with the instincts he relates from Earth. Through pain, he moves to a sprint towards the edge of the gap, and jumps in the air. He propels upward at a seemingly safe trajectory to fly across the gap towards Samantha. He lands with phantom feet over the sand, crumbling to a roll on top of Samantha.

The two lay on the sand for a moment, and look in to each other's eyes.

"Nice." He says out of breath.

Mark struggles to stand back up, fatigued from the jump, and weight of his gear. He presses his hands on the sand to push himself up and away. Samantha spins away, and dusts herself off. They move up, and forward towards another hill in the sand. Samantha leads the way. In the distance, off to the side, a bug aimlessly walks around the desert.

"Keep moving quietly." Mark whispers to Samantha, observing the bug.

They reach the peak of the dune, finding another treacherous canyon below.

"Slide down to gain momentum, and jump." Samantha recommends. She follows her instinct, sliding her feet down the sand hill. Jumping nice and high, she clears the gap, and turns around to wait for the Space Jumper.

Mark slides down the sand in a similar fashion, with the ghost vapor from his feet shooting sand away like a leaf blower. He plants the heavy spot of his vapor on the edge of the cliff, and springs across the gap with momentum. His feet feel heavy as he floats over the gap, landing on his butt on the other side of the canyon. He quickly looks up to Samantha, and smiles with the stars behind her.

They move up another sand hill to reveal the outskirts of the police base, and about ten bugs walking around outside. Before the main gate is another large gap, surrounding the base like a moat. "Let's make a run for the fence." Samantha says with excitement.

"Run?" Mark reiterates out of breath. "Yeah, we should run." Samantha says, beginning to jog to the fence towards the large, aimless bugs. Mark looks around the desert, takes a deep breath, lifting his heavy feet to lumber his body forward. He slowly drags his feet over the light sand, building momentum towards the rapidly increasing gap across the moat.

Samantha is ahead, sprinting full speed towards the fence. The bugs hear her steps, and gives chase from above and under the ground. They dig and burrow through the sand, revealing their heads at unpredictable locations. Samantha uses her agility to step around and over the large insects. She takes out her mini bat and stun gun to shoot with her left, and bash with her right at the approaching bugs from the side. She attacks the bugs with both weapons at the same time, stunning down the alien insects.

Mark is trying to build speed behind his faster ally, as he watches her jump high over the moat, leaving about five dead bugs behind. She holsters her bat mid-jump, and clings to the tall, chain-linked fence. One of the bulbous insects tries to jump at Samantha on the fence, but as she turns around, she takes notice, and blasts a single shot back at the bug. The bug falls away to base of the fence, and drops into the dark liquid below. The bug squirms in the water, appearing to cook in the volatile pool. It sinks all the way down into the moat.

Samantha climbs up the chain-linked fence, and stops about mid-way up. She turns around to find Mark, galloping over the dark sand.

"Run Space Jumper." She whispers loudly.

The bugs in the area surround Samantha near the fence, but move back underground. Mark casually approaches the edge of the moat, when two of the remaining bugs at the side of the sand take notice, and move up towards his location. Mark continues forward to a high point on the dune, and controls the energy from his feet to muster up a jump.

He floats over the moat with low energy, and grabs the absolute bottom rung of the chain-linked fence. He dangles with his gear from the metal fence, as the bugs across the gap take notice of the sound. One of the bugs makes a jump at the Space Jumper, who hears the shuffling descent of sand behind him without turning around. He clutches his gloves tight, and turns around to find the daunting enemy bug flying towards him in mid air.

"Whoa!" He exclaims, rolling his hand across his body to grab a different part of the fence. He spins again, moving away from the sluggish bug, as it crashes headfirst into the metal fence. It falls all the way down into the nasty water, and simmers within the volatile liquid. Mark climbs up the fence using only his arms, making his way up to Samantha, who sits at the peak.

"Nice move, Space Jumper." She says to Mark, continuing to climb the fence. The remaining bugs in the area retreat back into the sand. The Space Jumper clambers over the top of the fence, meeting Samantha at eye level. He takes a deep breath, siting on top of the fence. Samantha looks ahead at the base. "That garage is our best way in." She says.

"Let's move." He replies.

Samantha hops down from the fence, landing on hard, unforgiving dirt. "Space Jumper, be careful with your feet." She says up to him, who slowly climbs down with his hands and arms. He quietly touches down, where the two continue forward towards the base. Mark creeps low, as Samantha takes point ahead. The area outside the base is quiet and vacant. The air feels colder for Mark without his shoes.

Outside of the entrance to the base, a pair of guards patrol the front. Samantha looks at Mark, and points to the guard on the left. She nods to Mark, as he nods back, and creeps low towards the guards. Samantha sits low in front of a waist high barricade near the guard. She glances at Mark, who crouch walks to the other guard. She motions her hand, indicating attack. Mark wraps around the waist high concrete barricade, and chokes the guard with his arms. Samantha rises from a crouch, dangerously close to the enemy, and bashes his head into the barricade. Both guards fall unconscious, as Mark and Samantha begin to move inside the base.

A tall, dark cave leads down a small, paved hill for a few hundred feet. The concrete ground is stable, where the walls line with lights and dense granite. At the bottom of the hill is a gate, with another pair of guards on patrol behind.

Mark and Samantha take notice, and crouch behind concrete barricades. Samantha waits next to Mark for a moment for the right time to infiltrate. She moves around the cover, and jumps high over the sturdy gate towards the watchtower above. She bashes a guard in the back of his head with her club, knocking him out. The other guard appears to be female, where Samantha shoots her gun to incapacitate her. Samantha climbs through an open window in the watchtower to the top of the gate. She presses a button, opening the gate.

Guards from behind hear the commotion, and run towards the opening gate to investigate. Mark jogs forward on the ground through the gate in the garage to a parking lot within the walls. Similar police vehicles that arrested him in space are in the lot. Samantha jumps down to ground level from the top of the security gate.

The enemies approaching whip out retractable batons, batting them in their hands for intimidation. Mark jogs past Samantha from the back, and rushes the nearest guard in straight anger.

The guard tries to bash the Space Jumper, but Mark catches the baton with his hand, and throws the guard hard to the side, breaking his arm. The guard slides on the concrete towards a police cruiser in the garage, causing the alarm to go off. Mark walks to the next heavily armored security guard of another race than human, and dodges a punch. Mark counters by punching the guard in his side, cracking ribs through the heavy gear, finishing the combo with a left elbow to the head. Mark slashes the guards helmet off, knocking him to the ground.

Samantha runs past Mark and jumps head high to the final guard. She uses her legs to grapple his neck to the ground. The guard smashes his head to the concrete with force, knocking him unconscious. Samantha wipes her brow, and looks at Mark.

"Let's go find my shoes." He says to Samantha, his ally.

Beyond the garage is the main entrance to the base, where Mark and Samantha move forward. She kicks down a glass and metal framed door to a check-in area, with a guard standing behind a desk. The guard equips her gun and aims at Mark. Samantha slides down to her right, equips her gun, and takes shots at the front desk guard. The guard crouches behind her desk, when Samantha takes cover behind a wall. Mark walks forward to the desk, not scared of the opposition. The guard is oblivious of his move as she calls for reinforcements. He reaches over the desk and takes her gun from her hand as she looks down. He holds the gun to his side as the guard looks up to him.

"Where are my shoes?" He asks the small girl intensely. She slowly rises back to her feet from her crouch, and looks at Mark, surprised at his humility. "I know nothing of shoes, sir. Please don't hurt me." She says nervously in clean English. Mark quickly turns around towards the entrance, and throws her gun hard out of the front doors towards the parking lot. The gun sails past the gate, and slides on the ground. "Go get your gun." Mark says with an impatient tone. The guard takes the long way around her desk, and around Mark, where she runs out of the door towards the gate. Mark looks at Samantha, where they move forward through a hallway in the atrium.

A pair of doors are at the end of a white hallway, as Mark bursts through with aggression into a mall-like area. Numerous shops, kiosks, and a handful of guards appear, as the Space Jumper quickly hides behind a bush within the cave. Samantha joins in next to him in the small and cramped bush, where they wait and observe the scene. Their cover remains intact, noticing most of the guards reach for their communication systems to listen to a distress call, and rush towards the main gate. The guards are in too much of a hurry to notice Mark and Samantha inside the green bush.

As the guards exit, Mark moves left across the path towards the back wall behind the first shop. He browses the wares of the kiosk, noticing glasses are for sale or barter. He continues forward on the path, staying low beneath the stall. Samantha follows close behind moving towards the next kiosk over, selling body armor and defensive gear. They move forward together to the next stall selling shoes, socks, and gloves.

Mark notices a pair of rugged, black boots sitting on the counter. He takes a small rock from the ground and arcs it over his head like a grenade into the stall. It makes a small and subtle knock at the back of the kiosk to distract the worker. The Space Jumper reaches up from his low position, and swoops the boots from the kiosk. He crouch walks forward to an intersection in the mall and takes cover inside another bush off the beaten path.

He quickly slips the boots into his vapor feet, closing most of the vapor from his lower leg. The shoes match his original size nicely, from before, when he had feet. Ghostly vapors spew out from the breathing holes in front of the shoes.

"Better, but it's not the same." He says to himself, tying the laces.

He attempts to stand, feeling a weakness in his calves as he rises. The vapor calms and forms within the boots, providing a small threshold of comfortability.

"Hey, give me those back, Thief!" The alien clerk yells to Mark from his shop.

Mark runs around the back of the kiosk as the clerk whistles incredibly loud with his fingers in his mouth, catching the attention of the remaining police in the mall.

Mark looks at the clerk while leaning his right leg back. He slowly lifts his left leg up while springing forward with his right. He connects his left foot to the face of the clerk, knocking him surprisingly far back towards a patch of grass in the mall.

"What shoes?" Mark replies, lowering his kicking leg.

Samantha chuckles at Mark's proficiency, and rises up to fight the approaching guards. Mark turns around, finding Samantha grappling heavily armored police in front of the remaining three kiosks. Mark joins the scrum and starts swinging elbows at any security personnel. He drops low, leg sweeping two of the guards down. Samantha drops her foot on a guard, incapacitating his face. Mark throws the final guard into a stall, crashing through armor, gear, helmets, and pads.

Mark smiles at Samantha and begins to jog forward through the remainder of the mall. He carefully opens another pair of metallic doors, revealing an area with lockers and small jail cells.

A trio of large female police officers patrol the room. They are thick faced and bodied, as Mark sneaks behind one of the guards to his left, and chokes her out quickly. He wraps his arms around her dark, rough, and thick neck until she cannot breathe. The Space Jumper's legs spew out massive power. Samantha enters through the door, and shoots the guard behind the main desk, shocking her down and off her seat. Mark scoops up the guards heavy baton from the floor, and throws it at the final guard's head, turning her around.

The female guard stands around nine feet tall, weighing about a half a ton. Her skin complexion is mostly a dark tan, as she turns around with her weighty legs to find Mark and Samantha ready for a fight.

After the Space Jumper throws the baton at the back of her head, Samantha fires her gun from her hip and buzzes the remaining security guard. She stands still, obviously incapacitated. Mark takes notice, and springs towards her with the vapor from his feet shooting full blast within his new shoes. He jumps forward towards the large stunned guard, and lays back in the air while lifting his feet. He loads his knees back, quickly approaching the her. He connects the bottom of one foot, and the top of the other on her upper body, knocking her backwards a few feet, and down with a thud to clear the room of threats.

Moving forward to another room in the underground police base, the remainder of the police crew sit at their desks and do paperwork. The branch of police appear to derive from humanity, with alien forms mixed in. They have natural, human features, like arms and legs, but with an alien feel to them.

Together, Mark and Samantha run forward, shouldering through two separate desks, collapsing wood on top of a pair of officers. Continuing their warpath for answers, beating everything that stands in their way, Samantha is at the side of the room, shooting electronic lasers with her gun, while Mark is on the other side, dodging punches and grapples from the cops, working in tandem to eliminate the opposition in the room.

All of the enemies in the room are down, when the Space Jumper and Samantha meet up, and take notice of a glass door in the back, reading Captain. Mark walks quickly into the room, barging inside to find the captain of the base sitting comfortably behind a desk. The room is larger than anticipated, with books, antiques, and furniture splayed deeper around.

"Where are my shoes?" Mark demands from the captain with an annoyed tone in his voice. The police captain delays to answer, when Mark bangs his fists angrily on his desk. "Your shoes are not here, sir. What is wrong with the pair you are wearing?" The captain replies nervously. Mark looks down at his feet, and looks back up. "So where are they, guy?" Mark asks more passively. "How about you take a seat and we'll talk about it, Mark of Earth." The captain says. Mark quickly pulls out the leather chair in front, and aggressively takes a seat, looking straight into the captains eyes.

Samantha stands and listens from the back of the room, guarding the door from the inside. She peaks outside of the captain's room for a moment, and closes the door. Samantha remains calm, as Mark and the captain waste time with menial questions of each other's character. She leisurely tours the captain's office, browsing his vast memorabilia, and books of knowledge. While rummaging through the captains stuff, she notices a pair of petite gloves sitting on a shelf within the books. She quietly takes the gloves, and stashes them in her back pocket, as Mark and the captain continue a heated exchange. The gloves have wires and electronical components similar to the ones Mark wears. Samantha begins to walk closer to Mark, providing moral support.

"Your shoes are with a group that I know will keep them safe." The captain says. "That's not fair!" Mark replies calmly in frustration, and continues. "Why can't I get them back?" He asks. "Who the hell are you to posses that kind of power?" The captain asks the Space Jumper with a tough bravado. "Apparently somewhat important if they landed at my house." Mark replies. "Well by now, they are on another planet, in another galaxy, billions of lightyears away. There is no way you are going to get them back." The captain says.

Mark boils inside at the comments made by the captain, and does not reply for a moment. "First things first, Space Jumper." The captain says, calmly taking out a pistol of some kind from his desk. He points the weapon at Samantha before she has a chance to notice, and pulls the trigger. The gun shoots a sound wave across the room, hitting Samantha directly in her body. A swirl of air and gravity capture her, disrupting the space-time continuum. The air and sound behind Mark swirls around the room, as Samantha quickly implodes into a black hole.

Books and paper scatter across the room in a mysterious windstorm. Mark's mouth opens wide at the shocking turn of events, as he watches the black hole fade away. "What did you just do?" He yells at the captain, who smiles at his work. "You two need some time apart." He says from behind the desk. Mark quickly leaps forward over the captain's desk and uppercuts him in the chin with a stiff fist. The captain rolls back in his chair, and drops his gun on the desk.

Mark picks up the gun with haste and steps back from the desk. The captain regains his senses, and crouches over his desk to watch the Space Jumper shoot himself in the chest with the black hole gun, imploding into a swirl of altered gravity.

Chapter 3

Sword Forest

Everything is dark as the Space Jumper teleports through another dimension of empty, blank space. Awake, alive, but unable to move, see, or hear during his transport of presence, the Space Jumper hovers in darkness, until the familiar scent of Samantha catches his breath. He follows the closest thing he has to an ally in the new universe.

Moments later, the Space Jumper emerges from the darkness, into a bright light surrounded by soft sand and watery waves. He crumples down in the sand on his hands and knees.

"Where am I?" He questions out of breath with fatigue. He looks up, and stares out into the vast ocean, to study the waves of the water. He turns around to notice a dense group of trees in a forest. He circles around to his left on the beach, when he finds a body laying on the sand. Adjusting his vision through his glasses, he discovers the body is Samantha, unconscious or dead with her head down. He slowly rises up to a stand, and runs on the beach in exhaustion towards his ally.

He crashes down in the sand next to Samantha, removes his bag, and rolls her on her back. She lays completely still, soaking wet, as if the tide from the ocean brought her in. "Not now Samantha, please don't do this to me." He says with an increasing heartrate. He holds her head up from the sand, slightly raising her upper body. He tries to revive her as best as he can from what he remembers from Earth, providing air by blowing into her mouth, and pressing down on her chest. After the second press, she coughs, and quickly expels a small portion of water to her side. She coughs for a few more seconds, slowly regaining life.

"Please! Let me rest. I have no energy." Samantha says with her eyes closed, not knowing who she is talking to. "I'm glad you're alright. Do you know where we are?" Mark replies, thinking she does not know who he is. "I don't know. Not familiar with this universe." Samantha replies out of breath. "Great." Mark replies sarcastically, slowly standing up. He picks up his bag and board from the sand, and looks around the area.

Looking at Samantha, he sees she is completely exhausted. The teleportation from the black hole gun made her fatigued after swimming from the ocean. She lays on the sand, as Mark scoops her up, and walks her towards the dangerous looking forest ahead.

He grows fatigued, mostly in his legs, after walking some steps to a safer part of the sand. He places Samantha back on the beach, away from the tide, between the water and trees. "Wait here, I need to do reconnaissance." He says calmly to his unresponsive ally.

Approaching the trees, Mark notices the branches are made of metal swords. The trunks of the trees are bark, but the leaves are incredibly sharp and silver metal. Swords appear everywhere as Mark walks deeper through the brush. Daggers, swords, and blades of all kinds are above, below, and next to him.

"Sword Forest?" Mark asks himself, taking a medium sized blade from the ground by its dull end. He uses the blade to deflect the hanging blades from the trees. Clearing a path forward is a sword fight on the new planet in the unknown galaxy.

Information remains a crucial aspect in all forms of life, as Mark moves to recon the area, cautiously avoiding the edgy tree blades. A misstep or miss-jump could make him lose his head, as he swings the blade over and around to clear a safe path. As the wind blows, swords cling and clash at every moment around him.

After a mile of slowly battling away bladed tree branches, the forest reduces density, unveiling a tall mountain with a lake in front. The bladed trees remain scattered around the area, as Mark continues to move forward towards the peak of the mountain. A small village at the top connects buildings to the main, elevated path. The buildings are small sized shacks made of wood and swords. Mark raises his eyebrows after focusing on the discovery of the village, and continues forward with a long blade in hand.

The air and atmosphere is warm, with the galactic sun above providing light and heat. The Space Jumper treks forward around the side of the lake, following a beaten path in dirt and rocks. Approaching the base of the mountain, Mark prepares for a climb, not being able to utilize his jumping powers.

Despite not having the cool shoes, he believes they are still a part of him in spirit. The controlled spirit inside his police boots provides a slight power when he jumps.

He walks up the side of the mountain until it transitions to jagged rocks. He uses his blade from the forest for ground stability as he moves forward and up. As the dirt transitions to rock, Mark has to jump up the jagged parts of the mountain. He carries momentum by running and jumping in special spots, avoiding stray bladed trees in the area. He spears the blade into the mountain to anchor himself forward. The mountain grows steeper and jagged towards the village above. At one point during a jump, he spikes his sword into the mountain, but loses traction when the rocks collapse around the blade. He grabs the edge of a cliff, dropping the blade down the steep mountainside. Mark pulls himself up to a small space in the cliff, and takes a deep breath.

The final leg of the mountain requires either a grappling device, or a jump of around ten feet up. "Alright, we can do this." He says to himself, focusing strength to his legs where his body meets the exuding vapor. He springs down, and jumps up, soaring not very high into the air, but enough to grab and hang on the top of the mountain. He pulls himself up, and stands at a high spot. The village is now eye level, as Mark inspects the area for life.

Moving forward across the main, raised wooden platform tied together by thin rope, Mark carefully approaches the first building. He touches the side of the building to study its temperature, time, and texture, as he continues forward to the entrance. He checks the corner of the hut for signs of life, or any other developments, only to find more of the top of the mountain. He walks past the building, noticing a tarp as a door. He continues over a bridge, which dangerously overlooks the edge of the steep mountain. The sharp blades of the Sword Forest glisten in the sunlight below.

Mark cautiously walks across the raised sky bridge with wooden planks that look ready to break at any misstep. The wind blows stronger, as Mark continues forward. A pair of wooden huts connect to the main bridge from separate walkways. Mark glances at the buildings with closed doors and windows while traversing over the tall footbridge. The path moves up and down at times, complementing the angles of the mountain. Blades from the trees below clang in the breeze.

Growing weary, Mark moves forward to where the bridge connects back to land. He touches down on the dirt, grateful to be on solid ground. Walking to the right, Mark maneuvers around another building at the top of the mountain. He walks towards another bridge that continues over the cliffs.

Everything remains quiet, besides the Sword Forest, as he treks forward through a gusty wind. The community of houses and organization of bridges indicate that some kind of life has been here at some point. He continues to weave from bridge, to mountaintop, inspecting the exterior of the homes.

After walking about half a mile, Mark discovers the end of the line. He holds a handrail at the start of the final bridge, and moves down a path towards a building at a lower part of the mountain. He creeps around the larger sized hut, and quietly walks to an open window on the furthest side of the camp.

Looking inside, the building is spacious, but empty and dark. Towards the back of the room, stands a hairy creature with arms and legs, indigenous looking with the territory. It mauls a venison-like carcass, raw on a table. The creature is naked, with long, brown hair covering its entire body. Mark stands outside the window looking at the strange being inside. The hairy, naked creature feels Mark's presence, and quickly looks to the window, taking a break from its meal. It growls at the Space Jumper, looking at him with yellow eyes behind layers of dark hair.

Mark gasps at his blown cover, crouches low, and steps away from the window. The hairy creature walks defensively inside of its shack, making strange noises with its mouth. From the other side of the room, another indigenous and naked creature emerges into view. The first creature begins to make its way towards the makeshift door in front, as Mark moves backwards towards the path he came from.

The two hairy beings move outside, and scream out to their comrades, emerging into the light from behind the hut. They escort the Space Jumper up the path, as he walks defensively backwards.

The creatures stand around five feet tall with no clothes on, and different colored hair. Mark turns around and begins to run up the raised wooden path to where he came from. The two creatures make more loud noises, and begin to chase the intruder.

Mark runs up the path with limited speed past the previous huts where more of the indigenous creatures emerge. Some of the species carry spears, while most are unarmed. They all join the mob from the original two creatures, and run across the bridges towards the intruder. With every house and hut he passes, more of the tribal enemies run out and join the chase. Mark embraces his survival of the fittest mentality, and runs his best over the wooden footbridges. As he runs towards the first hut at the top of the mountain, he breaks several planks of wood on the bridge below his shoes. He catches his step and continues forward.

His legs grow weary approaching the first hut. With over twenty of the indigenous beings behind him, a spear rifles past his right leg, and off the mountain. Mark takes the sign of hostility that the creatures want him dead. Towards the final leg of the sky-bridge, Mark breaks a few more planks below him on accident, and falls down a steep part of the mountain. He slides feet first down the slanted, rocky face, struggling to maintain traction.

His shoes take a beating while sliding down the mountain, as he hops over angles and cliffs. The indigenous creatures continue to throw spears down the mountain, as Mark loses footing and begins to tumble. He tucks and rolls over the dense dirt, as the hairy enemies slowly wrap around the side of the mountain to flank the Space Jumper. They follow a path towards the base of the mountain.

Rolling down the mountain, Mark regains footage of the dirt, and quickly begins to run back down to the Sword Forest. The indigenous creatures are nipping at his heels, as he runs as fast as he can through the sharp blades of the forest. The Space Jumper ducks beneath the bladed branches while trying to maintain speed in his crummy shoes. The barefoot hairy creatures are nimble as they maneuver through the Sword Forest.

Mark makes it back to the beach, running out of breath, where he sees Samantha staring off into the horizon.

"Samantha!" Mark yells while running towards her on the sand with over twenty hairy creatures behind him. She stands up from the sand as Mark runs behind her for cover, hoping she knows how to handle the creatures. "Stop!" Samantha yells at the hairy creatures. The leading creatures in front halt in front of Samantha and Mark on the beach, and hold their spears up in an attack position. With silence between everyone, Samantha grabs the black hole gun from Mark's hip, and aims it at the aliens with a serious and intimidating look on her face.

"Huhh!" The hairy aliens gasp questionably at the anomaly. Samantha claps the gun in her hand, intimidating the aliens as they begin to move backwards towards the Sword Forest. "Go!" She yells, motioning to the forest. The hairy aliens look mad, as they remain defensive, and retreat to where they came from. They all back away into the Sword Forest, and out of sight.

"Thanks." Mark says out of breath to Samantha. "We need to get out of here." She says. "Let's just use the gun. Do you know how it works?" He replies. "Not really. How did you get that thing anyways?" Samantha asks. "I punched the captain at the police station after he shot you, and took it. I shot myself with it, hoping to find you." He answers. "You are brave, Space Jumper." Samantha replies, romantically holding Mark's hand. "I will call for reinforcements. My crew can pick us up." Samantha says. "Do you even know where we are?" Mark asks. "It doesn't matter. The beacon I will send to my group appears across the universe." She explains.

Samantha takes out her special, circular phone, and presses some buttons. "This shouldn't take long." She says with confidence.

Mark sits down on the beach, and watches the water, waiting for extraction. Samantha sits in front of him, and cuddles back on sand. Together, they sit on the unknown beach, on the unknown planet in an unknown galaxy.

A few minutes later, a large, metal pirate ship bursts through the upper atmosphere from warp speed, and approaches the beach. Mark checks his surroundings, noticing the hairy, naked, indigenous people from the planet observing what is going on from within the Sword Forest. The ship swoops in over the colorful beach, and lands on the off-white sand. Everything about the presence of the ship feels comfortable, from the smooth landing on the sand, to the water and sun in the background. Mark and Samantha stand on the sand, waiting for any form of similarity to rescue them. Samantha paces ahead on the damp sand, recognizing her company. Mark stands back and blocks the sun from his eyes, watching what is about to go down.

A door at the side of the ship quickly opens, when a ramp flips down to the sand. The ship stands tall at thirty to forty feet high from the ground. A pair of sails stand tall for turning, with a pair of large, hot-rod energy exhausts at the sides to provide power to lift off. The space ship has multiple windows on the side, for viewing and defense. The ship is mostly metal, with some wooden panels roughly armoring the outer hull. It has wings on both sides, indicating the seabird can fly.

A species similar looking to Samantha walks out the door, and down the ramp. Their gear looks comfortable, yet intimidating, with denim styling leather armor above. They stroll out of the ship and walk to Samantha, who continues down the beach to meet in the middle. Mark stands back on the sand for his own safety.

"Sam! I'm so glad you're okay." The lead person in front with a beard says to Samantha. He walks past her and says nothing, continuing his pace towards Mark. The crew behind the leader stop with Samantha and begin to engage in friendly small talk. She shakes hands, hugs her crew, and back looks at Mark.

"So you're the infamous Space Jumper." The human-like alien with the beard says, walking towards Mark with his hand out. The Space Jumper slows his time, and takes the friendly gesture, shaking hands, while staying an appropriate distance away. The bearded man's hand is rough, from journeys endured. Mark resonates well, connecting spiritual warmth, as they break.

"You should come with us Space Jumper." He says to Mark beneath the noise of his quiet ship. "What's the plan?" He asks. "We need to get your shoes back." The nameless alien with the beard says. "Yeah, that would be nice." Mark responds enthusiastically.

The dark green alien with the beard turns around, and walks back towards the ship. Mark gives a final inspection around the trees, and walks on the sand with his fake shoes and vapor feet. He moves next to Samantha and her crew, and looks at her. "I think he asked me to join." Mark says to Samantha. She smiles, and looks ahead to the ship. Mark feels relief, being around people who do not immediately want to kill him. The shoes on his feet provide little protection over his damaged spirit as he walks up the dense ramp into warmth from the ship.

The inside of the ship is well insulated and warm. The walls are metal and wood, utilizing an appropriate mix of luxury, and protection. Pipes and wires scatter around the roof, providing extra security. Mark follows Samantha through the interior towards the front cabin. In a new room, a large table with chairs around it take up most of the floor. Windows surround the room, exhibiting the beach at which they park. Mark looks out of the window as the ship takes off from the beach, and into the sky. It quickly accelerates for a few seconds, fully launching into outer space. Mark finds a moment of moderate stillness, sitting in a chair to join the bearded alien and Samantha.

Members of the crew enter the meeting room and join the bearded alien, Samantha, and the Space Jumper. The ship begins to reduce speed, yet flying fast through outer space. Mark looks out the windows, observing planets in the distance slowly rotating through space. "Samantha told us of your efforts in your home universe." The bearded man says to Mark, and continues. "She says your goal is to spread equality through out the universe?" He asks. "Yeah, I don't think it's turned out well so far, I should probably just go home." Mark jokes to the crew. "I don't think that's a good idea, Space Jumper." Samantha interjects. "And why is that?" Mark reiterates quickly. "We need your help."

The man with the beard says to Mark, crossing his arms from across the top of the large table.

"Who exactly are you guys?" Mark asks the crew. "We are Lineage, a mercenary group that takes from the bad, and shares it with those trying to increase the common good." The bearded man replies. Mark sits back in his chair with his bag and board, and looks at Samantha, then to the bearded man.

"Maybe we can do business. I need my shoes back to continue my journey." Mark replies. "So we're good then?" The bearded person asks. "That's one of the things I'm afraid of." Mark replies. The ship moves fast in space towards the next destination.

Chapter 4

Alphanauts

"We have an idea where your shoes may be located." The bearded member of Lineage says to Mark. "We think it is the Alphanauts, otherwise known as the A.N." He says.

"Let's go find them." Mark says to the table. "Well, that's the problem. The A.N are considered good guys here in this universe, and they are everywhere." The bearded captain replies, and continues. "We have coordinates to their headquarters, but it is incredibly far away, even with warp travel."

"Do you think this gun can help?" Mark replies, pulling out the black hole gun from his back hip. "What!" The bearded captain exclaims at the sight of the anomaly. "That's the newest model of the Splitter." A member of Lineage says from the side of the table. "How did you get that?" The bearded leader from Lineage asks Mark.

"After we broke out of jail, we visited the police captain regarding my shoes. He shot Samantha with it, so I leaped up, and punched him out. I shot myself where Samantha was shot, and ended up with her." The Space Jumper explains to Lineage.

"Amazing, we will utilize, sit tight Space Jumper." The bearded captain says, taking the gun from Mark's open hand. "You guys are dismissed." The bearded captain of Lineage says to the group. He takes the black hole gun to the pilots cabin of the ship, as Mark sits back in his seat, glad to be alive. Samantha remains in her chair and studies Mark.

Five minutes later, Mark is asleep in his chair in the meeting room next to the pilots cabin. Samantha is a few rooms over, fraternizing with the crew. The bearded man in charge walks over to Mark, and shakes his chair to wake the Space Jumper. Mark snaps awake and looks lost around the room.

"We combined the mechanism from the gun with our ships warp capabilities to control black holes in space. We can manipulate the space time continuum however we choose." The bearded captain explains. "Let's test it out." Mark replies, straight from of his nap. "Those were our intensions." The bearded captain replies.

"Hey, what should I call you?" Mark asks the bearded captain. "You can call me Captain, or Drake, or both, I lead this ship with objectives from my elders." The captain of Lineage says, walking back to the cockpit. "Check it out Space Jumper. Witness the power of space and science." He says to Mark.

The Space Jumper is slow to get up, and walks into the pilots cabin with buttons and knobs beneath a window to the stars and deep space behind. He looks down at the center console of electronics to find a replica of the black hole gun.

"Fantastic." Mark says to Drake and the pilot. They look at Mark, when the pilot presses several buttons on the console.

Drake moves things up and down on the console, assisting the pilot, when a swirl of black suddenly appears ahead of the ship, moving deeper back through space. The ship slowly follows the path inside the widening black hole, and disappears in to a deep dimension of black space.

Floating through cold black nothingness, the ship emerges fast into a forest of trees, plowing through dozens of heavily aged trees. The ship knocks them to the ground with ease, but knocks the pilots out cold.

Mark uses his arm strength to prevent himself from crashing through the front window, holding on to the backs of the chairs. He quickly notices the captain and the pilot are unconscious on the dash from the crash. The ship continues to plow through trees like pinball. Samantha comes running through the cabin.

"Space Jumper, help me control the ship." She says.

Mark slides his bag behind the seat, and leans in over the pilot of the ship, as Samantha does the same with Captain Drake. Samantha adjusts things on the console, flipping knobs and pressing buttons. "The engine is down, and needs time to cool! Turn the steering handle, Space Jumper, and try not to crash into the trees." Samantha exclaims. Mark begins to steer the front of the ship through wet grass, dirt and green trees with brown bark. He aims for smaller trees with thinner trunks to avoid further damage to the ship.

The heavy ship carries tremendous momentum through the dense forest. Mark steers the ship using a steering handle for the advanced rudder in the rear. He flicks the handles, aggressively avoiding trees and rocks, sliding the ship away from danger. After a minute of sliding, Samantha flips a switch, nosediving the ship to the ground, sending rocks and plants flying into the air. The Lineage ship decreases momentum to a smoky stop on the hot dirt and burnt plants amongst a dense brush of trees.

Mark and Samantha take a sigh of relief, as the ship settles in the dirt. Captain Drake and the pilot begin to regain consciousness. "Is everyone alright?" The captain says, looking around at the scenario. He shakes the pilot in his arm to wake him in his seat. Mark and Samantha aid Drake and the pilot to stand. "Where are we?" Mark asks the crew in the cabin. "I honestly have no idea. Let's hope we're closer to your shoes." Captain Drake says in pain. "Someone give me a status report!" He yells back to the rest of his crew.

"There's heavy damage, boss. The engine and hull require significant repairs." The crewmember replies from the back. Captain Drake places his palm to his face, quickly thinking of a new plan.

"Can you guys scope out the area?" Drake asks Mark and Samantha. "No problem. I have to get my shoes back on my feet." Mark replies, looking at Samantha. He picks up his backpack and space board from the back of the seat.

Mark and Samantha pivot away from the pilot seats, and walk through the damaged ship towards the opening exit hatch. The long and high door rise, when a pair of crewmembers approach from behind. "We have you covered, team." He says to Mark and Samantha.

The door fully opens, exposing the destructive path blazed behind. Smoke rises from the ground, leading beneath the ship. The air smells burnt from the scorched rocks and trees. Mark rubs his eyes behind his special glasses, adjusting to the light. The team walks out of the ship and spreads out to observe the area. Mark sticks with Samantha, trusting her experience.

"Let's move forward while they repair the ship." She whispers to Mark. The crew look at Mark and Samantha from the opposite side of the ship. "We see dislodged parts from the ship that we need to recover. Go on ahead with out us." The lead crewmember says to Samantha. She acknowledges back with a head nod, when the crewmembers walk the path back through the destruction.

Mark and Samantha move to the front of the ship through plants next to trees. Mark takes out his laser sword and tablet from his bag, and slices down annoying plants in his way while scanning for anomalies. They clear a path forward about half a mile with little change to their scenario. The Space Jumper cuts a short tree from its base, and kicks it away with his uncool shoes to continue forward. Samantha follows behind, aware of Mark's laser sword.

His scanner struggles to gain a clear signal through the dense trees. Samantha's scanner is on the same level as Mark, both lost in the forest, trying to find a way out as they move forward. Tired of not finding anything relevant, Mark walks to one of the large trees in the area.

"Give me your knife." He asks Samantha. She reaches to her side, as Mark takes his hatchet and Samantha's knife in each hand. He jumps up, and stabs the bark using the blades to hoist himself up. He stands on thick branches for stability while stabbing the tree to climb higher and higher.

Mark stands halfway up the large tree, jumping on branches to move up to particular spots. The climb up the tree is tiring on his arms and chest. He luckily maintains a solid and natural physique. Switching trees by branching branches, piercing bark with his blades, Mark reaches the peak of the forest. He continues upward over the shorter trees to the final sturdy branch above. He hooks the blade in the bark of the branch, and swings up to stand.

He looks over the canopy, finding a large break in the tree patterns ahead, indicating some kind of structure or property. He takes out his scanner, and sends a ping around the area. The signal is much clearer above than on the ground. The scanner collects the distance and image of the property, fenced off with a building in the middle. Mark stashes his tablet back to his bag, and absorbs the data.

He uses his blade to grind into the outside of the bark as he drops down through branches. He slows his speed by stabbing harder in a deeper angle. The tree grows wider as he moves down, slicing a scar across the brown wood. Towards the bottom of the tree, he unhinges his blade, and falls feet first on a thin branch. The Space Jumper's weight, speed and force is too much for the poor little branch. He snaps through the wood, and falls down the remainder of the tree, landing awkwardly on his back on the grass below. The ground shakes upon impact, sending stray leaves popping up like popcorn as his space board powers on for a moment.

"See anything?" Samantha asks, chuckling at Mark. She picks up her knife from the ground, and holsters it to her side. "Uhh, yeah, give me a sec." Mark replies in agonizing pain. He squirms around on the ground for a moment, and slowly rises to his feet.

"There's a base up ahead that could have my shoes." Mark continues out of breath, taking out his tablet in pain. He shows Samantha the saved location of the base from his scanner. Looking at Mark's tablet, she copies the location to her mobile device. "Let's keep moving, Space Jumper." She says, as Mark stretches his back in pain.

Samantha takes point, scouting ahead with the information from her phone. Mark limps behind, recovering from the fall from the tree. Pain does a good job at following the Space Jumper wherever he goes. Samantha walks forward through a section of the forest with a heavy presence of trees bunched together. Mark follows behind, bumping in to a few of the branches. He quickly equips his laser sword from his bag, and stretches an ache out of his side. He ignites the laser from his flashlight, and spins counter clockwise in a circle to cut down the trees.

Up ahead, Samantha hears the noise from Mark's laser, and turns around to watch a collection of small trees fall over him. The laser sword sticks out vertically from the shrubbery. Samantha giggles, and continues forward slowly through the dense brush. Skinny and fit, Samantha slips through the shrubs and prodding bushes, nearing the first fence ahead.

After some time of slicing trees and walking through bushes, Mark cautiously jogs up to Samantha with her phone in hand through an opening of trees. The reduction of trees unveils the fenced property ahead.

"Hey, up ahead." Mark says quietly to Samantha, pointing to the obvious fence. The two walk together towards the fence, when Samantha looks at Mark and his gear, and smiles. He looks back at her, and smiles, taking the hint that he needs to rip down the fence. He ignites his laser sword again, and carves an upward oval at the base of the fence, big enough for people to walk through. Mark walks through first after the metal drops. From the opposite side of the fence, the Space Jumper crouches down, and offers his hand through the hole for Samantha to accompany him on the other side.

Trees stand loose around the inside of the gated property. Mark and Samantha continue to trespass forward, until the roof of a large, domed building emerges between the trees. The building sits behind another layer of fence, guarded by actual people at a gate.

"Whoa." Mark exclaims quietly. He holds Samantha's arm back from moving forward, as she looks at him with confused eyebrows.

"How should we play this?" He asks her. "Why not walk through the front door?" She replies with a wink and a smile. She motions her head forward to Mark, and moves towards the guarded gate. Mark hesitates, and follows behind. A dirt road leads up a slight incline towards the building, where Samantha continues to walk. Mark picks up his pace to catch hers, and holds her hand. The two walk down the road together and smile, not worried about consequence in each other's presence.

"Can we help you strangers?" The guard at the gate asks. The two guards wear light green cone hats made of dense plastic, with vibrant safety vests over long sleeve t-shirts and armor. They look similar to humans, but have a tanner complexion and thicker skin density.

"Yeah, I'm looking for a pair of shoes that were stolen from me." Mark replies. "It looks like your wearing a perfectly good pair on your feet there, human." One of the guards says sarcastically. "The shoes were special to me." Mark replies. "What is this nice building, anyways? Are you guys A.N?" Samantha asks.

"Special shoes you say?" The other guard asks, looking at the main guard, who reaches up to his headset. "We have a two-fifteen out front." The guard mumbles through his radio.

"Two-fifteen?" Mark whispers to Samantha. "Wait here, freshman." The guard says to Mark. The two guards walk back inside the gate towards the building, leaving Mark and Samantha lost in front. After about a minute of standing alone in the jungle, strange looking machine guns come to life on the walls of the building and on the ground by the gate. "Take cover!" Samantha quickly yells.

Mark moves left, while Samantha moves right, as the guns in the area target both of them, and begin popping off rounds. Mark and Samantha take cover behind separate trees in the area, as small caliber bullets strike the ground next to where they stand, kicking up dirt and debris. Bullets strike the tree Mark uses as cover.

After a short pause, he slides on the ground headfirst towards the next closest tree. Samantha finds time to sneak away from the path of bullets tracking her on the opposite side of the domed base.

The gun emplacements lose sight of their targets, as the Space Jumper and Samantha swap cover behind the trees and rocks surrounding the walled property. Mark continues to wrap around the outer structure before reaching the back end of the property. He sits behind a large boulder as the machine guns take notice, and rain bullets down from above and ahead.

Moments later, Samantha slides behind a tree for fresh cover near Mark. She sits at the other side of the end of the dome. The gunfire is nonstop, as Mark notices Samantha move behind her cover. He whistles for her attention, and waves from behind his cover. Samantha finds Mark sitting behind a rock, and waves back to him as he peeks out. They smile at each other, remaining slammed by bullets from the roof of the main building. Mark is out of breath, with his feet hurting inside of his not-so-cool shoes. Samantha breathes deep, and regains her composure.

Mark waits for an opportunity to move closer to Samantha behind a tree towards the middle of the exterior of the base. Samantha does the same thing, moving together, until the two are nearly arms length away.

They pause during a break in the gunfire, where Mark counts to three on his fingers. On three, he runs forward towards the back gate, igniting his laser sword. He slices a hole in a fence while running, and charges through the metal. Samantha runs close behind, as the gunfire resumes.

She swerves left and right, dodging the path the mounted gun thinks she is going to take. Mark takes cover behind a heavy, metal shipping crate, and waits for his ally. Samantha jumps through the hole in the fence with a roll to beat the gun. She slides to cover next to Mark on the metal container. They look at each other in amazement over how extreme the scenario is. They are surprised at each other's resistance to death. Mark smiles, looking at Samantha's weapon.

She looks at him, and his lousy shoes, sitting down behind the large cover. Capable of continuing his quest, Mark looks back at her, with a perplexed look. Through the levity, Mark runs out of the cover towards a barricade of stacked sand bags. Samantha almost follows him across, but only peeks through the cover of the red shipping container. A hail of bullets begin to follow the Space Jumper's direction.

Samantha watches Mark roll out of the sand towards another dumpster in the distance. Opportunity strikes, as she takes out her stun gun. She rolls to the opposite corner of the container, and fires a set of shots at the heavy gun emplacement planted on the roof, focused on Mark. The mounted gun malfunctions, as smoke flares out of the mechanism. Samantha looks at Mark, and continues towards the dense wall of the main structure. Mark rolls out of his cover, and walks casually towards Samantha at the wall.

"The door is probably locked." Mark whispers out of breath next to Samantha. "Give me a boost, I'll go up." She says, stepping back from the door. Mark crouches at a proper dismount point, facing Samantha as she moves back to jump. He turns around, and looks away from her as she is about to go. He loads his legs, prepared to launch her upward. She runs forward, and uses Mark's back as a springboard to the roof of the cold clay exterior of the base. She does parkour up the roof, and lands flush against the glass dome.

Mark moves back from the crate, and looks up to the roof. Samantha looks down from the roof, motioning Mark on the ground, who notices her at the base of the dome.

Samantha takes a moment to study her path, and form a plan. She takes a deep breath, figuring it is time to break out the special skates on her bag. She sits atop a dense part of the roof at the base of the dome, and tightens the straps of her skates over her shoes. Her skates glow green and white, with her veins glowing green and white with the sound of her soul.

The skates immediately feel like magic on her feet, with strength deriving from a mysterious source. She clings her wheels to the roof with tremendous strength, maintaining a comfortable balance.

"I'm not doing this for too long." She whispers to herself in her native tongue. Samantha stands on the roof, and begins to climb the glass dome of the building with power from her skates. She rolls up the steep face, increasing momentum as if it were nothing.

Her wheels exhaust a thin layer of glass as she climbs the dome. She takes out her gun, the boa constrictor, and shoots another shot at the downed turret, killing any remaining power. She rolls over the glass dome with her skates like a blade over ice.

Samantha veers left over the large dome towards another gun emplacement, and shoots a pair of shots at it. She zaps the gun, slicing her blades right up the dome. The mounted gun catches fire behind her as she skates up the glass towards the opposite end.

Mark puts his ear to the heavily locked door ahead, and listens for commotion. Samantha glides over the glass through the silence of stealth. The gun emplacements are incapable of turning up above the dome, as she maneuvers away from their path. She glides quickly on the three in-line wheels beneath her bright green feet. The wheels carry momentum, with power rolling through Samantha.

She moves up the glass with fast momentum, providing a smooth surface to ride on. The gun she moves towards rises, and begins to aim at Mark, taking cover at the end of the door.

She skids her skates next to the weapon, and kicks the mounted gun off its hinges in Mark's direction. The gun rolls down the glass, crashes onto the concrete base, and rolls off the side of the building. Mark looks up from the ground, and watches a large machine gun fall in his direction. It skids over the concrete surface, as sparks shoot from the metal.

The Space Jumper looks up at Samantha, noticing how bright she looks with her skates as her eyes glow green. Excited and confident, Mark quickly salutes her, and drags the gun behind the crate, away from view. Mark takes out his tablet, and scans the weapon for information. Nothing of relevance occurs on the screen. Mark looks down at the gun, and finds a set of cut wires. He smiles, and sits next to the gun by the door.

Samantha continues to skate up the smooth glass towards the peak of the dome. She rolls hard, gaining momentum by slowly moving left and right. She senses the peak of the dome, and stops her speed by rolling on the back wheels. She quickly stands straight, empowered by the juice from her shoes. She sits down at the peak of the dome, and begins to remove her skates. She clings the laces together, and throws them on the special hook behind her bag. She stands up on the glass with her regular military boots on.

The peak of the dome feels weak and flimsy beneath her feet, as she takes notice to take advantage. The very peak of the dome is obvious with subtle lines from the glass. Like an orange and its slices, the dome has a central point. Samantha jumps up moderately high, and powers downward, trying to crash through the glass. The central point of the dome cracks in several directions, appearing as if one more jump would break it.

Samantha crouches over the crack, and jumps up in place, even higher than the first. She spins around a full turn on the descent, where she crashes through the remainder of the glass. She drops through small and medium sized pieces of pulverized glass, scattering in mid air. She slowly falls into the dome towards a central workstation.

Samantha lands on top of a comfortable security agent with armor, gear and clothes providing support. The dome appears bigger from the outside, as she scans around for threats. There are three other security and work aliens at the far side of the dome where Mark is waiting. Samantha regains composure after the drop, and equips her gun while running through the workplace within the building.

The interior of the dome was well air-conditioned before the gaping hole on the roof. The large lab is scattered with large machines and tools to develop things for the Alphanauts. Samantha jumps across tables, and moves around cover near the three guards walking towards Mark at the other end of the door. She gains momentum to a sprint, harnessing left over energy from her skates.

She jumps from the cold ground of the development base, and kicks the first guard in the back of the head with tremendous power. He flies forward, crashing into a desk and workstation. She regains balance, and shoots the remaining two guards approaching the dense hatch door to the dome. As they turn around, Samantha stuns them both with the power of her boa constrictor. She continues momentum towards the door outside, and spins the hatch. She pops the door open with her shoulder, and looks at Mark while out of breath.

Mark grabs the heavy turret gun from the ground, and carries it inside. He walks forward, and flicks the loose cables to try to spark a connection. Nothing happens, as he continues forward into the quiet lab. He places the gun on the ground as the dome expands wider around him. He uses both hands to connect the cables together, which powers the guns rotating chambers. He picks the gun up from the ground, and looks around the room as the chambers slowly spin, manipulated by Mark controlling the cables.

"I've got a weird feeling about this place." He says to Samantha as she re-enters the dome. Samantha runs across the floor in the research lab to check the area. Mark walks forward, absorbing the rapid change of environment. Tech is everywhere, on the ground, on tables, on the wall. The amount of potential in the room dwarves anything the Space Jumper has seen so far. Thrilled with adventure, Mark walks to the center of the lab with the heavy turret spinning in his hands.

A pinging noise startles Mark at the side of the room. Moments later, a second ping echoes across the floor. Mark and Samantha check the noise, noticing a set of opening doors from the side of the dome. Five similar looking military personnel walk out to the floor with advanced guns, armor, and gadgets. Mark turns to the elevator, and begins firing in to the group of Alphanauts.

His heavy machine gun unleashes around ten bullets, quickly running out of ammo. His shots do little damage to a couple of the guards, as Mark frantically attaches and detaches the cables on the gun, finally realizing it is out of ammo. He places the gun on top of a desk ahead of him, and crouches down to hide.

Samantha is across the room watching Mark take action. She fires charges from her boa constrictor, knocking two of the guards unconscious. She takes cover behind a desk, awaiting a hail of gunfire. A few shots whiz over her head as she wraps around the corner of the desk to look at Mark. He takes heat and gunfire as well from one of the guards, when she watches him take out his gun.

Mark equips his BB gun, and wraps his hand around the particle accelerator to adjust the size of the bullet. He takes a deep breath, and turns his head around the corner of the desk to inspect the threat, noticing two guards ahead. His attention sways to the side of the dome to watch another elevator door open, releasing another five guards into the room. Mark takes advantage of awareness, moving to another desk with a glowing artifact on top.

Staying low, Mark slides on his knees to the desk with the glowing thing on it. He quickly checks over the desk, and grabs the test artifact from its holding apparatus. A blue and silver glowing disk electrifies in his hand. Mark presses a button on the center of the device, unleashing an aura of magnetic energy, propelling away loose and miscellaneous things.

Enwrapped in an anonymous shield, Mark stands obliviously from a crouch, and inspects what he is holding. Feeling invincible, he stands from his cover, where the Alphanauts notice his position. "Space Jumper!" Samantha yells to Mark, standing out like a sore thumb in the lab.

His force field glows blue, purple, and pink, with white air blended within. He looks down at the silent device in his hand. The Alphanauts shoot bullets at the Space Jumper, but deflect away from the physical force field of color. The shield looks like liquid when struck by projectiles.

He studies the device for a moment within a blissful state of peace and quiet. Vibrations ripple around him from the deflecting projectiles. He finally remembers where he is, and calmly crouches back down behind the desk, as the device runs out of power in his hand. The color and blankness of sound exaggerate around him, making him wish he were back in that blank state again.

Samantha reloads a charge to her weapon, and switches out of her shot up cover. She moves right, towards the oncoming gunfire near Mark, and crouches behind a desk. Focusing her breath, she moves up from cover, and fires at a guard. Feeling let down against the five other guards remaining, Samantha retreats down and figures out her next play.

She moves to another cover away from the action, finding herself at the walls of the dome. She wraps around the enemies location, and flanks a pair of Alphanauts. Mark takes notice of her positive progression, and plays with the particle accelerator on his gun. He aims at the crowd of enemies occupied by

Samantha's harassment, focusing on the movement of one target, switching to the second, and to the final target.

He fires a shot at the first guard, striking as directed, firing a second bullet to the second Alphanaut's leg. He fires the third shot to the final Alphanaut as Samantha clambers over him with her legs, slamming him down to end the damaging combo. The room is clear, taken care of in nearly a flash, as the enemies fall to the ground.

"Hey, grab a shield." Mark says to Samantha, throwing her one of the prototype disks from a table. She quickly places it in her back pocket without hesitation to what it does. "Let's make our way down." Samantha says, walking towards one of the opened elevators. Mark does a final inspection of the room, and backpedals towards Samantha to the entrance of the elevator. They step inside the large, silver elevator, where Mark presses the lowest button on the side of the wall. The doors close, and the elevator slowly drops.

Mark and Samantha loosen their limbs during the hiatus of action. Mark stretches side to side, where Samantha reaches for the sky. They smile and giggle at each other's movements, feeling better about everything. The elevator begins to slow down towards the bottom.

The doors slowly open, unveiling a bright, narrow hallway ahead with doors to the side. At the middle of the hall is a crossroad to another hall, with a guard standing at the end. Mark and Samantha take cover to the side of the elevator, as the guard looks up at the opening doors, figuring the people who came down have already exited. He puts his head back down to his desk, when Mark and Samantha creep out, and walk forward towards him. Mark walks up to the front of the desk, and slams the guards head into the glass top. The guard slips out of his chair, and slides to the ground. "Clear." Mark whispers to Samantha at the crossroad.

"Which way should we go?" Samantha asks Mark. "Wait here." He whispers back. Mark jogs down the hallway, and carefully glances around the corner. An Alphanaut guard is patrolling the area, wearing armor on his arms, legs and chest. Mark turns back and walks low to Samantha. He motions his hand forward to the opposite end of the hall, not saying anything. Samantha waits to meet Mark, as he walks normally in front of the desk towards the next corridor. He glances around less stealthily than the other corner, revealing too much of his head and some of his body for another guard to notice the odd commotion.

The Alphanaut guard walks down the narrow, business-looking hall towards Mark and the front desk. Hugging the corner, Mark and Samantha hear the guards breathing, and wait until he walks close. At the mirrors edge of the corridor, Mark grabs the guard by the back of his neck, and slams him headfirst to the ground. He elbows the nearly human looking guard in the back of the head to subdue him.

"Let's go." Mark whispers after checking the guard for tools and keys. Not finding anything relevant, they hop over the guard and continue down the hall.

At the next corner, Samantha crouches low, and notices a door in the center of the hallway. She turns the corner with Mark, as the two walk towards a high tech door. Samantha touches a button at the side, quickly opening the door. Behind the door, a monster sized guard stands behind a desk, watching security monitors of the building. He hears the door close, and turns around to see Samantha and Mark, standing in the center of the room.

Samantha inches to the right, as Mark stands still. She moves low around the large guards desk as he is walking out, and kicks him in the leg. He lowers down in pain, as Samantha retreats back towards the wall. Mark takes advantage, and moves toward the downed guard. He jumps on top of the desk, and performs an uppercut on the guards jaw, sending him back unconscious to the corner of the control room. The floor shakes as the three hundred pound guard falls down. His keys slide on the floor towards Samantha at the side of the room.

"Those keys might help." Samantha says, pointing to the set after they slide across the floor. She walks to the keys, and scoops them up from the large ring. "Nice, but where do they go?" Mark asks. "It's got to be somewhere close." She responds. The two search the room for a moment, as the large guard lays unconscious.

As they explore, the downed guard from the opposite side of the wall wakes up, and hears the commotion. He investigates the area, turning the corner to the main room. The guard walks in on Mark and Samantha as they obliviously look for another door.

Mark looks back at the hallway to find the guard he originally saw standing outside the doorway. The guard takes out his weapon and points it at Samantha and Mark, switching rapidly between them. "Freeze you two, don't move." He says with authority. Mark and Samantha stand up straight, and look at the funny dressed guard. His gun is no joke, but the ensemble he wears beneath it is not very intimidating.

"Hey, don't shoot. We don't have a problem with you." Mark says to the Alphanaut in a calm tone. "What are you guys doing here?" The guard asks nervously. "Can you help me find my shoes? I don't want to cause any more trouble." Mark reiterates to the Alphanaut. The guard takes a moment to comprehend what the Space Jumper means by shoes. "I heard we weren't supposed to talk about those shoes." The Alphanaut replies. "Can you point me in the right direction? This can end easily for you." Mark threatens the Alphanaut. The guard lowers his weapon, and looks at his unconscious ally in the room.

"Looks like Berto dropped his keys, again. Check the hatch at the side of the room." The guard says to Mark and Samantha. They look over to where the guard is looking, and notices the locked basement on the floor towards the metallic wall. Mark and Samantha say nothing to the guard, and walk quickly to the small lock with the keys. "Space Jumper is here at control, looking for the shoes." The Alphanaut says in his radio device. He gives Mark and Samantha a dirty look, and turns the corner out of the room where he came from.

Mark and Samantha look at each other, and continue to try to open the lock with one of the many keys on the ring. They open the lock and lift the heavy metal hatch, unveiling a lit staircase down several levels. A cool breeze flows from the basement. They look at each other, and move down the steps. Mark leads the way, wielding his flashlight. Samantha creeps close behind, excited for what may be next.

The stairs are cold and dark, with only minor lighting from a set of bulbs on the wall. Nearing the bottom of the steps, Mark looks down a long, lit hallway about a football fields length away. Open corridors line the outer walls to the end of the room, where Mark sees a person holding a pair of shoes with a familiar set of rings around them.

"Hey, those are mine." Mark yells down the hall. The mysterious person stands still for a moment, slowly turns around, and smiles at Mark and Samantha with rotating eyes. "You don't deserve the power." The mysterious person says calmly from far away.

The strange being with blonde, spiky hair and camouflage armor runs down the remainder of the hallway. At the end of the long hall, he throws something on the ground. A small, circular black hole opens up. He gives a final look back at Mark and Samantha, who are running down the long hallway next to the open corridors with barrels stacked to the ceiling against the walls. The mysterious, tattooed wielder of the cool shoes jumps through the black hole, as it immediately disappears behind him. As Mark is about to grab the guard, he escapes with the shoes.

"Nooo!" Mark yells on his knees in front of a raised sanctuary. He cups the air that used to be the black hole. Moments later, Captain Drake and some of the crew from the ship come barging down the steps, and run down the hallway towards Mark. He slowly walks next to Mark, who crouches beneath the remnants of the warp. Drake takes out an empty, glass vial, and scoops some of the air from the black hole inside. He closes a top on the vial, and quickly sticks it in his pocket. Mark remains on the ground, disappointed at how close he came, only to come up with empty feet, once again.

"Let's get back to the ship!" Captain Drake says to the crew. "We got him, Space Jumper." He says down to the sorrowed human. Captain Drake begins to walk down the cold, concrete hallway. The remainder of the crew stop searching the basement, and follow the bearded captain up the steps. "C'mon, Space Jumper, we'll get them." Samantha encourages Mark in the quiet cellar of the Alphanaut base.

Mark is down in the cellar, as Captain Drake hastily walks back up to the ship, carrying the location of Mark's shoes. He is the first one aboard the ship, parked at the main entrance to the front of the dome, as most of the crew follow behind. He walks to the engine room in the ship, and places the vial of black hole air inside a hose on a large, benched machine. The large device absorbs the gas and air from the wormhole, sending it to the computers in the ship. Captain Drake walks up the ship to the pilots seat, and checks the navigation device. With the assistance of the black hole gun, the ship locates the exit path of the wormhole. Captain Drake chuckles at the location, and turns around to watch the crew enter the ship.

Mark and Samantha take a moment longer to exit, as the Space Jumper remains uninspired after everything. The crew watch Mark and Samantha emerge from the dome from the ship, parked at an open lot in front. Mark recognizes the ship after minor adjustments to the damage. The engine looks mostly together, missing a few panels and pieces of metal. Tape is everywhere on the broken ship, securing the shaken parts. The entrance is open, as Mark and Samantha walk inside.

They see Drake and some of the crew in the operations room behind the pilots cabin. Mark and Samantha walk to a pair of open chairs next to the captain, drop their gear to the floor, and plop down with exhaustion.

"So where is he?" Mark asks impatiently. "You're probably not going to like it." Captain Drake replies. A pause surrounds the room, as Drake continues. "He's far away, in the heart of the biggest city in this universe."

"So where did he go?" Mark asks again. "The place is in the Fireball galaxy, on a set of connected planets called Radium." Captain Drake responds. "Not Radium." Samantha sighs to the crew. "Radium is where everyone stays. It's the coolest place in the universe." Captain Drake adds. He sits back in his chair as if ready to drop another bombshell on Mark. "The real problem is our crew is banned from Radium." Drake says to Mark and the crew.

"That explains why he would take the shoes there." Mark responds eagerly. "We can fly the ship over the planets, but you must jump down to the surface." Captain Drake pitches to Mark, observing the eyes of his crew. "You'll need a space helmet, and a parachute." Samantha says to Mark, looking to Drake, who looks back at Samantha with a smile. "Let's get started." Mark says to everyone.

Chapter 5

Fireball

The Space Jumper sits with Samantha and the crew in the crew quarters of the ship. Warping through space, they wait for the word from above to drop in to their next mission. The ship has a few holes in it from the previous warp jump to the mysterious Alphanaut planet. A small breeze flows through the loosely taped holes of the broken wood and metal.

"What's this place like?" Mark asks the crewmembers next to him. "The Fireball galaxy is very much alive. Three core planets and multiple suns orbit Radium in the middle. It is the most powerful set of planets in the universe." Samantha explains. "You guys have vehicles on the ship?" Mark asks the crew. "Yeah, we've got some things, and we see you have that board." One of the crewmembers says to Mark. "Let's start suiting up." Samantha says to Mark and the crew.

Everyone follows Samantha down a spiral staircase through the crew quarters, engine room, and to the garage, where four all terrain vehicles park inside.

"What are those called?" Mark asks random members of the crew, assuming they all know the name. "These are Hedgehogs. They go sort of fast over most solid terrains." A member of Lineage says from ahead, as Mark walks down the final step of the short staircase to the garage. The ATVs have wheels that are larger than the engine and body of the actual vehicles, and can only hold one rider. Mark walks towards a bench to the side of the garage and studies the vehicles.

"You'll need this helmet to breathe, Space Jumper, sorry." Samantha says to Mark, handing him a compact helmet for his head. The helmet is made of a light plastic, with a light blue breathing apparatus in front. Mark removes his bag from his shoulders, and sits on the bench to the side of the spacious garage. He leans down in his seat, and organizes the remaining tools in his bag.

He digs around his gear, realizing he is missing one of his lighters from Earth, also some of his explosive devices. He had around thirty explosives with special EMP attachments obtained from the Cigar galaxy in his home universe, now he has around ten.

Jail was rough on his gear, giving everything a strange smell and feel. He removes the gear from his bag, cuts his losses, and counts his blessings. The Space Jumper takes a deep breath, and reorganizes his belongings as the Lineage crew watches on. Mark's space board is the only thing on the floor in front of him as the ship begins to slow down. The breeze coming from the loosely patched holes makes less noise with the decrease in momentum.

A bright light shines on the outside of the pirate ship, creating heavy glares through the windows. Mark turns away, allowing a moment for his eyes to adjust to the daylight.

"We're here guys. Mount up on the Hedgehog, and get ready." Captain Drake says to Mark and Samantha over the speaker from the pilots cabin.

Emerging from a wormhole of black space with yellow sparks shooting behind, the pirate ship enters the new galaxy via warp. The space is not black, but dark green, as the aura surrounds a magnificent trio of planets connected by a set of bridges. The three planets are different colors within the strange green haze in space. The Eastern planet is blue and purple, while the Northern planet contains multiple shades of green. The South Western planet is a dry yellow and brown. Mark watches the planets emerge, slightly rotating while hanging on to each other.

"I'm driving." Samantha says to Mark who rises from his seat. Of the four vehicles scattered around the garage, Samantha jogs to the one ahead, and climbs into the drivers seat. She activates the Hedgehog, as Mark walks behind. He attaches a special electronic winch to his board, connected to the bumper of the vehicle. The board automatically powers on, and hovers at a head high level over the ground of the ship. The Space Jumper watches his board float in the middle of the air, connected to the four wheeled power outlet. The crew take notice, and watch the space board.

Mark walks close to the board, and uses his hand to touch the metallic top. When his fingers make contact, the board sends a strong jolt of electricity through his body. Mark stands shocked in the ship, forcing the board down to the surface, fighting its anti-magnetic strength. His body vibrates heavily from the shock, yet he remains focused and unfazed. He continues to power the board down to where his foot is able to help keep it on the ground.

The Space Jumper begins to cringe in pain, holding the space board down without his cool shoes. His bare ghost feet react to the board through his janky, rubber shoes. Continuing to hold down the anti magnetic strength of the board for a moment, Mark's rubber boot begins to slide away from the vapors shooting from his foot.

His phantom foot moves and muscles out of the shoe, blasting a bright white aura across the ship. His ghost foot continues to hold down the powered board, low enough to turn the power off by hand with the button on the side. The board drops down a couple of feet, and sits on the floor of the ship.

The crew look around at each other, as Mark stands on one shoe, and a white vapor. He walks awkwardly to the shoe at the side of the floor, and picks it up.

"Looks like I don't need these." He says, looking at the shoe. He walks to another nearby bench, and removes his other shoe from his foot. The white vapor shoots light out strong from his ankles. He throws the shoes in his bag, takes a deep breath, and looks at the board.

"Don't forget this, Space Jumper. I think you'll need it." A member of Lineage says to Mark, handing him a paper-thin backpack. "What is it?" Mark asks the crewmember. "That's your chute." He says.

"Oh, you got me there." Mark says with gloom to the crewmember, as he puts the bag over his backpack.

"So how is this going down?" Mark asks the crewmembers next to him. "Samantha's Hedgehog is equipped with a similar parachute to yours. When she activates the chute for the Hedgehog, yours should open as well. Stay hooked in to your space board and float down to the surface." The crewmember explains with ease. The same crewmember walks around the Hedgehog to look at Samantha and Mark. "You're going to be noticed immediately, so you've got to be on the move upon landing." The light-skinned crewmember says to the both of them. Mark puts his headphones on, and connects his tablet to Lineage's radio system.

"We've tracked a rough location of the target. He's on the Eastern planet of Radium." Captain Drake says over the ships radio. "This sounds like fun. I'm ready to go." Samantha replies to the crew through microphone communication.

Placing his helmet on his head, the Space Jumper synchronizes his glasses to his tablet for the new world below. A fast-paced guitar song with a ton of emotion strums through his earbuds. His scarf sits mellow and lifeless under his jacket without the power of his cool shoes. The crew follows Mark's lead, and dawn their personalized helmets, when an alarm rings around the ship.

The bay doors in the back begin to open, unveiling the trio of colorful, connected planets within the bright, green space. Everything good to go, Mark holds on to a metal bar connected to the winch connecting to his board. He hooks his ghostly feet into the space board, and powers it back on by pressing the button.

His hair stands up from the jolts of lightning shooting from the board. The hairs on his legs stand as he quickly rises over the ground, hovering around five feet above the floor of the garage.

The busted bay door slowly opens nearly halfway down, when Samantha accelerates the Hedgehog. The wheels skid over the metal surface, and roll quickly out of the ship, jumping the vehicle off the receding bay door ramp to space. The Hedgehog floats in space for a moment above the trio of colorful planets.

Mark holds the metal bar connected to the winch, maintaining slack. He lowers his level, maintaining a rough electronic shock across his legs and body. Sensing the end of the rope, he quickly slingshots out of the ship, riding off the same ramp Samantha hit with the Hedgehog. The board has a familiar magnetic traction in space, as Mark adjusts his vapors. Samantha carries momentum down through space, as the nose of the Hedgehog tips nearly vertical.

The outer space is warm, as Mark follows the rear lights of the Hedgehog on his board. Samantha steers the Hedgehog through low gravity, optimizing thrusters beneath the vehicle towards East Radium, blue and purple, marked on her map.

Her speed increases tremendously as the vehicle plummets. Mark maintains a natural connection to the space board through the vapor from his legs, and the electronics from the board. He stays centered, falling through space. A warm breeze flows through his layers of clothes. He almost believes his cool shoes are on, but feels only the empty pain of them not being there.

Samantha follows the path displayed inside the Hedgehog, veering the ATV through space to break through the atmosphere of the targeted Eastern planet. Dark purple clouds fade away around the vehicle, unveiling a variety of water, land, and vegetation. The grass looks green, where the dirt appears naturally brown. The water is blue and purple, surrounded by lakes and rivers scattered across the globe. The trio of planets appear more natural as the scale from space reduces, giving clearer perspective to everything.

The weather is warm and clear as day on East Radium. Samantha looks over the back of the Hedgehog at Mark, and gives him a thumb up. Moments later, she activates the parachute on the vehicle, activating Mark's chute at the same time. Warm air and heavy clouds flow up the curved parachutes, slowing their drop speed before the ground below. Mark feels the weight of the board begin to slip from his vapored lock. He grabs the metal board with his hand, and tucks it close, embracing the heavy shock on his skin through his gloves.

Samantha gently drops the Hedgehog into an open canyon, broad and beautiful, with trees and wildlife everywhere. The Space Jumper holds the board tight, as his parachute drops him slowly to the ground, forcing weight back up to his space board. Upon touchdown, the parachutes attached to Mark and the Hedgehog detach, and fly away.

Everything is rough, pointy, and natural on the new planet, from the high walls of the canyon, to the rocky ground below. Mark's heart begins to race as Samantha speeds up the Hedgehog over the ground. He struggles to stand, maintaining stability with all of the speed, wobbling his unsteady ghost feet on the board. With a deep breath, Mark remembers his skills, and veers the space board side to side to manage stability.

The ground is sandy and rocky, light in color and density. The Hedgehog crushes over the ground and sand dunes ahead. It climbs up steep hills with fantastic torque and acceleration, as Mark cruises behind on the board. They move up and down hills and ridges, jumping over gaps in the sand with speed. Jagged rocks spear out of the ground, as the Hedgehog either climbs over, or moves around them. Samantha controls the tempo of the Hedgehog, which dictates the Space Jumper's safety behind.

The Hedgehog hops over sandy hurdles ahead with its thick and durable wheels, climbing over the toughest terrain. Mark holds the slacked rope behind, floating over the same hurdles with his space board. No signs of life come into their path, as they trek forward to the last known location of the shoes. The walls of the canyon they ride between grow larger beyond the nature of water and trees, as they speed ahead.

The Hedgehog catches air ahead, and drops down into a dune of sand, when Samantha and Mark notice a mile high hill in their path. Samantha accelerates the vehicle, and begins to move up the steep and smooth sand hill.

Mark holds the slack, staying low on the steep incline. The Hedgehog runs fast to the peak of the hill.

Samantha controls the speed off a small jump, leading to a much larger jump. She lands the vehicle on sand, and rides the speed down another small hill, where she further gasses the Hedgehog. Mark hits the jump moments later and catches a cool air, holding the board close to his legs with his hand to the downpour of sand below.

Samantha drives forward, and hits the next ramp off the large cliff, catching immense airtime forward. Mark holds on to the rope after the previous jump while holding on to the board with his hand, embracing the painful shock on his body. He hovers high, following the Hedgehog off the ramp, trailing its path down in mid-air. The air is warm in the clear day as Mark and Samantha fall off the sandy mountain. Samantha steers the vehicle down to safety, balancing acceleration to land on a curved sand hill.

Mark's trajectory alters in mid-air when the vehicle lands on the sand. He follows the slack of rope towards the wall of the mountain. He looks down face first as his board forces him outward. He rides the transition of mountain to hill, speeding forward down the sandy ramp. The Hedgehog moves fast for its size, as Samantha struggles to maintain balance, steering down the sand.

She gradually slows the heavy, singular vehicle, regaining stability as the ground begins to even out. She carries good speed forward. Mark struggles to maintain stability on the board as the remaining sand blows plenty of debris forward. His special glasses from his allies on Andromeda protect his eyes from the sand during the descent.

He slams down the tail of the board to slow the speed of his momentum, and some of the momentum from the Hedgehog. Sand shoots down the transition of mountain to grass like fireworks, as the Space Jumper breaks a little bit of speed.

The two move forward across a dirt path leading to a grassy and forested area ahead. The vegetation is lush, healthy, and natural, as the forest ahead is a relief for Mark, recently coming from a planet with metal swords for branches. Green bushes and trees are to the left and right of the wide dirt path, as the Hedgehog rolls around forty miles per hour over the mix of dirt and grass. They ride through a beaten path straight ahead for a couple of miles.

The wind blows through Samantha's hair, as she checks to make sure Mark is still behind. He hangs on over the space board, keeping everything up and right.

Samantha rolls the Hedgehog over a dirt hill, revealing a tall city in the distance ahead. Trees continue to surround the road, but subside when the large canyon walls begin to lower around them. The city becomes tunnel vision through the wide canyon, from the outside moving in. Mark's eyebrows raise as he peaks over the hill to see the city, a landmark on the foreign planet. The trees reduce in size and population.

Samantha follows the path forward to a large, metallic bridge, with a deep drop, and waterfalls to the side. The bridge spans miles across the width of the canyon. On both sides of the bridge are two waterfalls at different heights, with two different looks.

Mark begins to cross the bridge behind the Hedgehog, when time slows down on Radium. Flickers of water from the waterfall hit his uniform, hitting his face where he tastes the water, at least to his knowledge of what water actually is. A strong static shocks his face from the mix of moisture and high voltage coming from his board. Glares of light strike through the water at the falls, creating a mix of colors, as Mark takes in the pleasance of the planet's natural beauty. The bridge holds strong beneath his board as he hovers over with ease. The air remains warm, as all seems well.

The Hedgehog crosses the bridge as Mark soon follows on the hovering bungie board. They travel down another dirt path through the forest.

The vegetation ahead reduces to plains, as the canyon heights drop towards ground level. The Hedgehog rumbles along dirt as Mark's space board maintains height and speed with ease over the bumpy ground. The land is plain and deserted to the left and right as the day remains bright. The trees to the side lower and disappear, as the trio of connecting planets grows present beyond the horizon. Mark's heart skips a beat, stumbling upon a place so beautiful.

Since landing, it appears little time has passed, as Mark and Samantha approach the enlarging city fast over the wrinkled terrain. The wheels of the Hedgehog absorb the rippled distortions from dirt on the way forward, as Mark bounces up and down quickly while pulling from the vehicle. Multiple suns over the trio of planets bash Mark in the face, as his prescription glasses adjust like a camera's lens.

About two miles out from the city, a large highway circles around the buildings ahead. Vehicles drive fast around the raised, grey highway. Some of the vehicles hover, while some have wheels. The inhabitants of the planet appear to jump over cars with wheels, to land safely back on the road.

Mark feels Samantha slow the Hedgehog down as they take shade under the highway from the high sun. Organized streets lead between the buildings made of glass, concrete, and metal. The buildings vary in texture, but grow in size.

The Space Jumper raises the nose of the board as the Hedgehog parks next to a large skyscraper. He crouches low, and flicks the kill switch on the side of the board, dropping it immediately to solid ground. Mark slides slow on dirt and rubble. His knees shake as he hops off the board.

Samantha jumps out of the Hedgehog to her left, and begins to collect her gear from a storage box to the side. Mark unhinges his board from the winch, and connects it back to his bag. The winch automatically rolls back into the Hedgehog. Mark hooks the board back to his bag, and walks toward Samantha on the sidewalk.

"That was fun." He says, rubbing his hands together to create friction. "I don't think anyone noticed the drop." Samantha says to Mark, organizing her gear. "Where do we go from here?" Mark asks. "The map says we should move forward into the city." Samantha replies, slamming the storage door closed on the Hedgehog. "Let's get my shoes back." Mark says enthusiastically to Samantha. He stands on the ground, shooting vapor from his feet.

The city is an oasis in the middle of a broad desert, away from the mountainous canyons. The buildings are tall, scraping the sky. Pedestrians begin to emerge from street corners and businesses. The inhabitants of the planet appear human, but have oval shaped heads. They wear fancy, neutral colored suits with sharp dress shoes, where the women wear colorful dresses. The city is high tech, and modern. Vehicles begin to drive down the streets as Mark and Samantha move forward. The vehicles are small and sleek, ready to transport people around Radium.

Mark and Samantha walk forward through the warm city streets towards a roaring intersection of fast moving vehicles. "Be careful around these cars." Mark says to Samantha. He waits for an opportunity to move across the vehicles speeding down the street. Moving forward, Mark dodges cars in multiple lanes. The drivers of the vehicles do not seem to care about pedestrians, as they continue to drive fast. At one point near the middle of the street, Mark jumps over a vehicle with the little strength he has in his feet. He lands to a roll at the sidewalk ahead, where Samantha is waiting for him. He looks up to her from a kneel with a confused look on his face, when she offers her hand as a car comes roaring down the road towards him.

Samantha pulls Mark up from the street to the safety of the sidewalk. She pulls too hard, causing their gear, her skates, and Mark's space board to crash over each other on the dirty sidewalk. Mark continues to hold her hand as they collapse on the ground. Not caring about the traffic around them, Mark looks down at Samantha, and smiles close. She looks to Mark, and smiles back. He maintains grip of her hand, and pulls her up to her feet as he rises to a stand. She kneels for a moment, and quickly pulls her skates from behind her bag. She sits on the ground, and ties the straps around her feet. A tall skyscraper stands next to the sidewalk, with a paved road to her left.

"Good idea." Mark says, as Samantha stands upright on her special blades. "Use your board Space Jumper. Try and stay above the traffic." She says, circling around Mark as he stands on the ground. She rolls a few laps around the Space Jumper, as he takes his board off his back. He stands above his metallic plank, allowing a moment for the vapor on his feet to synchronize. He crouches down, and presses the power button.

Hostility from the environment inspires the Space Jumper's soul as he sends shockwaves of power to his ghost feet, sparking the board. Danger becomes irrelevant to him when he has to defend his life.

Rising up from the cold and dense ground, Mark stabilizes the space board in the air, maintaining a safe height and angle. The board pushes him up, requiring more strength from his legs, and the feet he does not have. Samantha watches him control the board, as her skin glows with the power of her rollerblades. "Let's keep moving." She says, checking the map on her mobile device.

Traffic continues to roar through the intersections of East Radium for several blocks. Mark hovers back towards the previous street, and stabilizes level. He forces the board down to increase momentum forward past Samantha. Forcing down harder, he releases tension from his legs before the street to hop up using the antimagnetic force. He floats above the street, gaining enough momentum to rise over the traffic. He lands across the street on the sidewalk, carrying momentum while picking up speed.

Samantha rolls her blades back to the end of the first street, and glides fast towards the curb. She crouches down and jumps high in the air over the street with rushing cars. Air flows through her brown hair as she flies forward. She lands smooth on her wheels, on the opposite side of the street. Mark continues ahead, jumping his space board over the dangerous blocks of traffic. Samantha carries momentum over the sidewalk, and jumps over the street.

The bleak buildings to the side of the street block what really is going on in the city. After several blocks of street jumping, Mark reaches a fenced building, similar looking to the building from the previous galaxy. He slows his space board, powering it down over the sidewalk. The board has a low battery, not being able to recharge with the power from Mark's cool shoes. He takes cover next to a building on the same block as the fence. He checks behind to find Samantha flying in over the rushing cars. She looks at Mark taking cover at the edge of the building ahead, noticing the similarity to the one on the other planet. She slows momentum on her skates, and quickly joins him at the side of the building.

"This building looks familiar." She whispers, rolling next to him. "We're heading in the right direction. Let's check it out." Mark replies in a whisper. "There's no way you can get over that wall." Samantha says softly, taking a seat on the dense ground. She looks up at the tall metal fence, beginning to unstrap her skates from her feet. She ties them together, and slings them around her bag, standing up next to Mark.

"I'm thinking we take a more direct approach." He replies, leaving the cover of the building with a smile. Mark casually walks down the sidewalk with his board on his back. Samantha follows a short distance behind. The building has a rectangular base with a large dome on top, not as camouflaged as the one in the forest. The dome in the city is more civilian friendly to the eye. It is obviously a high security place with a blacked out dome. Above the dome is a set of walkways connecting the buildings and skyscrapers in the area together.

Approaching the metallic gate ahead, Mark walks casually to a pair of male security guards. The guards take a moment to discover it is the Space Jumper. Mark notices the guards turn their heads to the radios on their chest. They reach for their guns, where Mark quickly does the same with his. He quickly fires four small shots at the legs of the guards, forcing them down and out in pain.

Mark continues his pace forward, walking through the guards on the ground. Alarms surround the domed building with a horn-like sound. Samantha follows Mark with her gun in hand. The Space Jumper walks forward to the entrance with a determined look on his face. He stands in front of a pair of heavy metallic doors, and tinkers with the radius of the particle accelerator on his gun. He sets the diaphragm to fire large sized bullets, aims at the center of the door, and pulls the trigger.

The heavy metal doors crash to the ground inside, and slide across the floor, where smoke and debris cover the entrance. Mark walks inside the building, noticing a significant difference to the interior compared to the other dome. The first floor is a small atrium with several rooms behind doors. A set of stairs are to the right of the atrium.

"Let's move up." He says to Samantha as she enters the building behind him. She nods to Mark, where he nods back. They move to the stairs and climb the flight up one floor. Mark and Samantha turn a corner on the second floor to find a group of Alphanauts standing in front of an oval map of the solar system. The dome is a planetarium, displaying a map of planets and stars. The guards hear Mark and Samantha scurry into the room from the corner, and raise their flashlights and guns at them. Mark reaches into his pocket and holds on to his new shielding device taken from the Alphanauts. He presses the button to activate a force field around his body.

The shielded Space Jumper takes out his hatchet, and runs to the first guard in the pack, taking several shots to his head and body. The lasers fired at him deal no damage, and ripple off the shield. Mark uses his hatchet to cut through the first guards armor, slicing a gash on his shooting arm. He continues forward across the floor of the planetarium to the second guard. Mark crouches low, and slices her leg down.

He activates the special attachment on his blade that expands the pointed tip to a large, blue blade. The hatchet transforms into a glowing axe. Mark uses the blade to deflect a shot back to another guard. He throws the hatchet like a boomerang over the floor, and over a guardrail, hitting one of the Alphanauts on his helmet, knocking him down and unconscious. The boomerang circles back quickly, and returns to his hand, synchronizing locations with his special glasses.

One guard remains behind a set of boxes at the end of the planetarium. Mark walks to the guard as his shield drops, leaving him vulnerable. The guard aims his gun at the Space Jumper in a panic. Before he pulls the trigger, Samantha fires a laser at him to knock him back into a rolling chair in the room.

Mark turns around and looks at Samantha out of breath. Her gun smokes after the precise shot. Mark relaxes, and stands up straight. He sits in the first level of seats in the planetarium. He sits for a moment, and looks up at the fake stars on the ceiling. He takes his time reflecting on everything he was and could be. The stars clear his head of the things around him, except Samantha, who he owes the universe to, who is a distinct part of his universe.

Noise erupts from above, and moves down like a breeze to the floor of the planetarium. Samantha looks up as Mark remains lost in reflection. She notices another set of guards emerge from a door at the ceiling, connected to a maintenance walkway. She opens fire at the guards with her laser gun, the boa constrictor. Mark continues to look up at the display of lights in the planetarium, lost in thought. He sees Samantha's shots soar over the room, paranoid if it is a projection of a shooting star, or an actual laser.

Mark snaps out of his tranquil trance, and hears the exchange of gunfire between Samantha and the fresh guards. He crouches low, and circles around the remainder of the planetarium to meet Samantha at another set of stairs leading up. She shoots one of the guards down the stairs, as several more move on the raised walkway. Mark takes out his gun, and twists the particle accelerator to shoot smaller bullets. He aims the gun, tracking the movement above, taking time to steady his breath. He pulls the trigger, shooting one of the Alphanaut guards off the raised walkway.

The Alphanaut crashes hard to the floor as Mark and Samantha begin to move up the steps. One of the last guards moves down the steps, meeting Mark in the middle. They grapple for position, as Mark forces his gun out of the Alphanaut's hand. The guard attempts to punch Mark with a straight arm, but misses. Mark ducks down to dodge the punch. He quickly kicks the guard sideways off the middle part of the stairs. The guard falls down, and crashes through a computer console at the center of the planetarium. The Alphanaut crushes the technology that creates the galactic map overhead.

Mark and Samantha stay close, moving up to the top of the steps, as the room turns dark. They move forward across the dark catwalk towards the open door leading outside. On the way to the door, Mark is able to see the final Alphanaut guard struggling to find his way around the darkness. He elbow checks the guard in the side of the head as they creep by, knocking him off the scaffold. The guard flips over the guardrail, and falls to the ground. Mark reaches for the door before the guard has time to hit the floor.

Mark and Samantha emerge outside at the top of the planetarium. The weather is warm as they stand at the beginning of a metal bridge connected to the center of a building across the street. The bridge is rusty, with unsteady hinges connecting to a dangerous brick opening in the building from the concrete roof of the planetarium.

Samantha leads the way towards the bridge, holding her mobile device up with a map of Radium. They step up to the bridge and begin to jog across. Mark continues to bear a tremendous limp in his step, spewing his soul and strength through his empty feet. Samantha holds her gun, the boa constrictor, and looks down at the street from the center of the bridge. She pays no mind to the ordinary nature of civilization.

She crouches down off the bridge, and approaches the brick opening in the wall. She holds her gun up in search of danger, sounds, and smells. Mark clambers down from the bridge behind and jogs to the brick opening. They slowly walk inside the building to a dark wooden hallway. A set of stairs lead up a floor, and down a floor at the end of the hallway.

"Let's keep moving." Samantha whispers to Mark. "Let's go." Mark replies quickly. Samantha crouches low, holding her gun up stealthily. She stays low, moving forward across the old, wooden hallway. The interior is faded and deoxygenized.

Samantha is determined to go for the shoes, where Mark stands at the stairs leading down. Samantha realizes Mark has options, and checks back, noticing he is making his way down the stairs.

Samantha remains low, and creeps to a sliver in the wall that meets the stairs. Mark looks up at Samantha and puts his finger over his mouth, indicating silence as he walks casually down the stairs with no weapons equipped. The wooden steps and walls have dim bulbs of light around the hall, indicating deep decay from the warm air outside. Towards the bottom of the steps, the natural wood begins to rejuvenate to a considerable glow.

Samantha remains up high, and walks towards the end of her hallway. She stays chill on the wall, and awaits danger.

Mark turns the corner at the bottom of the steps, and walks down the hallway of apartments. Looking for an opening to add closure, the Space Jumper studies the cracks in the doors, as he moves quietly across the floor.

His gear remains dull and lifeless without the electric spark and synchronization of the cool shoes. The lack of spark creates silence as he moves forward to the next set of stairs down. He walks towards the first door in the hallway and listens to what may be going on inside.

Nobody is home, as Mark continues towards the stairs. He listens to the second door in the hallway for a moment, and walks to the stairs, where he quickly turns the corner to creep his way down.

Moving down another floor, the wooden interior grows more luxurious. At the end of the hall is an open door, glowing of golden decadence. Furniture lines the interior of the hallway, with trims of gold and red. Mark cautiously moves past a couch, and an end table, towards the open door down the hall. A set of stairs lead down, most likely to a more luxurious interior than the current floor. The Space Jumper is too intrigued at what is behind the golden door number one.

He approaches the corner of the door, and angles his head slightly around the wall. Inside the room is a clean apartment structure with a lovely view of the plains beyond the city. The large canyon grows to the left, where mountains linger further in the horizon. The interior of the room is a marbled white, with plenty of stone on the floor and walls. The furniture looks comfortable, and expensive. The person who lives here lives a comfortable life.

On a table inside of the apartment, sits a pair of high tech gloves with circles in the palms. Mark focuses his eyes with his special lenses to the prize on the fancy table.

Because the building connects to the planetarium run by Alphanauts, Mark finds it morally neutral to take something from them, of what they have stole from him.

He surveys the gloves behind the doorway, when a couple of wealthy business aliens walk towards the window at the end of the room. They talk about something inaudible to Mark as he crouches low, and enters the room. He moves to cover himself behind a loveseat in front of the table with the gloves.

The two aliens continue to talk a numbers game, as Mark stays low. He moves slowly, anticipating the words the two aliens are saying. He blocks his body with as much of the low sitting table as he can. Staying low, he moves against the table, and snatches the gloves from the smooth surface.

He swoops the loot, and retreats slowly behind the seat. The two aliens at the broad window continue to talk at a high volume while the Space Jumper catches his breath. As Mark sits behind the chair, blocking his body, he attempts to merge his powerless gloves with the new ones. His fingers glide through rigid friction between the two sets of gloves.

Palm to palm, the new gloves have an advanced, protective layer around the fibrous material he wears. He looks at his hands, feeling a chill around his body. Utilizing friction, he rubs his hands together with the new gloves attached, and powers the palms within the new outer pair.

Rings around his palms glow bright, with a miniature fire in each hand. The warmth of the gloves power his spirit ahead of his cold face. He remains low, and moves across the floor, with the new gloves burning holes in the surface. He continues to crawl slowly, awkwardly, and quietly, swooping his body to the side of the room. He quickly moves out of the apartment to the gold lined hallway. As he turns the corner from the door, he clenches a fist with his hand, accidentally powering fire in his palm.

Heat in the Space Jumper's hand engulfs into a flame before he finally notices the fire. He aims his hand around the corner of the hallway at a plant sitting on an end table. The fire from the Space Jumper's hand burns the plant to cinder. The fire from Mark's hand dissipates, but continues to empower the circular rings of the gloves. "Fire!" Mark whispers as he exits the floor towards the rising steps at the end of the hall.

He turns the corner, and climbs up the dense wood to a rougher, dryer floor. He continues up to the next level, with goods in hand. The new gloves heat his hands, as he cruises up and across the floor of the old hallway. More decayed than the previous floor, Mark continues to move towards Samantha, hoping she is waiting at the top of the stairs.

Controlling the fire in his hands, he moves as fast as he can through the halls of the apartment, up the stairs. He runs through the floors of the building to stairs at the end of the hallways, quickly turning and rising up. Samantha stands at the wall at the end of the hall with her finger pointed over her mouth. Mark continues to rise up the stairs at a slow and cautious pace, noticing her motion with his new fire gloves and spirit feet.

Samantha points up, motioning to the floor above. The floor creaks with the movement of people or things in the hallway. Samantha holds her gun in hand, as Mark begins to approach her. He looks at his hands, as the circular fire raises and lowers at the strength of his fist, creating a fire less dense, and quite intense. He motions Samantha to stay, and let him take the lead with the new fire attachment on hand.

Mark walks close to Samantha, and looks deep in her eyes. The fire in his hands burns close to the skin on her leg, as he guides himself up the steps. He cautiously walks up the steps as Samantha follows close behind. Mark rises towards the next floor, one-step at a time. At the top, he notices more enemies dangerously close at an arms length away.

The Alphanaut guards are quickly making their way down the building, when Mark turns the corner at the top of the steps. He raises his hand with the new gloves, and clenches a fireball in his palm. He throws the ball of hot energy at the guard, igniting his gear. The guard rolls around on the wall to try to suffocate the flames, but finds little relief. Mark walks forward to the guard behind trying to help his friend, and punches him in the face. The first guard rolls around on the ground to extinguish the flame. He remains on the ground as white and black smoke rises from his burnt body and gear.

Mark and Samantha continue forward over the downed guards on the top floor. At the end of the hall, a similar opening to the floor below connects a sky bridge to another separate building. Mark continues to take the lead, moving forward across the narrow, metal bridge. Alphanauts begin to pour out of the building ahead. Four guards stand at the end of the bridge, and begin to shoot heavy projectiles across.

Mark puts his hand in his pocket, and activates his new shield upgrade. The energy covers his body the moment bullets make contact. Samantha takes cover behind Mark, using him as a human shield, as they continue forward to the building. She uses her gun to shoot two of the Alphanauts at the right time. The remaining two guards approach the center of the rusty bridge. Mark's shield loses strength, with the guards at arms length.

The Space Jumper ducks beneath a punch, and dodges a kick from the guard, stepping backwards. He clenches a fist to load a flame in his hand. He unleashes a fiery hook to the Alphanauts face, knocking him off the tall building. The guard falls down and slams hard on the ground, far below. Mark finishes the combo with a kick to the second guard approaching behind. The kick forces the Alphanaut back to the start of the bridge.

Mark's legs continue to weaken after all of the action. Together, Mark and Samantha walk to end of the bridge over the downed Alphanaut agents, high and low. They walk into the new building, colored with a different interior and design from the opposite skyscraper. They continue forward to walk up a set of steps at the end of the hall. They move up another set of steps to the next floor, where at the top of the steps, another pair of Alphanauts guard the room ahead.

Upon noticing Samantha and the Space Jumper, the Alphanaut agent runs into the room at the end of hall, at the end of the line. Mark and Samantha attack the single, scared guard outside of the room, knocking him down. Mark and Samantha glance at each other, and follow the guard into the room. They move into the building to find another lovely view outside. A group of guards with guns, mixing of males and females, are inside the apartment. The Alphanauts aim their large weapons at the intruders, and open fire.

Mark takes cover behind a green couch in front of the living area. Samantha moves to an edge in the wall and takes cover. She holds her gun tight in her green hands, and waits for an opportunity to strike. Mark holds his gun, and checks his bullets while being shot at by the enemy.

The apartment is warm colored, with luscious upholstery scattered around. Feathers and cloth fly into the air from damaged tables, chairs, and seats. Mark looks up at Samantha, standing next to him at the end of the wall, and waits for movement, or silence.

With silence, he looks up from his torn cover, and shoots three quick, large shots at an Alphanaut enemy by the window. The first shot hits the large glass window behind the guard, shattering it into thousands of pieces. The second and third shot hit the guard in her body, sending her flying out of the opening. She falls back and down into the lovely view behind.

Two guards to the right of the room, including the guard from outside, rush Mark behind the couch. Samantha fires a shot from the boa constrictor, incapacitating the closest enemy with an electric shock. Mark rises up, and loads fire into a punch at the second guards body, knocking him into the second guard behind, making him lose his weapon. The guards fumble around the apartment, as Samantha runs ahead to finish them off. She kicks the stunned guard in the face, putting him to sleep, and uses her hands to force the second guards head into the floor. The room is clear, as Mark and Samantha catch their breath.

A single door is at the end of the room with an emergency bar in the center, indicating it must go outside. Mark kicks the bar on the door, revealing a covered bridge with another door at the end. The bridge is glass, surrounding a wide, red carpet.

A pair of guards sit on furniture on the bridge. Mark moves forward, not looking at the Alphanauts. Samantha follows close behind, and quickly shoots the two guards down to knock them out. Mark moves to the door at the end of the short bridge, and kicks it in.

The metallic emergency door slams into the wall behind, where Mark walks into a similarly luxurious apartment room. An Alphanaut guard sits in front of a television with headphones covering his ears. He plays some kind of game on his TV, unaware of the intruders in his space. Mark and Samantha look at each other for a second, and continue to sneak around the guards sights. They quietly exit the room at the opposite side to avoid a potential fight.

In a new building on Radium, Mark walks out of the room on the top floor to a hallway, finding another Alphanaut guard on patrol. Mark sneaks behind the guard, and elbows him in the back of the head, knocking him down a set of stairs. The guard falls down the steps like a sack of potatoes, as Mark and Samantha watch the calamity from the top. They wait a moment, using the noise as bait to lure other potential guards. They hear the jingle jangle of heavy gear running towards the commotion below. A pair of guards crouch next to their fallen comrade, and look up the steps. Both Mark and Samantha aim their weapons down at them. They fire separate shots, taking out the two guards, with one attack violently removing an arm. Samantha's attacks remain nonviolent. The guards fall to the ground at the bottom of the steps.

Moving down, Mark jumps over the bodies and a small pool of red blood on the ground. Together, Mark and Samantha move down the new apartment. They follow another set of steps down, continuing to follow the path ahead. They move across a vacant hallway down another set of stairs. Continuing the trend, they move down the apartment.

On a new floor, Samantha points to a sign on the wall that indicates an exit is nearby. They move forward across another longer hallway towards the exit sign. The sign tells them to move up a separate set of steps. They progress up wooden steps to find another vacant hallway with an opening to another bridge. The bridge moves upwards and across at a deceiving angle.

Mark moves to the start of the bridge at the end of the hallway. Samantha follows behind, observing everything around her. The bridge starts moving up, but straightens out a short distance later. As Mark moves forward up the slant of the bridge, a pair of Alphanauts emerge from the opposite end. Heavily geared, the guards carry electrified batons. Mark walks at a brisk pace towards the Alphanauts, annoyed at their continued presence. Not carrying any weapons, Mark approaches the guards, and awaits an attack. The two Alphanauts look at each other, and swing their batons at Mark at the same time.

Reading the attacks, the Space Jumper activates his new shield attachment. The electronic batons of the enemies strike Mark's head on both sides. His shield deflects the attacks, sending an explosive shockwave through the two Alphanaut's batons. The guards fry to the side from the strong force, repelling them off the side of the bridge. They fall at the same time, at the same velocity down to the ground. Mark stands still for a moment as the shield around him crumbles and disintegrates.

Mark looks back to Samantha and smiles. "Let's keep moving Space Jumper, we are almost there." Samantha says. Mark concludes his sarcastic smile, and nods in affirmation. Together, they move across the warm, open bridge to the new building ahead.

Crossing the bridge, entering the building, Mark notices another bridge ahead at the end of the hall, connecting to another planetarium. The planetarium has a much bigger dome than the last, providing a larger secret inside.

The weather remains clear and bright, as Mark and Samantha emerge from the apartment building. A pair of Alphanaut snipers stand perched on a walkway around the top of the dome. Mark crouches low, and motions to Samantha to do the same.

Staying low, they move over the small bridge towards the raised walkway at the dome. The walkway circles the entire large dome, as Mark moves left, and Samantha stays still. Flanking the snipers, Mark circles the outside of the dome to reach the opposite side without notifying the enemies. Mark looks to Samantha on the other side of the dome, when the guard closest to him turns, and notices him. Mark quickly rushes the guard, and wrestles his large electronic sniper rifle away from him. Samantha shoots the other sniper with her boa constrictor, knocking him to the cold, rusty floor of the walkway.

Mark forces the snipers gun off the building, clanging off the side of the dome to land in a bush below. The sniper is strong, and pushes Mark over the edge of the walkway. Before falling down, Mark grabs a safety pipe on the walkway, and hangs on for dear life as his legs dangle in the air. The guard takes action, and tries to stomp on Mark's hands. Mark moves his hands at the right time for a couple of kicks. He looks around to Samantha, who runs over the raised walkway towards the guard. She jumps up with momentum, and kicks the Alphanaut sniper off the raised walkway. He falls into a grouping of plants below. Samantha helps pull Mark up from the edge. They dust themselves off, and check the environment. Everything is quiet, as Samantha takes out her mobile device.

"I think we're here." Samantha says. "These doors lead inside the building." Mark replies calmly out of breath, pointing to one of the two doors on the dome. He catches his breath and stays low, moving towards the metal door closest to him. Samantha crouches low, and stays close. Mark pushes a lever, and opens the door to the top of the dome.

Mark and Samantha quickly walk into the building, and close the door behind them, turning invisible in the dark. They crouch low over transparent metallic rafters, shadowed in darkness to maintain ambience for the stage below. As the light grows, the indoor coliseum unveils a lecture hall. The room is filled with around twenty or thirty people, all circled around a familiar face who stares at a familiar pair of shoes sitting on a table, with lights pointed down at them.

Mark continues to circle around the rafters above to get a better perspective. The darkness cloaks him as he cautiously moves forward. Samantha stays near the door behind a crucial spot in the rafters. Mark is hunting for a suitable spot to drop down to the stage, hoping the shoes below have the power to bring him back to life.

Centered at a suitable spot, Mark sits on the rafters, and listens to the lecture about to begin. The presenter is the same spiked hair military goon Lineage has been chasing across several galaxies. He may or may not have noticed the Space Jumper sitting above, looking down at the stage.

"He calls these cool shoes. They connect to the host to a point where they neurologically familiarize. The air they breathe, the smells of their surroundings, and tastes of the universe all go through these shoes. These shoes are a shield from space, providing too much power to the owner. Our job here today, is to break these things down, and utilize that power." The spiky haired lecturer says to the audience. Everyone in the room smiles in anticipation to get to work.

Samantha slowly walks on the high-rise towards Mark, where he feels the vibrations of the situation. He climbs to his feet to clamber over the guardrail. He activates his board in his hand, and looks at Samantha for a moment.

"Let's party." He says to her, holding his electrified board forward in his hand. He jumps from the balcony down towards his shoes. Samantha leans over the rail to watch.

Mark interrupts the break in the lecture, dropping in on his board to provide comfort on his already injured legs and ghost feet. He bounces slightly on the flat surface in front of the stage at the end of the lecture desk, right next to his shoes. He maintains an uncanny stillness, quickly deactivating the low powered board, as he slings it to his back.

"Well, look who it is everyone. The Space Jumper, in the flesh, coming to take his shoes back." The blonde, spiked haired military person says with volume. The audience watches the two perspectives openly, not advancing to action. The good favor leans towards Mark.

"I need my shoes back." Mark says, recovering from the tall fall, and all of the tall falls from his past. He stands motionless, with his hands in his jacket pocket. His index finger gently hovers a sensation over the button of the shield, hoping the enemies do not take notice.

"You think these are your shoes?" The spiked haired military person asks Mark, looking to the audience of students and scientists, with a few business people mixed around the lot of guards.

"Yeah, you can't just take things that you don't think belong to someone." The Space Jumper says in frustration, getting comfortable on stage, constantly watching his shoes.

"Do you think you can just, master the universe wearing these? Nice try, there are rules to space, Space Jumper." The lead speaker says casually to Mark.

"You think I don't know that? You should talk to the ones who plan to harm the universe. My intentions have always been clean." Mark replies, moving slightly closer to his shoes. The crowd sits patiently behind and around the center of the stage, where Mark and the spiked haired Alphanaut circle the shoes.

"I've read your rap sheet, Space Jumper. You think what you are doing is good, but you are actually ruining centuries of organization." He says to Mark, trying to persuade him to give his shoes over.

"Good to know, but I need those shoes to stay alive. They are literally mine." Mark says to the military person, moving closer to his shoes.

Samantha leaps over the guardrail, and drops in on the lecture. She flies down fast, aiming her body to land on the spiked hair guards back. She breaks a lot of her speed on the leader's back, who crumples down on the stage. With a knee on his back, Samantha locks her arms around the blonde Alphanaut's neck.

"Space Jumper, now!" She yells to Mark, who makes a quick break for his shoes.

He stands before the table where his shoes observe the crowd. He swoops the pair together, and flips the wooden table over for cover. He sits behind the table, and faces Samantha and the blonde military guard, blocking view from the crowd.

Mark finesses the first shoe into his ghost foot and awaits a connection. The vapor from his leg slowly transfers through the opening of the shoe. Mark's actual foot begins to materialize back to actual mass inside of the cool shoe. With the quick development of his foot, the shoe powers on with glowing rings, and tight straps. He quickly performs the same action with his opposite foot, awaiting synchronization. His foot grows like a leaf into the shoe. The rings glow bright, as power courses through the Space Jumper.

The lead Alphanaut guard with the spiked blonde hair awkwardly rises from the ground, breaking Samantha's lock on him. He flips her away to the side of the stage, where she rolls on the ground, and takes some time getting back up. The Alphanaut turns to Mark who has his left leg back, ready for a kick with electricity, sparks and fire bursting off his ensemble. He lowers his leg, striking the blonde Alphanaut guard in the face to send him sliding back across the wooden stage. He stops sliding after twenty feet, and lays motionless on stage.

Everything on Mark's ensemble turns on, quickly charging to maximum power in no time as he rises to his feet. His scarf flows of electricity, as his base gloves glow below the new fire gloves on his palms. Mark clenches a set of powerful fists, and looks up at the blonde military person opposite the stage. The lead Alphanaut speaker slowly begins to stand in a daze, and moves to the side of the stage. He pulls an assault rifle up from the floor, aims it at Mark, and slightly at Samantha.

Mark unleashes a strong force from his hand, throwing an energetic fireball combined with electricity towards the head Alphanaut. Lights begin to flicker and fluctuate across the domed auditorium. The electric fireball singes the blonde guards face, losing energy on the wall behind. The Alphanaut falls dramatically backwards off the stage.

Samantha crouches down on the ground, and watches Mark knock the Alphanaut back with the fireball. She dusts herself off, and looks at Mark, glowing bright in his cool shoes. He walks up to the presentation table, and looks at the group of Alphanaut guards, scientists, and mechanics in the auditorium. Some of the guards tickle their weapons on their sides, ready to bust a retaliated cap in the reborn Space Jumper.

Samantha quickly notices the hostility in the crowd, and reaches for a special grenade at her side. She presses a button with her thumb, and throws the grenade forward between Mark and the crowd. The special grenade falls to the feet of the crowd, detonating an electric blast shocking several hostile guards reaching for their guns.

The Alphanaut guards not affected by the blast run forward to Mark on the stage. Samantha joins the Space Jumper, ready for a fight. Standing back to back, Mark and Samantha slowly rotate on stage to deter enemies away from the blonde, spiked haired Alphanaut, and the audience.

Dancing with death, Mark takes his gun from his side, and checks the ammo in the cylinder. He has a full clip to empty on the enemies around his circle of defense. He swings behind Samantha, unintentionally bumping backsides. She aims at several targets in the crowd to put them in check. A guard approaches the stage, where Samantha uses the butt of her pistol to smack the guard away. Mark aims his gun up, using the sights and particle accelerator to focus on threats using small caliber bullets.

Alphanauts are everywhere, emerging from the other end of the stage, and swarm the Space Jumper at the same time. Mark and Samantha use all the tools in their arsenal to defend their life, their position, and their belongings. While shooting and sweeping Alphanauts off the stage, Mark notices the spiky haired Alphanaut, lingering around the back of the approaching guards.

Mark makes eye contact with him, kicking and shoving away powerless Alphanauts. He watches the blonde guards eyes slowly rotating inside his head. He thinks about the rotating eye in his possession from the alliance he helped create in his home galaxy. The rotating eyes represent a powerful trend from Mark's foes across the universes, as he looks away from the lead Alphanaut.

The Alphanauts will not go away, as Mark whips a counterclockwise roundhouse kick across several of the guards heads and bodies. Samantha blasts people with her gun, rolling and dodging away from attacks. Together, Mark and Samantha hold their ground on stage, and chip away health from the Alphanauts. After some time, less enemies rush the stage, until Mark and Samantha are the last ones standing.

The blonde, spiked haired Alphanaut approaches the end of the stage. "What makes you think you are capable of securing peace in the universes? Do you think you are a god?" He asks Mark and Samantha, high fiving and touching hands at the center stage.

"These days, I don't know what makes a god anymore. I only wish to continue being a good and positive example of humanity, and to spread those good and positive morals to those who need it most." Mark explains, walking closer to the only remaining Alphanaut in the room.

"I hate you." The Alphanaut says quietly in pain, with a bloody smile in front of Mark. "I hate you too." Mark replies with enthusiasm, and a genuine smile. The two stand at center stage, with empty seats in the planetarium surrounding the room.

A blade slowly slides down the hand of the blonde Alphanaut. Mark notices the move, and takes half a step back, ready to retreat. Instead, he lunges forward at an incredible speed with the power of his shoes. Time slows as he lifts his leg up quickly towards the mouth of the blonde guard while sliding forward. Moving too fast, causing time to slow down, Mark kicks the Alphanaut back on his mouth, knocking his eyes forward, and out of his head in slow motion. The Space Jumper bends his leg back, moving his body closer to his raised leg with his foot still on the guards mouth. He moves forward enough to reach for the rotating eyes popping out of the blonde Alphanauts head. Mark snatches the eyes from the air, ripping them away from metal wires connected to the Alphanauts head. He thrusts his leg forward, resuming time to power the Alphanaut forward and across the room.

The blonde haired Alphanaut smashes his back into a dense seat in the audience, falling unconscious, and maybe dead. Red and black blood begins to pour from his mouth, as Mark stands on the stage with his leg in the air. Smoke and electricity puff and pulse off the rings of his shoes.

Holding a new pair of rotating eyes, Mark turns towards Samantha and shows her the pair like holding trophies. "Congratulations Space Jumper." She says with a smile. He smiles back to her, and says nothing. He kneels down to place the new rotating eyes next to the other one in his bag.

"We need to get out of here." Mark says from a kneel, zipping his bag closed as he looks up to Samantha. He scans the room to find an observation deck behind the rows of seats.

Mark jumps up from the stage to the control room in the back, and walks inside. Multiple computer terminals and sound changing devices beep and buzz as he looks around. He takes his tablet from his bag, and connects it to the terminal with his own cable. After a few seconds, a large display in the auditorium displays a map of the current universe, smaller than his home universe, but large enough to have plenty to do and see. The map is holographic, and slowly rotates, coordinating his location on Fireball. Mark uses the computer to update the maps on his tablet, where the process is mostly automatic, and easy.

Mark uses the computer terminal to zoom in to the largest galactic masses in the universe, setting up a new itinerary to help him discover where his shoes came from. The current universe, known as Universe Four, appears smaller than his home universe. He uses knobs and levers to zoom and spread the map in the planetarium.

Shifting through galactic mass in the new universe, Mark spreads the map outward enough to discover the transfer point between universes, or Alter Zone, referenced from the prior universe. Heavy fog encompasses the map the further he spreads out. His hands begin to tingle while holding the handles of the planetarium map.

Reminiscing of the blank space of white nothing from the Alter Zone, and being under arrest right after, Mark's instincts jitter the remote forward within the refrains of the current universe.

"What are you going to do now Space Jumper?" Samantha asks Mark from the top level of the auditorium seats. He continues to zoom in on galaxies while checking his tablet. "The eyes I've been collecting indicate an interesting species patterned within my path. My next objective could be somewhere in this universe. I have to keep tracking the answer to where my shoes came from. I've got space jumping to do." He says, scrolling through the map, as if pressed for time.

"Can you meet us on the ship to say goodbye to the crew?" Samantha asks, as if it were going to be the last time. He scopes the map in the planetarium, and unhooks his tablet from the console in the programmers chair. "Let's go." He replies, feeling hints of blue in his soul.

"I'll secure the Hedgehog. Do you have the keys?" Mark asks Samantha. She tosses him a key with a heart connected to a ring. He snags the key out of the air, and feels its warmth in his hand. "Make your way back down to the street. I'm going to go back up." Mark says. "I think I might do the same." She replies, moving towards the stairs at the back of the auditorium.

Mark and Samantha backtrack to the roof, closing the door to the planetarium behind them. Standing on a windy catwalk, Mark is eager to jump back into the clouds. He feels the shoes adapt to the air around him. Breathing becomes easier, as the airways are clear. He waits with Samantha, and carefully inspects the surroundings. Mark walks forward to the end of the balcony, and looks around for a moment. He scratches his head, and looks back to Samantha.

"Stay here for a minute. I'll be back." Mark quietly whispers to Samantha. He activates the shield in his pocket, engulfing himself in an electric cloak.

He runs a few steps over the catwalk, and attempts to jump on the roof next door. He springs normally off the ground, and launches up at an incredible trajectory. Moving up the air, Radium quickly transitions to clouds, where his shoes absorb a tremendous amount of power. The rings light up to overdrive as he angles his body down to cut trajectory, landing on a cloud.

Sliding over the cloud, Mark positions his body above the Hedgehog a few blocks back. He dives through the cloud headfirst towards the surface of Radium. The coolness of the fog transitions to warmth from the air. Mark lands hard on the street next to the car, launching a fiery explosion of electricity and forced air. His feet and legs comfortably absorb the impact. He looks up to check the surroundings. Everything is clear, including the traffic ahead.

Mark jumps in the Hedgehog, and ignites the engine. He pushes a handle forward, like accelerating a plane to increase speed. The front tires quickly lose traction as the vehicle squirms left and right on the road. Mark maintains control of the Hedgehog using the steering wheel, and moves down the block towards the first security checkpoint. Mark runs through the vacant intersections he originally jumped over with his board towards the wooden roadblock on the street at the first planetarium.

He accelerates the hedgehog to increase the height and width of the tires. He runs through a wooden roadblock into another vacant part of the city, continuing forward to the second planetarium. Mark notices signs leading to a bridge to the next connected planet, as he slows the Hedgehog, and parks ahead of the planetarium where Samantha said she would be. He stops the Hedgehog in front of the vacant, dry, planetarium, as Samantha runs from the side of a fence.

Standing on the balcony of the roof of the planetarium, Samantha watches the Space Jumper leap up and sail through the clouds. Mark is gone in an instant, as she catches her breath. Everything remains clear, quiet, and complete. The Space Jumper has his shoes, nearly completing a successful mission. Samantha walks across the circular balcony of the dome to a set of buildings nearby. She smells the scent of something cooking in the air, looking back at the door to the roof. She stares blankly into the sky where the Space Jumper may be.

The door to the roof opens, alerting Samantha. She crouches forward around the circular catwalk on the roof, above a thin figure eight metal pattern. She moves around the dome to a safe spot away from trouble. She sits opposite of what looks like an Alphanaut guard a far distance away. As she crouches still over the metal, Samantha is able to feel the location of the enemy through her depth of sense.

She sits on the metal catwalk, and straps her skates over her feet. She stands up, and flexes her muscles, gleaming her green skin across the air of the island city. She pushes off the rusty handrail, carrying traction with her durable, but worn gloves.

Samantha rolls quickly and quietly over the metal pattern of the roof, gliding at a careful pace to flank the guards. She circles around the metal roof, slightly beneath the top of the dome. The wheels of her skates roll smooth and melodic over the catwalk towards the squad ahead. She carefully adjusts her momentum, and sneaks up on the encircling guard. She rolls behind the last guard, physically throws him out of the way, and off the railing to the side. Samantha rolls slowly, and carefully kicks the next guard in front through the opposite door of the roof.

The final guard finally notices the commotion, and lifts his gun to aim back at Samantha. When he has a shot, she rolls low on her skates, and ducks beneath his lifted rifle. She skids her skates to stop her slight momentum, and uppercuts the final remaining guard in the side of his head. His body flies up and over the side railing like a rocket, off the planetarium.

Samantha utilizes her skates to build momentum around the raised metal catwalk of the planetarium. She circles a lap around the catwalk with some good speed, and jumps off the roof towards a neighboring circular metal silo to the side. She angles her legs in midair, landing the wheels of her skates on the wall. Her blades adhere to the surface of the silo as she carries speed around the circle. She remains low, and rolls herself around the silo, manipulating the weight of her body to the light gravity of the planet. She concludes her merry-go-round exit in front of the silo, and rolls on concrete ground next to a fence surrounding the planetarium. She slows pace, and rolls towards a bush by a house near the street.

She sits on the ground within a leafy bush, next to a small house in front of the farm and silo. She unstraps her skates and throws them on her backpack, takes a deep breath, and looks up at the roof of the planetarium. More guards are on patrol, looking for the girl who rolls. They carry heavy alien rifles, and circle the roof.

Commotion runs amuck on the other side of the wall. Seconds later, Samantha hears the sound of a familiar engine rolling up the street. She peaks out of the bush, and looks at Mark, parked perpendicular to her on the side of the street. She runs quickly to the Hedgehog, where Mark exits the vehicle, and powers on his board.

Mark and Samantha say nothing as she climbs into the singular seated Hedgehog. Mark hooks himself to the winch behind the Hedgehog, cutting himself some slack from the cable. He slaps the dense frame a couple of times, where Samantha quickly accelerates forward.

Spinning the wheels to create smoke, the Hedgehog rolls forward down the street with Mark on the back, connected with his shoes, his board, and his gear.

On the final leg of the mission, Samantha carries top speed forward down the mostly vacant street on East Radium. Skyscrapers line up the side of the streets as the Hedgehog pierces through the heart of downtown. The buildings appear luxurious and high tech, with another language of the universe worth noticing.

Ahead, Mark notices a smooth vehicle appearing to be undercover. He swivels his head on his board to notice the alien vehicle begin to follow behind. Moving down the street ahead, Mark notices several more cars pull up from quiet cross streets, and give chase. The trailing vehicles increase speed to the semi-slow Hedgehog. The passengers of the vehicles aim their heads and arms out, and begin to fire weapons at Mark and Samantha.

Startled by the pop of gunfire headed in his direction, Mark maneuvers his body around the street using his movement as cover. He adjusts the slack of the cable connected to the Hedgehog, and moves closer to the driver of the first car. He jumps the board up to the hood of the vehicle, hovering to the front window to crack the glass. The power from the anti magnetic board blasts the drivers face, disrupting his vision. Mark hops the board off the hood with great power connected to his shoes, and back to the ground. The Alphanaut car turns, and crashes into a building to the side.

Several more cars begin to approach from behind, moving fast down the street. One of the black cars with wheels continues to accelerate as if they wants to move through the Hedgehog. Mark hops his board up and over the quickly approaching vehicle, as it crashes into the back of the Hedgehog. The vehicle slows, as smoke begins to spew from its engine. The Hedgehog continues forward, faster and un-phased. Mark moves to the side of the broke down vehicle, using quick maneuvers on the hovering board to evade damage.

Three cars, some black, and one blue, all with wheels, continue to trail the Hedgehog, as Mark and Samantha move through smaller buildings in a more suburban part of the city. The Hedgehog rolls steady over the concrete on the main road. Mark hangs on to the cable at the back with his antimagnetic space board, while Samantha controls knobs and the wheel in the Hedgehog.

The Alphanauts want to stop the Space Jumper from taking his shoes back, and to stop him from continuing his path of good. They maneuver their vehicles behind the Hedgehog and shoot side arms at him.

Mark takes out his BB gun, while holding on to the bar connected to the cable. He uses his stomach to manipulate the scope of his particle accelerator to shoot larger bullets. He aims his arm back, and sights the vehicles behind. He pulls the trigger, firing a large bullet in the direction of the vehicle.

The bullet is horrifyingly huge at the size of a bowling ball. The projectile strikes the lower hood of the car, sending the nose down to lift the back tires off the ground. The car looses traction, and front flips off the road in a fiery explosion.

Two vehicles remain behind, as Mark fires another large shot at the Alphanauts. The blue vehicle trails to the side of the Space Jumper, where the passenger shoots his gun at him. Mark evades side to side from bullets whizzing around him. He aims his gun up to the car, and pulls the trigger. The dull click of an empty gun shakes his heart, raising hairs on his arms. He pockets the gun back to his side, and pulls one of his explosive devices from his pocket. He clicks on the small battery to activate the electronic components. He cooks the grenade in his pocket, and waits for the right time to let it fly.

He drops the cooked electro-magnetic pulse on the ground in front of the car. The remaining Alphanaut vehicle drives over the bomb, unaware of its presence and action. The bomb magnetically clings beneath the lead vehicle, and explodes, launching it up in a small, fiery explosion with a mix of electronic disruption. The Alphanaut vehicle is gone beyond repair.

Mark remains calm, taking a moment on the board to load a few more BBs into his gun, and holster it to his belt strap. He moves side to side on the board over the ground behind the Hedgehog.

The large, metal bridge connected to the neighboring planet of Radium is ahead, not far in the distance. North Radium appears mostly green and blue, with very little dry ground within.

The Hedgehog moves forward towards the metallic foundation in the ground. Heavy planks of metal build upward to a large metal archway over the road. Mark crouches low on the board, hovering at a variable three to four feet in the air, as they speed up the road through a strange archway expelling energy. The road expands several lanes out, where heavy cables rise up to provide support for the metal bridge. As the grade of the hill increases, the surface of the road transitions to transparent glass.

The Hedgehog powers up the increasingly steep hill towards the sky, where the ground grows miles away below the glassed road. Mark's space board collects power over the strange surface of the road. The density of the glass provides a monumental amount of anti magnetic force for the board, leading to an increase in speed. Connecting to the power of his shoes, the battery on the board remains full. The bridge gains altitude, as the air grows thin.

Nearing the height of space, the bridge loses its foundation to the ground, and holds together with cables, a sidewall, and the transparent road. Samantha continues forward on the Hedgehog, while Mark maintains stability on the board.

A metallic road sign indicates the gravity will drop to zero ahead. The bridge transitions to a glass tunnel in space in order to preserve air to travelers. Beyond the tunnel is a loop in the road, going full vertical. Samantha and Mark speed into the tunnel, continuing to gain altitude up a semi steep incline. The tunneled road is cold, but well lit, and insolated with oxygen.

Only a couple other vehicles are on the road, as travelers are scarce between the planets. The road is vacant and open, as Samantha continues the Hedgehog forward towards the short loop.

"Punch it." Mark yells up to Samantha in the drivers seat. She looks back to Mark out the window, hearing what he said, as if she was not already going full speed. Mark sighs, and grows worried at the lack of speed before the loop.

He presses down hard on the board, forcing it close to the ground. He accelerates forward, and begins to push the back of the Hedgehog.

Mark continues to force the space board down to increase speed, where he uses his strength to push the Hedgehog forward with a turbo charge. He leans his weight on the back of the Hedgehog, and pushes it up several more miles per hour.

"Get ready." He says to Samantha through an opening in the Hedgehog.

Approaching the transparent loop, Mark continues to push the Hedgehog to a speed that can safely clear the hill. They roll forward up the loop, upside down in zero gravity to find an increase in speed with more traction, less weight, and less resistance. The Hedgehog picks up speed as it rolls down the loop to a short straightaway. Another short ramp launches the two up to the tunnel, and down to the road to another long straightaway. The road arches up and down like riding over large humps, as Mark holds on to the handle of the winch, letting go of the Hedgehog. The vehicle returns to normal speed as they roll over the spacebridge towards the Northern planet of Radium.

Security personnel for the bridge post at checkpoints to the side. The security does not appear to be Alphanauts, but for the planet. Mark and Samantha drive by, as the bridge police frantically run to a set of vehicles at the side of the road. Mark takes out one of his last electronic grenades, and holds it tight as the police vehicles approach the slow Hedgehog. The police coordinate behind the Hedgehog on the transparent ground, where Mark releases of the grenade. A blue explosion propels three of the vehicles around the translucent tunnel. They crash to the side, where a hole opens the glass ground from the explosion.

One of the cars from the back of the pack survives, and steers away from the chaos. Mark takes his gun out and fires a large BB through space into the ground in front of the vehicles path. The bullet pierces through the road, opening another hole in the bridge. The remaining police vehicle falls through the hole, and floats into the open gravity of space below. The driver of the car jumps out of the vehicle, and floats up towards the bridge. The Hedgehog rolls over the bumpy, transparent road towards North Radium. Lights flicker on and off in the tunnel, creating a sense of emptiness in outer space.

Reaching the middle part of the bridge, space appears even more empty and beautiful with the absence of two of the three planets in the cluster. To the left, South Radium sits away in the distance, with two bridges connecting it from each end. The road remains wavy, moving up and down for stability in space. Samantha keeps a steady pace with the vehicle, as Mark trails from a rope on his board behind.

After moving up a small incline, a larger decline unveils more of the surface of the second planet. Another loop sits in space after a small hill, circling down for travelers to increase speed. The Space Jumper smiles on the board, feeling at peace with the universe again.

Samantha rolls down the transparent hill towards the loop, increasing speed. She rolls up the ramp and circles over the loop, increasing speed at the drop with an increase of friction. At the descent from space over the bridge, Mark and Samantha got what they came for, and are looking for a clean escape.

The second planet of the set in the Fireball galaxy contains multiple large islands, with a main road connecting to each of them. Samantha drives the Hedgehog down the road for several more miles until reaching the first archway grounded on the planet. Mark hangs on tight, controlling speed on the board behind the Hedgehog.

The road transitions from transparent glass to concrete. An increase of cables appear to the left and right of the road, indicating they are moving closer to the ground. They break through a set of clouds, where the weather on the planet is humid and warm.

Dry air and windy vapors flow across Mark's face. The islands on the planet appear endless over the horizon, with various commodities growing on each one. Some of the islands have tall skyscrapers across a wide space, while some have skyscrapers across a smaller space. Some of the islands have clouds over them, raining down on small towns within, while some of the islands are empty, only containing water, sand, and dirt.

Samantha rolls down the bridge towards the transition to ground. She moves through multiple support arches where the bridge begins to feel more grounded. As the arch of the bridge levels out to the first island, no one is really around to see it. Mark and Samantha notice the emptiness of the land.

"We have the shoes, and are ready for extraction." Samantha says inside the Hedgehog. "We're on our way, we need to make this quick." Captain Drake says from the ship. Mark hears the call through the synchronized radio channel. "Meet us on the next island ahead, check your map." Captain Drake says to Samantha over the radio. She checks the map in the Hedgehog, where a blip indicates the location.

The Lineage ship activates its engines in space, and dive bombs towards Radium.

Samantha steers the Hedgehog over the twisty roads on the island. She maneuvers left and right, safely across the vacant road. The island they ride over is empty, with no signs of life nearby. The waves from the water gently crash on the sandy dunes below the concrete highway.

Rolling down the concrete road across the islands, Mark hangs on to the Hedgehog when he hears a swift movement from behind and above. The Lineage ship flies over the road, and lands at the beach of the next island.

Samantha continues to roll forward over a bridge to the next island. A heavy fog lingers from the left to the right of the islands. The water is dark blue, rough, and treacherous for travelers.

Mark and Samantha travel over the low bridge to the next island for extraction. Once crossed, they veer from the road to a dirt path with trees surrounding. Samantha moves left and right, as Mark follows close behind on the space board.

The ship flies down from the sky and parks at the edge of the sand and water. The Lineage ship opens the bay doors to the garage, where the Hedgehog rolls in with speed, sliding to a halt behind the ramp. Mark slides the board up the ramp, and presses his hands on the bumper of the Hedgehog. The large door swings up to close as the ship rises out of the sand.

Lineage flies up and out of the atmosphere into the depths of space, leaving the trilogy of planets behind. The crew applaud Mark and Samantha as they park there vehicles, and move through the ship. They shake hands and hug the crew, moving up the stairs of the garage to the crew quarters. Mark's shoes glow bright and strong beneath his feet as someone hands him a bottle of something to drink.

They meet with the rest of the crew, already celebrating the successful mission. Mark places the bottle on the pool table, and climbs up next to the bottle. Standing on the middle of the pool table, the Space Jumper kicks the top of the bottle with his shoe, popping the cap. The bottle stays perfectly still on the pool table, and does not spill a drop. After a couple of seconds of silence, laughter erupts around the room when the metal cap from the bottle hits the metallic surface. The Space Jumper grabs the bottle, takes a swig, and jumps down from the table, spilling some of the beverage.

The Space Jumper walks to a member of Lineage with a closed bottle in his hand. He leans back, and kicks the cap off his bottle using the heel of his right cool shoe, arousing more cheer and laughter around the cabin.

Captain Drake hears the commotion from the pilots cabin as he flies the ship into a deep section of the galaxy. Radium becomes far from a star at the speed they travel using advanced warp technology. Drake walks out of the cabin holding a bottle of the same thing the crew is drinking. He slowly emerges towards the ruckus with the crew.

"Good work, Space Jumper." Captain Drake says, walking towards Mark. They clink their bottles together, where Drake takes a drink. "It needed to be done." Mark replies with a sigh, taking a drink as he sits on the edge of the pool table.

Mark kneels down to his side, reaches into his bag, and takes out the new set of rotating eyes. He rolls the eyes on the pool table, where they clang next to the two ball and the cue ball. Mark walks over to a stick rack on the wall and chooses a well-proportioned stick. He grabs the stick, and walks confidently back to the table with his cool shoes blaring. Samantha sits at the side of the room and watches with several other members of Lineage.

Mark walks back to the table, and takes an odd, upright shot of pool using one of the eyes as a cue. He banks the rotating eye off several soft bumpers, where it deflects off another ball. The eye appears unfazed, with only a small dent on the small, metal backing plates.

"So what do you guys have planned?" Mark asks Drake from the side of the room. Captain Drake slowly walks to the table, holding the bottle in his hand. The co-pilot emerges from the cockpit, where Mark acknowledges him with a salute of the bottle.

"We have plenty to do. I see you have some rotating eyes." Captain Drake replies, watching the eyes on the pool table. A crewmember from Lineage hits the cue to break the balls, and the eyes. Everything circular bangs on the table, and spreads out wide. Mark remains seated on the side of the table, when he snatches one of the eyes before it sinks into the side pocket. He holds the eye in front of Captain Drake, and briefly studies it.

"These are not the only ones I found. I helped create peace between my neighbor galaxies, Andromeda and Cigar, back in my home universe. We formed a strong truce between man and machine, symbolized by the pair of rotating eyes." Mark says, holding the eye up in front of his face.

"You gonna keep both of those?" A crewmember next to Samantha asks Mark from across the room.

Mark looks up at the person who asked the question, and throws one of the rotating eyes in his direction. The eye floats through the air inside the ship, as the crewmember catches it, and grasps it smoothly in his hand.

"Make peace Lineage." Mark says to the crew, where he takes a drink from the bottle of bubbly. The crewmember looks at the eye like treasure, as the rest of the crew cheer, Mark smiles while drinking.

Captain Drake walks to the crewmember holding the eye, and quickly snatches it out of his hand. Drake looks at the eye, and looks to the Space Jumper. He flips the eye up in the air, catching it back in his hand, symbolizing a locked friendship. The crew whistle and cheer, as they drink from their bottles and glasses. Mark grabs the other eye from the pool table, and sticks it back in his bag. He stands from the pool table, and walks towards Samantha, as Captain Drake shows the eye to the crew around the quarters. Mark walks in front of Samantha and smiles, holding his bottle down at his side.

"I need to continue my quest on my own." Mark says to Samantha with a heavyhearted tone. "I understand, Space Jumper." She replies, as a tear rolls down her cheek. Mark uses his finger to scoop the tear from her cheek.

"My crew will have your back if you need help." She replies in an upset tone. "Thank you Samantha, for everything you and the crew have done, to help me get back on my feet." Mark says, reaching for her hand. Captain Drake walks to Samantha, and looks at the Space Jumper. "Any ideas on where I should start looking where my shoes came from?" Mark asks Captain Drake. "You should try the Café galaxy, not too far from here. The tech there is insane, almost magical." Drake replies. "Thanks, I'll keep that in mind." Mark says, sticking his hand out for Drake to shake. The two clasp hands and grasp, symbolizing unity. Mark lets go of Drake's hand, and gives Samantha a big, tight hug. He embraces her feeling and smell, never forgetting the people who sprung him free.

Mark begins to walk up the steps that lead to the top deck of the ship. Samantha, Drake, and the rest of the crew follow the Space Jumper up the stairs. Mark opens a wooden hatch on the ceiling, and walks to the top deck of the ship in the middle of space. Some of the crew wear space helmets, while some, like Captain Drake and Samantha are able to breathe naturally. Mark shakes Captain Drake's hand again, and walks to Samantha to give her a kiss on the cheek. He walks to the side of the wooden pirate ship, climbs the side of the waist high guard wall, and looks back at the crew. He salutes Lineage for a few seconds, and backflips hard off the ship, leaping miles away into deep space.

Chapter 6

Café

In the new universe, space is equally cold to humanities home universe. Stars remain to be the surroundings of the Space Jumper, moving, rising, and climbing through varied gravity densities. Gravity fields are warm as Mark continues to jump away from Lineage. He moves up at a high speed, spinning his body like a torpedo to gain a monumental amount of momentum. During rotation, he takes his tablet from his bag, and checks the updated map from Radium, on Fireball. The universe expands similarly to the projection from the auditorium. He expands the current galaxy to track the fresh lead known as Café.

Scrolling through his tablet, the Space Jumper discovers his documents and pictures remain intact. His tablet device activated a failsafe before powering off, protecting his applications. He takes joy in knowing his notes of travel remain a part of him. He browses through the tablet, discovering Samantha sent Mark a link to a special application to Lineage. He scrolls through the application, which has a direct hotline to the Lineage ship. He takes a deep breath, and follows the new waypoint set on his glasses towards the Café galaxy, fifty thousand lightyears away.

Stacks of momentum lead Mark to warp speed through an open path of space. Gravity fields feel irrelevant beneath his cool shoes, where his focus centers on the waypoint from his glasses. The heads up display contains many features when connected to an electrical source. Temperature, the distance to hotspots, heart rate, wave varieties, speed, and a compass are measured.

Travelling over fifty thousand miles per hour, Mark condenses time into a tunnel of space swirling around him. Colors of green and blue surround a heavy white from the surrounding stars. His tunnel of speed looks like a shooting star from afar.

Balancing his speed with careful jumps through green and orange gravity fields, Mark takes time to observe his surroundings, remaining in the Fireball galaxy.

With fifty BBs in his pocket, enough for five full clips for his gun, Mark soars though space through a warp tunnel. He remains focused on the waypoint in his glasses. Everything in his arsenal of tools and apparel synchronize, yet he feels more light than comfortable. He wishes to have a more comfortable armament, being even further away from Earth. Mark's home universe is at a no turning back point from where he stands. With his gear and the lack of ammo, food, and drinks, he will barely stand a chance.

The upgrades he continues to acquire fill the gaps for his lost consumables. His new gloves can replace the lost explosives and lighters, connected with his shield that temporarily deflects projectiles.

Ammo can alternate with electronic fireballs, but distance is always relevant in space. His hatchet hinges on his worn out backpack, with his journal next to his laser sword inside. Ammunition for the BB gun continues to worry the Space Jumper.

Travelling at warp speed, a strange vibration mixed with heat sneaks into his pant leg, alarming his senses. He moderates speed, and turns around for a second to find a set of five spaceships behind him, struggling to keep pace. He turns around again, looking down in a position resembling laying in bed, and seeing something between one's feet. He twists his particle accelerator to its maximum setting, ready to shoot cannonballs at the attackers.

He maintains a speed nearly at warp, when he opens fire at the first silver ship. He shoots a single shot ahead of the direction the circular ship is going, and strikes it with the large bullet, obliterating it from view.

Assuming the ships following him belong to the Alphanauts, Mark continues to take defensive maneuvers by swerving left and right though his warp tunnel. He takes his ammo count to consideration for the fight ahead. He tracks the movement of the enemies behind, quickly switching between the varied looking targets. Some vehicles are pitch black, and hard to see, while most are silver and circular.

Space is warm at such a high speed, with molecules of friction providing a subtle heat through the Space Jumper's gear. As the Alphanaut enemies twist and turn beneath his feet, Mark aims his gun through his legs while jumping fast on gravity fields towards his destination, the Café galaxy. He focuses on the movement patterns of the space ships, growing irritated at their persistent presence. The pursuing ships begin firing blue and red lasers at Mark.

Continuing to move up at a high speed, Mark jumps on gravity fields to outrun the ships, and their lasers. He continues to jump backwards while looking down to observe the enemies movements. A stray ship approaches, as Mark finds time to angle a line with the sights of his gun. He fires another shot, missing the approaching ship, but hitting another in the group behind. Once hit, the enemy spaceship stops moving and sinks down through the empty space.

Spinning and moving through space, avoiding lasers and fast ships, Mark continues towards Café. He fires quick shots beneath his feet, striking another two ships. Running out of ammo, and enemies, Mark takes each shot carefully, not to waste bullets. Shy on ranged projectiles, Mark's only hope right now is his BB gun. His boomerang hatchet would be lost behind at the speed he propels himself.

With one more ship trailing behind, Mark evades the lasers in deep space, veering left and right after jumping from an abundance of gravity fields. Controlling speed, Mark turns around to aim at the final Alphanaut enemy, when he sees a squad of four more ships move fast from behind. The reinforcements appear sleeker and stronger than the spaceships he previously fought.

Random planets within the Fireball galaxy come into view ahead and behind the Space Jumper, as he focuses on the movement of the reinforcements. His legs grow tired, running on gravity fields at such a high velocity.

"I should have stretched before jumping." He says to himself, catching a second wind in space. He fires several shots quickly towards the approaching enemies, striking two of the ships hard with big bullets. The ships fall out of space like dead flies.

Three enemies remain, as Mark slows some of his speed, and carefully reloads his gun. He moves side to side, avoiding fast lasers as he loads the final bullet into the chamber. He snaps the gun back and quickly fires a burst of three large shots at the ships. Mark takes out the reinforcement ship in front, where its engine sputters, sending its flightpath awry. It crashes into one of the ships behind, as two more Alphanaut space ships are down, with one remaining.

Mark uses his shoes to jump from a gravity field in a hard angle to the side. He turns his body with speed, handling intense and astronomical g-forces to circle around the remaining ship. He moves forward behind the ship, as they realize they lost their target. The ship slows its pace to nearly a standstill in space, as Mark stands a hundred yards behind. He aims his gun up, and fires a single shot directly into the rear section of the silver, oval spaceship. The large BB pierces through the metallic hull of the ship, sending bits and pieces across the near space. The spaceship explodes, as Mark uses his hand to cover his face from debris and heat.

The Space Jumper looks around, and listens to the silence of space. A cold chill rattles his spine at the depth of his isolation. He reestablishes connection with his path to the Café galaxy, and builds momentum through space. He shakes off his passive cobwebs, realizing he is all alone again, and must fight for survival. Warp speed comes easily, wrapping around his body like a colorful blanket of gravity.

Halfway to Café, Mark blasts through space when he hears an odd vibration to his side that tickles the hair on his earlobes. Slowing speed, he looks around the space ahead to find an odd-looking anomaly sitting still. As Mark approaches the side of the anomaly, he notices it is either vibrating up and down, or spinning around incredibly fast. The moment he takes time to determine what the anomaly is, he finds it spinning fast in his direction.

"What the hell is that thing?" He asks rhetorically to space, jumping upward. Breaking his line to Café for a moment, he looks down to find a saw blade the size of a house spinning fast in his direction. The blade appears thick, spinning unbelievably fast up space towards him like a magnet. The crazy blade makes its way towards the Space Jumper as he moves forward above.

He tries to pick up speed on gravity fields, but finds no evasion from the dangerous, spinning blade. Picking up speed at a tremendous pace, Mark flies forward towards Café. He turns his head to find the blade continuing to move dangerously close to him. He fires a couple of large BBs back at the anomaly, but the blade spins the projectiles away. The spinning blade circling around its core has teeth that expand in width, protecting the anomaly. Mark continues to build speed when he feels the vibration of the blade directly behind his shoes. The Space Jumper adjusts his angle of velocity at the next gravity field beneath the flight path of the blade. Having only a short moment to breathe, Mark continues to move forward through gravity fields towards Café.

Moving up and down through space to a wavelength at a consistent pace makes the blade lose Mark's magnetic chase. He focuses on gravity fields ahead, angling his velocity while maintaining speed. Breaking away from the grasp of the blade, Mark finds warp speed while cutting space, up and down. Deflecting his location from varied gravity fields, the Space Jumper creates some distance from the anomaly. The blade loses its magnetic interest, as Mark powers forward. The blade randomly rips away somewhere else into space.

After a few more minutes of jumping, gliding, and soaring off gravity fields, the Café galaxy begins to exude multiple bright colors around his warp tunnel. He slows some speed from his warp to look around the space for attackers. The distance to Café grows near over his glasses. He takes a moment to look around, approaching the fresh galaxy.

Café grows wide, and more colorful, as the lightyears shrink in front of his eyes. He maintains warp a little while longer before feeling an increasing warmth in the air. Auras of green, blue and yellow engulf his immediate space. Mark slows down from warp, and crashes hard into a force field in front of a set of planets within the galaxy. His face and body are smushed into the glass-like barrier, like a bug hitting a windshield.

"I did not see that coming." He says with his face stuck to the force field. He pushes his body off the barrier, and floats around the outside of the Café galaxy. Several planets sit inside the green and yellow force field, all with different sizes, shapes, and colors.

"Hello?" Mark says to the shield. He knocks his fist on the force field like knocking on some ones front door. As he knocks on the shield, a mild distortion disrupts the flow of the force field. Mark moves back, and scratches his head at the distortion.

He moves close to the shield, and punches it with his fists. He mixes in kicks to fight the force field. The combos from his fists and kicks create a wider disruption across the shield. He takes a second, and equips his hatchet from his bag. He bashes the shield with the blade, incorporating punches with his free hand, and mixing heavy kicks to continue to disrupt the shield.

The green force field transitions to red, indicating damage across its plane. Swelling like a bruise, the force field turns bright red where Mark continues to attack. After a swift strike with the hatchet, the force field breaks apart like a ripped bag of groceries, and opens a hole around. Taking a breather, Mark stands before the open barrier, and veers forward into the galaxy, where the shield quickly reestablishes a full connection. The color transitions from red, to yellow, and quickly back to green.

Mark drifts down through the space, and veers toward a gravity field ahead. He plants his shoes over the brown and yellow plot of gravity, and prepares to jump. Mark attempts to jump, locking his legs, but finds he is stuck on the gravity field. He stands upright, and looks around the space to find three ships ahead, shooting consistent, individual beams of energy at him. The three beams connect to his body, freezing him in place.

Unable to move, Mark eases tension, and comes in peace. "State your business here?" A deep voice gargles from the vehicle from a loudspeaker. "I'm here to find where my shoes came from, and to explore the Café galaxy." Mark replies to the security.

Stuck behind the police's blue force field in front of the large green force field, Mark awaits a response from his captors. "Meet King Rox on Crystal. He may be able to help you. Don't cause any trouble, traveler." The security guard says behind the loudspeaker. The police back away from Mark, and lower their beams. The force field around Mark deteriorates as the three unidentified space vehicles fly away into the center of the galaxy. Mark frees himself from the deteriorating force field, standing on a gravity field.

"Now I have to find Crystal." He says to himself.

Free to explore the galaxy, Mark keeps his tablet close, and updates his scanner with the new planets nearby. Mark jumps from his current gravity field towards the first closest planet. He jumps cautiously towards the green and purple planet, watching his speed as if there is a limit that would get him in trouble with the authorities. His glasses scan the details of the planets, indicating mass, temperature, gravity, population, and other facts.

Moving forward towards the next planet in the galaxy, Mark scans the surface, checking the name. Again, not Crystal, Mark moves away in the opposite direction, following the path of planets. He scans over the next three planets before finding the obvious Crystal planet, all the way in the back of the set.

Crystal looks like an actual crystal, with two pointed tips at the northern and southern poles. The color is a light, jagged pink, mixed with a rose gold.

Mark approaches the large, obscure planet, and breaks into the atmosphere. The Space Jumper lands on the first set of fluffy clouds above the surface. He takes a moment to follow his updated map to King Rox, and jumps off the side of the cloud, bouncing over the pointed planet towards the location.

Approaching his waypoint, Mark breaks down through the clouds, finding a thinner layer of small clouds beneath. The weather in the planet is warm and smoky, almost foggy. The surface appears jagged and rocky like crystals covered with more pink, transparent crystals.

The city has buildings and houses where the inhabitants live. Lakes and rivers spread across large mountains of crystal, colored brown and salmon.

Dropping down to the surface, Mark lands on the ground next to a mountain, crunching the tips of the crystalized surface with his cool shoes. His glasses tell him to move forward over the mountain to find King Rox. Mark jumps up the extremely jagged terrain through a light haze in the air.

Reaching a small peak on the mountain, a group of creatures made of crystal stand on a small hill. The creatures are the same color and texture as the surface, making it look like the ground is moving. Mark does not know whether to engage the beings, or pass overhead. He decides to jump down the rigid hill behind the inhabitants, arousing their attention. The creatures turn around to look at Mark with jagged faces, limbs, and bodies. They begin to walk slowly towards Mark, when the first creature puts his head down to focus. After a few seconds, Mark notices shards of crystals growing from its body.

The Space Jumper puts his hand in his pocket, and quickly activates his shield. The blue shield covers his body when the crystalized enemy shoots out crystals like a porcupine. The shards of crystal deflect hard off Mark's shield. The two crystalized enemies behind rush past the lead enemy and throw slow punches at Mark.

The Space Jumper dodges the punches, treading carefully over the pointy mountain. He takes his hatchet from his bag, and swings it at the first guards head, slicing parts of its crystals off. The enemy looks unfazed, and angrier, as it moves closer to Mark. Taking a step back, Mark utilizes his blade to slash the legs off the crystalized guards before his shield turns off.

Vulnerable on the foreign mountain on the Crystal planet in the Café galaxy, Mark discovers he is unable to kill the enemies ahead of him. He cuts the rock people down to bits, and jumps forward over them to the next part of the large mountain. He hops off jagged edges of the dirty pink colored crystal mountain, gaining elevation towards the peak.

Landing on the peak of the mountain, Mark discovers another couple of crystal enemies posting up. The Space Jumper quickly rushes forward, using his special thrust kick to launch one of the crystal enemies off the mountain. The enemy shatters to bits on the way down, becoming one with the world. The second enemy swings a punch around its body, where Mark blocks it with his arms. The jagged fist of the enemy stabs through Mark's gear and jacket, causing him to bleed. Shards of broken crystals stick out from Mark's arm.

The Space Jumper utilizes a similar attack, swinging his hatchet around his body to slice the crystal enemy in half. The creature crawls on the ground, and continues to attack Mark. The Space Jumper jumps off the head of the crystal enemy towards the next forward part of the mountain, entering a small city with crystal houses.

Jumping up and down the crystal mountain, Mark notices that not all of the crystalized inhabitants are hostile. He looks inside some of the crystal houses, where some of the creatures watch him move forward. He waves to a family of crystals inside their home, and jumps forward up the jagged mountain. The crystal inhabitants look back with red eyes, and continue to live next to their fireplace.

More inhabitants of the mountain casually work on projects, harvest materials, and build structures. They are focused on their work, and do not want to fight. Mark walks casually through the mountain city with his hands up, indicating peace to the crystal creatures. Moving up a jagged hill, Mark reaches another peak, overlooking a steep and treacherous drop. Homes continue to line the side of the mountain, with civilians casually walking by.

Mark jumps down from the mountain towards a flat, jagged section below. Before landing, he notices a couple more crystal people below him. They quickly look up at him as if ready to fight. Mark carries momentum down, and lands a kick on the crystal enemy. He flexes his foot before impact, using his braking technique to prevent the spikes from puncturing his foot. He plants the enemy down to the ground, and punches his friend away with a strong, electric and fiery fist. The combination of electricity and fire from the gloves secure Mark's hand.

The terrain remains pointy and jagged with alien crystals. Houses line up the side of the next mountain to the left and right as Mark continues to move forward towards his location. He moves up another small hill atop the crystal mountain, where the air remains hazy and smoky with a lingering burning smell.

As Mark approaches the top of the small hill, two more of the crystal bullies grow out of the ground from nothing. They stand tall, materializing from the surface they stand on. One of the crystalized enemies throws a large, single shard of itself at Mark, who leans to the side to dodge it.

The Space Jumper throws his hatchet at the same crystal enemy, striking it in the face to shatter its body back into little pieces. Mark runs over to his hatchet, and scoops it off the ground. He quickly uses a backhand slice at the second crystal enemy, cutting it down to the ground. Growing tired of the dense durability of the crystal creatures, Mark jumps forward, closer towards the waypoint on his glasses.

Standing on a small cliff on another mountain, Mark scans ahead, looking for the location. On his map, the location of King Rox is behind a final mountain ahead. As the Space Jumper is about to jump up, a shard of glass strikes his calf, stunting his jump. He rolls forward down the mountain, and splashes in to a lake of alien liquid. The lake has a pink glaze, where Mark is in pain under the water. He continues to sink into the strange water, falling deeper and deeper down.

The liquid is sweet like candy and syrup, but light like water. Landing on the surface of the lake, Mark begins to walk forward, holding his breath.

His shoes support his breathing while under the water, as his glasses maintain a clear view ahead. A set of three strange fish creatures swim in front as Mark moves forward. His glasses highlight the shape of the mysterious lake critters moving closer. The fish have spikes jutting out of their figures, similar to the crystal creatures above.

The crystalized fish notice Mark's presence, and grin sharp, menacing teeth at him. The fish swim fast towards Mark, moving left and right to build speed until they are in front of the human. Mark stands on the floor of the lake, and jumps upward under the water. He carries little momentum up through the strange density of liquid, but enough to have the fish swim right past him. He swims forward under the water, carrying momentum to reach a rising sand bar towards a beach.

As he walks up the sand, the set of crystal fish swim fast behind him, ready to take a bite. Mark equips his special hatchet, and swings it around his body under the water, cutting one of the crystal fish in half from its face. It sinks to the bottom of the lake, where the other two fish spread out.

Mark climbs out of the dense, sweet water to the bottom of a hill, leading to the tallest mountain on the planet. He flexes his hands, igniting fire to his gloves, sending shockwaves around his body to dissipate the water. He shakes off the heated vibe, and decreases power.

The terrain remains sharp, with piercing crystals jutting out of the floor. The Space Jumper leaps up to move across the mountain range, jumping over several hills, before a major climb up the tallest crystal mountain in the region.

Mark springs off the durable, protruding crystals, snapping some loose as he jumps towards the peak. He controls his body on the sharp crystals upon landing to avoid stabbing himself. After a couple of hard jumps through the hazy weather, Mark lands on a flat spot at the top of the tallest mountain. Before he has a chance to appreciate the view, a pair of crystalized thugs rise from the ground, and form bodies with crystalized appendages.

Mark's eyebrows raise at the sight of the enemies at such a great height. He quickly crouches beneath a swinging arm of sharp crystals, and roundhouse kicks the enemy off the side of the mountain. He remains crouched low, and activates the shield in his pocket. He flexes his hands to shoot a ball of fire and electricity at point blank range at the second crystal bully, shattering it to pieces.

A shard of crystal lodges into Mark's cheek upon the explosion of the enemy. The shard contains an electronic pulse, sending a shockwave through his face. He pulls the shard from his cheek, stretching his face in pain. Holding the crystal in his hand, he watches it branch out, and grow from the air around them. With a mix of anger and pain, he clenches a fist, and shatters the shard in his glove.

Mark compresses blood from his cheek with his glove, sealing the wound with fire from his hand. He slowly walks over to the edge of the crystal cliff and looks down from the height. Below, an unforgiving gap between canyons rises up to a smaller hill. With the terrain being sharp and dangerous, Mark must choose his path carefully.

The path ahead remains unclear with the dense haze in the air. The waypoint is only a mile ahead. Mark jumps off the edge of the cliff with slightly enough power to clear the dangerous gap between the mountains. He drops down with some speed, nervous about landing on sharp crystals. The air is sweet as he inhales quickly through his nose, dropping down fast to the surface.

He lands on a steep cliff at the opposite side of the canyon, crushing through crystal shards extending out of the mountain. His shoes crash through the crystals to slow his speed, sending small shards across the mountainous cliff. His speed decreases, smoothing the side of the mountain like scraping corn off a cob.

He carries pace to a run over the flat part of the terrain, moving forward towards his objective. He jumps up another small hill, landing at the peak above. Scoping out the environment with his glasses, another lake sits below his altitude. Mark jumps up high, and aims for the center of the wide lake. He drops down, and splashes into the water.

Similar in taste and texture to the last lake, the Space Jumper quickly sinks down, slowly dropping towards another school of treacherous crystal fish.

The fish smell him in the water, and circle around his position like sharks. Mark touches down at the base of the lake, and checks his surroundings. His glasses highlight the enemies while underwater, marking their locations as they close in on him. The sweet water he walks through sends a special power through his shoes to energize his body. He focuses on the first fish approaching fast.

The Space Jumper juts his hand out before the fish opens its mouth. Electricity glows around Mark's hand as the fish tries to swallow it whole. The crystal fish clamps down on Mark's wrist, sending a shock of pain to his arm. The crystal fish locks it jaws on his hand as another two fish approach.

With full control of the fish on his fist, Mark uses it as a weapon against the other fish. Throwing a punch in the enemies direction, Mark clashes the two crystal fish together, causing them to smash, and explode. Shards from the connected fish's teeth remain attached to Mark's wrist, and spread beneath his glove. His hand grows numb, standing under the sweet water of the crystalized lake.

The Space Jumper flexes his hand, as the teeth of the crystal fish spread a germ through his wrist. A sharp pain extrudes from his fingers through his gloves as the final fish swims in his direction. He clenches his fist, when shards of crystals grow out of his hand, knuckles and fingers. The shards grow to around six inches long through the weave of his glove as the fish swims headfirst into his hand. The collision of crystals knocks pieces off the fish, deterring it in another direction. Mark flexes his hand again, breaking the shards off, as his knuckles pop under the water.

He continues to walk forward across the strange surface of the lake, with excruciating pain in his right hand. Unable to swim in the strange density of liquid, Mark walks on the surface of the lake, where he drops down a hole into a pit of sharp crystals. He lands hands first, where his non-crystal infused hand pierces through a set of sharp shards.

A separate infection begins to spread through his opposite hand as he lifts his body from the base of the lake. Carrying splinters of crystals in his hands, Mark grows shards from his fingers as he walks towards his objective growing closer ahead.

His breathing is natural under the water, with oxygen flowing through his shoes, protected by his mysterious spiritual barrier. He continues to walk over crystalized hills underwater before reaching another bank in the sand. He climbs the bank, finally emerging out of the lake.

He walks a few steps on the beach, and collapses on the crystalized ground. He inspects his hands, and flexes a fist.

Electricity, fire and crystal shards grow on his gloves. The harder he flexes his hands, the longer the crystal shards grow. The longer the shards grow, the more pain he inflicts. When he holds a fist as hard as he can, the shards shoot out in front of his body, where the pain subsides.

He kneels down before the beach, fatigued from walking underwater, and the pain of his new upgrade. His breathing is heavy, struggling to catch a breath. Liquid from the lake drips off his heavy clothes with his fist to the ground.

Catching his breath after the underwater fight, Mark flexes his muscles, empowering his shoes to charge his gadgets to heat his body. Feeling refreshed and ready to go, like drinking a cup of café, Mark notices his waypoint is over the next hill. He stands back up, loosening stress from his legs and body. He picks up a jog up a semi-steep hill over the strange, jagged surface on the crystal planet.

At the peak of the hill, he notices a large mansion made of crystal at the end of a path. The weather remains hazy, making it difficult to see the mansion. He runs forward towards the plaza, when another crystalized enemy rises from the ground. Mark stops in place and awaits for the thug to stop growing. Catching his breath, Mark continues to watch the enemy grow taller, wider, and sharper in front of the manor.

Standing over twenty feet tall, the crystal enemy grows a pair of arms and legs from its body. From its arm, the crystal creature grows a crystal bat, and loads back, ready to smack the Space Jumper to space.

Mark notices the spiked crystal bat swinging in his direction, and evades towards the goliath. The Space Jumper takes his hatchet from his side, and runs beneath the gap in-between the enemy's legs. Behind the monster, Mark jumps up, turns one hundred and eighty degrees, and slashes his blade in the back of the beast as he rises. The blade follows the Space Jumper's upward momentum, slicing a gap from the crystal goliath's lower back, to its head. As Mark peaks his jump, he continues to slash his hatchet over the monster, slicing its crystalized head, down to its chest. His falling momentum carries speed down, finishing the circular slice around the enemies lower front torso.

On the ground, Mark kicks the leg of the crystal beast to the side, knocking the goliath over in two separate directions. The split beast tilts over, and crashes both sides of its crystal body on the jagged ground, shattering into smaller pieces. Separated into four smaller sections, the monster stays alive and generally large. Its own bat turns into a separate monster, where the crystal creatures rise from the fall, and look at the Space Jumper. They slowly walk towards Mark, and surround his position. Two of the creatures swing appendages at Mark, where he ducks beneath the crystal arms.

As the second monster attacks, Mark grows crystals from his fists, and clashes with the punch. Blocking the attack, he uses his shoes to thrust kick the enemy away. The other parts of the crystal goliath walk near Mark and throw attacks at him.

With two crystal fists of his own, Mark deflects punches away from his body, leaving the enemies open. A heavy thrust kick destroys another portion of the goliath, sending shards flying into the smoky air. Mark turns his body, and throws a spinning back fist at another part of the broken goliath. Crystals, electricity, and fire from his hands overpower the slow creature. Mark knocks the enemy in half from the top, as it shatters down like glass.

Two more parts of the crystal goliath approach Mark, where he uses his hatchet to slice one down to small pieces. The destroyed parts of the crystalized goliath continue to mesh with the ground he walks over.

With one final portion of the goliath remaining to the side, Mark is eager to end the fight, and find the mysterious King Rox. He walks towards the fatigued crystal enemy, and stands face to glass. Mark grows a new set of crystals from his fists, fighting the pain, and unleashes a two handed punch to the final enemy. Upon contact, the final monster shatters into smaller shards of crystal.

Everything around the Space Jumper is quiet as he stands on the path in front of the spooky mansion, where King Rox resides.

Mark walks to the front doors, and swings them open. The building is architecturally accurate, with clean angles from wall to window, despite how jagged the rest of the planet is.

Mark enters the manor to a large crystal foyer, with art pieces made of crystal on wood and marble displays, spreading around the small room. Obscure paintings hang on the smooth crystal walls surrounding doors to the left, right, and front, where a host behind a desk stands behind.

The host is a similar crystal creature to everyone else, but is a darker shade of rose gold. Mark approaches the wooden desk slowly, and smiles at the host.

"Hi, I'm the Space Jumper. I'm looking to see if King Rox can tell me where my shoes came from?" Mark asks. "Ah yes, right this way, if you would follow me." The thin crystal host says to Mark in a deep and mumbled accent.

The host opens the wooden door behind him. Mark walks around the wooden desk to follow. They enter a beautiful, open room with vastly more art pieces spread out over two stories. The room is a nexus to many more rooms surrounding the mansion. The host continues to move forward, where he manipulates a special key from his hand to open a wooden door at the end of the central nexus. The door opens to a set of stairs leading down.

Mark slowly follows the crystal host, observing the art around the room. They walk down a wooden staircase to a dimly lit basement with barrels to the left and right. Large crystal pillars support the foundation of the building, as Mark and the host continue across the smooth floor. The cellar is chilly and vacant, with hundreds of wooden barrels containing some kind of special liquid inside. The host remains quiet, not asking Mark any questions.

After the cellar, they walk through another wooden door to a kitchen, with walls of icy crystals. Cabinets, shelves, and special refrigerators line the room, shaved down for special use, and smells like a variety of spiced meat, like salami, bacon, steak, and pastrami. Nobody is in the room, as Mark and the host continue to walk through the kitchen.

At the end of the icy, marbled kitchen, is an elevator made completely of smooth crystal. Everything in the mansion is smooth, compared to the outside world. The elevator is small and cramped, meant for only three or four people, or crystal creatures. The host forms another special key, and activates a button on the wall inside the elevator, as Mark stands calmly next to him. Wooden doors close vertically, as the elevator begins to rise up.

After a few seconds of rising up the crystal elevator, the door opens up to another hallway with a pair of rooms to the left and right. The host continues to walk down the hall to another door. He opens the door to a set of small stairs down another short, smooth, crystal hallway. They walk down the hallway towards the door at the end of the room.

"Our king is through these doors, allow me." The crystalized host says to Mark, opening the door for him. King Rox stands behind his desk, a similar looking crystal creature, stressed and worried, as Mark enters the luxurious, old-fashioned room. The king looks like an ordinary citizen of the planet, but wears a gold crown over his head. He has a red robe draped behind his back, as his body gleams of crystalized material.

"Sir, the Space Jumper." The crystal host says to the king, presenting Mark. "Whoa, you look capable of helping me." King Rox says to Mark as he looks across the wood and crystalized room.

"What do you need help with?" Mark asks the king with a smile. The door behind Mark closes as the butler exits. "The position of king is always up for grabs on this planet. Crystals are coming here right now to storm the manor. They think you are trying to take the throne from me. Are you trying to take the throne?" The king explains, asking Mark.

"No, I don't want to be king." Mark replies quickly. "Excellent, can you help me defend the castle?" King Rox asks the Space Jumper. "Yeah, but I need ammo for my gun. Is there anything you can do? Mark asks. "May I see your weapon?" The king asks Mark, presenting his crystal hand to the desk.

The Space Jumper rummages his hand around his pocket, takes out a single BB, and his gun. "This is your ammunition?" The king asks Mark. "They are bigger than you think." Mark replies.

King Rox holds the bullet in his crystal hand, and clutches a fist. In his other hand, he clenches another fist, and crushes parts of his crystal hand. He exhales after a deep breath, and opens his hand. In his palm is a large set of crystals nearly the same diameter as the bullet in his other hand. He cuts the ends of a few bullets at a time, and rolls them on to his desk. Mark picks up one of the crystal bullets, and examines the dimensions closely. He compares the diameter to one of his BBs, noticing the size is spot on.

"Alright, how many more can you make?" Mark asks the king. The king looks at Mark, and smirks, crushing another fist to release double the number of bullets than the first time.

The Space Jumper cleans the new crystal bullets with his glove, and places a handful in his pocket. He reloads his gun with the new ammunition, having more than needed. He dumps the rest of the bullets into the ammo sack in his bag. The air that fires the BB gun remains full in space. The intake of carbon from the atmosphere gives the Space Jumper plenty to shoot.

"Hey, can you tell me where my shoes came from?" Mark asks. "Throw your leg on the table." King Rox says easily to Mark, understanding his language with the power of his glasses and tablet.

The Space Jumper lifts one of his legs on to the king's desk. His shoe sits normally on the smooth wooden desk. The king moves his face close to the shoes to get a better look. He touches the shoe with a protruding crystal claw. The king's hand pops with an explosion of energy upon contact with the Space Jumper's shoe.

"Whoa, these are definitely not from here. This looks to be the work of a human. You should try your luck on Mega." King Rox says, stepping away from Mark's shoe, rubbing his crystal hand. Mark moves his leg from the desk, and stands back on the ground.

"Check back with my host to help defend the castle." King Rox says with his dry and craggily voice. Mark looks at the king, and nods in affirmation at the conclusion of dialogue, and the start of something much bigger.

The Space Jumper steps back outside of the room to find the Crystal host. They walk back to the front of the mansion through the door from the central nexus of the manor, and stand at the host table.

Mark stands patiently next to the host, and stares at the front door with his hatchet in hand. The host looks at Mark as they prepare for battle. "I hope you are ready for this Space Jumper." He says in a calm, dry voice. Mark nods at the host without looking at him, and walks closer to the front door.

He takes one of his explosive devices from his pocket, and plants it in front of the large set of double doors. Mark walks back to the host, and stands behind the desk, holding his hatchet. Together, Mark and the host watch the front door and listen for noise.

Minutes later, the front doors bang with a loud knock. The crystal aliens try to break the door down using their brute strength. The door bangs loud, three more times, and pauses after a few more seconds. The doors swing open, unveiling a large group of crystalized enemies. They begin to pour through the open door, when the explosive device Mark placed explodes, sending fire and shockwaves out the door. The first set of crystalized enemies explode out of sight.

The Space Jumper looks out of the door, and readies his BB gun in his opposite hand while holding his hatchet. Over a hundred crystal creatures slowly move towards the castle.

The windows to the left and right of the entrance crash open, and shatter on the smooth marble floor. Crystalized creatures climb through the open windows with jagged appendages. Mark aims his gun up to the window, and fires his new bullets at the creatures.

The first crystal he fires is incredibly large, separating several enemies back out the window. He tinkers with the particle accelerator, shrinking the bullets to a quicker, less obvious size. He continues to fire the gun at the windows, switching to the door at the swarm of crystal creatures.

The host of the castle wields a large crystalized sword, as he slashes through attackers, faster than most of the regular crystal enemies. He evades brute punches, swinging his blade at the enemies attacks. Mark runs ahead from behind the host stand to the floor to help push back the opposition. He uses his hatchet to swing and chop down enemies as they try to make their way into the entrance.

After hacking down over fifteen enemies with his blade, and shooting dozens more to empty the chamber to his gun, Mark is out of breath. A sea of crystalized enemies move in through the castle entrance outside the main door.

"We must retreat to the main hall." The crystal host says to Mark while fighting off a pair of enemies. The host slashes the pair of his fellow crystal creatures before opening the locked door to the nexus room. Mark nods to the host, and takes more bullets from his pocket. He loads his gun while moving towards the door. He hinges his hatchet back to his side, and takes out his laser sword. He pops out the light to manipulate a laser while holding his gun.

The Space Jumper runs to the center of the main hall as the crystal host closes the door to the atrium behind. The room is quiet for a few seconds, until the walls begin banging from all sides. Glass begins to break again, when the crystal creatures pour through the first and second floor. Their dense, crystal bodies hit the marble floor, when the door to the entrance room crashes open. The enemies slowly walk and tumble inside.

Mark continues to stand at the center of the wide floor of the nexus room near the stairs leading up to the second floor. Crystal enemies approach him from all angles, breaking through more doors and windows. The Space Jumper circles around to count all of the enemies, as his light sword shines a spectrum of bright colors. He approaches the most menacing crystal creature closest to him, and engages battle. He walks to the crystal enemy, and quickly slashes the helpless being in half.

Mark picks out targets approaching him at the center of the marble floor. He spins the light sword around his body, defensively attacking multiple crystal attackers. Bits of warm, cut glass crash on the floor as the Space Jumper moves around a large pillar.

Over fifty crystal creatures fill the main room as Mark moves around the floor towards available openings. He fights off crystals, as the host stands at the corner of the room near the door to the cellar. He uses his crystal sword to cut the enemies down to smaller sizes. Mark runs around the floor, shooting select enemies with his gun as they enter through windows.

One at a time, the crystal enemies fall, with only minor scrapes on the Space Jumper. Mark climbs the marble stairs to the second floor of the nexus, and runs past the many rooms to the side, listening for noise. Some of the crystal creatures stand on the balcony, waiting for Mark to approach.

The Space Jumper slashes through the slower, crystal enemies, finding time to reload his gun from the mob beneath him. The crystal enemies climb the steps to the left of the floor, and swarm the balcony above.

Mark is on the opposite side of the balcony, standing and watching the movement of the mob. He continues to jog around the long end of the balcony, shooting large crystals at the enemies pouring through the window. Crystal creatures surround Mark on both sides of the long end of the balcony next to the windows outside.

Before the crystals have a chance to grab him, Mark holsters his gun, and jumps over the wooden railing of the balcony, falling to the floor into a large mob of enemies. He clenches a fist on the way down, and pounds the ground hard through a small, jagged opening in the crowd. A deep and heavy shockwave ripples across the floor, shattering a large portion of the enemies.

Mark cleans up the remainder of crystal enemies near the cellar door as the host begins to open it. The crystal creatures on the balcony break the railing, and fall to the dense marble ground, shattering upon impact. The smart crystals move back to the steps, and slowly make their way back down.

Mark and the host retreat to the cellar beneath the house. They close the door, lock it behind, and stand guard at the bottom of the steps. They hear enemies crash and shatter on the floor above. "They are not worthy to poses the crown." The crystal host says to Mark, who smiles back, clutching his laser sword.

The door to the cellar bangs loud and consistent, quickly breaking open. Several crystal enemies tumble down the stairs, cracking off parts of their bodies.

As the crystalized creatures pile up at the bottom of the steps, Mark and the host start slashing the closest enemies. The light in the cellar is dim, with bits and pieces of glass flinging everywhere. After slashing over ten more enemies, Mark's laser sword begins to sputter. The interference of the glassed creatures disrupts the electronics in his flashlight. Mark's flashlight is the same one he brought from Earth, but with upgraded batteries from the Andromeda galaxy, and an alien crystal attached to the bulb.

Noticing the sputter, Mark lowers the laser, and takes out his hatchet. He uses the natural end of the metal hatchet to cut down pieces of glass from the consistently approaching enemies. The crystal host slashes several enemies into the stacked barrels of liquid, spilling the mysterious fluid over the floor. Wooden desks and casks flip and crash as the careless enemies move forward in the cellar.

Mark conserves his crystal ammo for special occasions, only firing when needed. He wields his gun and his hatchet, utilizing melee attacks from the blade, along with his arsenal of fight moves. He combines heavy slashes from the blade with thrust kicks and two fist punches, shattering the crystal enemies back. As one of the enemies fall, another five walk up from behind the pack. The cellar is now swarming with crystal enemies, overwhelming Mark and the host as they find themselves moving backwards towards the kitchen.

"Will they ever give up?" Mark asks the host out of breath. "We can only hope, human." The host replies, closing the door to the kitchen. Mark grabs a frying pan hanging from a rack of other cooking tools, and watches the door, awaiting the enemies to barge through.

A few seconds later, with one knock, the wooden door comes crashing down from its hinges, as the crystal enemies barge through. Mark throws the kitchen pan at the first enemy he sees, hoping to discourage them with creativity. The pan does little damage, as the enemies continue to push forward, and throw attacks. Mark uses his hatchet to deflect punches from the dense crystals, stepping back for stability.

The kitchen is quickly lost, as Mark and the host run back to the elevator to retreat. The crystal enemies continue to rush down the Space Jumper all the way to the closing elevator door. As the door is closing, Mark has to kick several crystalized enemies back. The elevator door closes, and begins to move up the building from the cellar. Mark and the crystal host of the manor are out of breath and injured with cuts and fractures. The luxurious elevator provides a calm atmosphere for Mark as he regains stamina.

The elevator doors open to the final hallway before King Rox's office. Everything is quiet on the top floor of King Rox's castle, until a window to the side of the hallway breaks. Glass falls to the dark red carpet of the lowered part of the hallway. Mark and the crystal host look over to inspect the commotion, noticing a random crystal creature beginning to crawl through. The crystal enemy climbs through the window, and falls to the floor, losing some parts of its body on impact. The crystal enemy looks at Mark and the host when several more windows begin to break one by one.

The persistent crystal creatures flood the final hallway in front of King Rox's office. Mark and the host walk forward, ready for another fight. Mark wields his BB gun and hatchet with the boomerang tip expanded. The crystal host wields his crystal sword defensively. Mark walks down the steps to the front of the doors leading left and right. He throws the hatchet forward at a moderate speed. It spins in the air, slicing through several crystal enemies. It hits the small staircase leading up to King Rox's office, and reflects back towards him. As the hatchet flies, Mark fires a few small sized crystal bullets at the attackers limbs before they can attack the host. Mark kicks several more enemies down and away from the action, as he catches his blade with one hand.

Crystal creatures continue to crawl through cracks in the windows around the red hallway. Mark and the host are almost in front of King Rox's office, as they climb the small staircase away from the guest rooms. They face away from the king's office, defending the space between. Mark fights off several enemies at once using fight moves and his hatchet, as the crystal host knocks on King Rox's door.

"Sir, the time has come." The host says to the king from behind the door.

The door to the kings office opens a crack. Mark kicks one of the crystal enemies into a larger group of enemies below the stairs, shattering some of them to smaller pieces. Mark turns the corner of the door, and enters the office. The Space Jumper and the host quickly enter the room after eliminating the closest enemies. Closing the door behind, Mark looks around the room and finds the closest, largest items around. He clutches a large, wooden bookshelf, and tips it over in front of the door to block the entrance. He grabs a heavy, wooden chiferobe along the wall of the office, and slides it behind the downed bookshelf. Mark throws an end table in the pile, and organizes the blockade for stability.

"They're coming." Mark says out of breath to the king, as he reloads special bullets into his gun. The king stands behind his desk, and takes a sword from the wall behind him. The king says nothing, when the door to his office begins to knock heavily. After a few more seconds of heavy knocking, the door breaks down from its hinges, and falls over the blockade of furniture. Crystal creatures try to pour through the ramped door in front of the office.

King Rox grows annoyed at the destruction of his manor, and walks forward to the door. Before the first crystal enemies have a chance to slip through the narrow crack, the king slashes their heads off, sliding the rest of their crystal bodies back.

The king camps by the door, waiting for the crystal creatures to enter. The burly king stands poised at the front door to his office, when a barrage of crystal shards come flying into the room over the barricade. The king blocks some of the shards, absorbing them into his own body.

Several more crystal enemies rip apart the barricade, smashing the door in half, and chopping the wood furniture to planks. They walk and slide through the entrance into the office, where the king stands awaiting. King Rox slashes his sword through the first approaching enemy, cutting it in half. He moves to the next enemy, continuing the violent combo with his sword. The King mows down over five enemies as they enter the room. Mark and the host watch the king vent his frustration out on his enemies, cutting the crystal creatures down to pieces.

One of the larger crystal enemies finds an opportunity to slash his weapon at the king, striking him in the chest. King Rox moves back a few paces, stunned from the attack. Mark notices the fall, and moves forward to defend the King of Crystal.

The Space Jumper fires a medium sized BB through the open gap of the king's office, sending back several crystal enemies, destroying many more. The room is partially clear, as Mark walks in front of the king. He looks outside the room to find a flood of crystal enemies pouring through all of the windows in the hall. King Rox walks next to Mark with his sword in front of his body, as Mark holds his gun and his blade.

Crystalized enemies climb over the debris from the barricade, fighting for a chance to take the crown. King Rox and the Space Jumper work together, defending the final room in the mansion. King Rox moves quickly and comfortably around the room, dodging attacks from the encroaching crystal creatures. Mark and the crystal host move towards the action to take some heat off the king. The crystal host slashes enemies with his big sword, while Mark utilizes fight moves and his hatchet.

The crystal enemies are persistent with their attack, rebuilding their bodies from the ground after being shattered in defeat. Most of the enemies Mark fights have already been defeated earlier in a different part of the house. The crystal creatures do not die under their safe circumstances, they reincarnate to a smarter form of their previous self. The way to defeat the crystal creatures would be to destroy their nucleus somewhere inside the genetics of their deep, rigid crystal form.

As Mark recognizes some of the enemies from prior, he realizes his efforts are futile. The Space Jumper does not have the proper armament to destroy all of the crystal creatures on the planet.

The enemies enjoy combat and confrontation, knowing they can respawn with an advantage. Mark takes a few steps back from battle, and watches King Rox and the crystal host fight the opposition with all their might.

"I don't know how much more I can take." Mark says to the king and the host. "They are relentless, but my host and I can defend ourselves from here." King Rox says to Mark, looking back at him as he tosses a crystal enemy against the wall. Mark kicks an approaching crystal enemy back towards the door, shattering it upon contact with the wall.

"You can escape through the window behind my desk." King Rox says to Mark during a short break in the fight. Mark nods to the host, and slowly walks to the window behind the desk. He looks outside, and checks down to the ground, finding more crystal enemies climbing the wall up towards the room. Mark takes a step back, and waits for the enemies to enter.

The host and the king notice Mark standing by the window and wonder what he is waiting for. Mark continues to stand patiently, as the first crystal enemy tries to crawl through the window. The Space Jumper uses the bottom of his foot to kick the crystal creature back out of the window before it makes its way inside.

Mark looks out the window again, finding a long line of enemies making their way towards the back wall. He stands back and punches the next enemy out of the window. Mark fights off the next few approaching enemies out the window as King Rox and the crystal host fight enemies at the door. Surrounded, Mark feels inclined to escape with his life, but does not want to leave the king surrounded.

Remaining persistent like the enemy, the Space Jumper continues to fight, helping the king preserve his crown, and his life.

The Space Jumper bashes the top of a crystal creature from the window, knocking down all of the enemies climbing up. The crystal creatures at the window shatter on the crystal ground below, requiring time to reform their bodies. Mark turns to the king and the host to watch them fight off the remaining two crystal enemies in the area.

"Now is my chance King. I'm off to Mega." Mark says to King Rox. "I hope you find what you are looking for, Space Jumper." The king replies, slashing down an approaching, injured enemy.

Mark walks to the window, and climbs on the ledge with one foot. He turns around, and waves back to the king and the host, as they lift their weapons back to him. Mark smiles, and faces outside, where he launches out of the window into the hazy sky. Catching a cloud, Mark charges a crouch, and blasts high into space.

Fed up with crystals, Mark jumps quickly out of the atmosphere to the zero gravity of space. Catching gravity fields over the planet, Mark retraces his steps to leave the galaxy.

Mega on his mind, feeling the curiosity for discovery, the Space Jumper catches gravity fields to warp past planets, jumping towards the colorful barrier of the galaxy in the distance.

Slowing before the colorful wall of energy, not trying to smash his face again, Mark inches towards the edge of the galaxy, and takes his tablet from his bag. Relaxing in zero gravity next to the security of the barrier, Mark expands the map of the universe, searching for Mega. He finds the galaxy, fifty million light years away.

Mark shrugs his face in disbelief at the distance of the galaxy, and sets the marker on his glasses. The direction to Mega displays in front of his eyes on his glasses.

"Maybe Lineage can help." Mark says to himself. He exits the map application on his tablet, and switches to his contacts list. He scrolls through familiar names of allies and enemies, dead and alive. Roger Clark from the International Space Station near Earth, Detective Ahura and Detective Torque from Andromeda, Officer Bill from Cigar, and the Wizard from Tengine, are some of the names he reflects back upon before finding Samantha's number.

The tablet rings as Mark calls Samantha from Lineage. "Is this you, Space Jumper?" She asks through her radio. "Hey Samantha, do you think you can break me out of the Café galaxy?" Mark asks. "Yeah, we'll be there in a minute." She replies. "Thanks, I'll send you my coordinates." Mark says. "See you soon." She concludes, as Mark ends the transmission.

Mark messages his astronomical whereabouts to Samantha, and places his tablet back into his bag. He takes time to catch his breath, relaxing his body in the zero gravity.

The Space Jumper closes his eyes, and doses off.

Finding himself over heating, Mark opens his eyes, discovering he is standing on a planet scorched by fire and destruction. Nothing is around but burnt trees, a smoky ground, and fire in the distance. He looks around, and takes a deep breath, smelling the heavy smoke of burnt trees, plants, and people. He looks to his right to find his mom, brother and ex-girlfriend standing a short distance away. They look at him and slowly wave with a smile. Mark looks to his left to find more of his allies, and random aliens from his home universe. Astronauts from the International Space Station, bartenders from Mars and Andromeda, peace officers, and doctors, all surround the Space Jumper on the burning planet. Mark looks back to his right to find his mom, his brother, and ex-girlfriend dissolve into ash, fading away in the wind. A tear rolls from his eye, feeling the pain of losing people who still have him in thought. He walks to the ash of his family, and frantically looks back to his left to find his allies burn away in a fire from the planet. The friends and family surrounding him burn into oblivion as a heavy vibration shakes his body.

Everything turns white around Mark, when he opens his eyes in real life to find the Lineage ship warp out of a spiraling black hole. The ship moves close to the barrier, as Mark sheds a tear in real life, shaking off another heavy dream.

Mark rubs away the tear of sadness from his eye. He watches the Lineage ship back in to the barrier. The hatch from the garage lowers from the back, as a member of Lineage walks out, carrying an electric prod. The Lineage member pokes the green and blue force field with the prod, activating an electric current to disrupt the shield. Mark takes advantage of the small window, and floats through the opening towards the ship.

"Cool tool, thanks for the save buddy." Mark says to the crewmember, requesting a handshake. The crewmember is stunned at the humility of the Space Jumper, and shakes his hand. "Samantha wishes to see you inside." The crewmember says to Mark. The two walk up the hatch, and into the garage of the Lineage ship.

Chapter 7

Listeria

"It's always good to see you Samantha." Mark says, walking up the ramp of the garage into the ship. Samantha stands next to the Hedgehogs, accompanied by a few members of Lineage. "Great to have you back, Space Jumper." Samantha replies, gushing to Mark with a smile. She walks towards the Space Jumper and gives him a big hug. He has his hand out ready for a handshake to keep things professional, but she squeezes him tight as if she does not want him to go again. Mark smells the familiar scent of her vibrant, green skin, as she lets go. "I'm looking for the galaxy known as Mega." Mark asks the crew.

"Mega?" Samantha reiterates to the crew with a smile. She looks back to Mark, and shrugs her shoulders up, not knowing about the galaxy. "Do you think Captain Drake knows anything about Mega?" Mark asks Samantha. "Drake is on a mission right now with some members of the crew. Let me try and radio him." She replies, moving up through the garage towards the stairs to the pilots cabin. The doors to the ship finally close all the way behind, as they take off, away from the Café galaxy. The ship cruises through space at a moderate pace.

"Captain, are you there?" Samantha whispers over the radio, sitting with Mark in the pilots chairs. "This is Drake, over." The captain responds with a normal tone. "Captain, the Space Jumper is back in our company, and is looking for the galaxy called Mega." Samantha explains to Drake over the radio. She sits back in her chair for a moment, as Mark leans in, eager for a response. "Our reconnaissance here is almost complete. Make your way to our location for extraction." Drake responds over the radio. "Affirmative Captain, we are on the way to Listeria." Samantha replies to the radio.

"Hi Captain." Mark says into the radio, sneaking into the conversation. "Good to hear from you Space Jumper. We could use your help here on Listeria." Drake says over the radio. "Affirmative, we'll see you soon." Mark replies, leaning back in his chair. "Over and out." Samantha concludes to Drake.

"Where is Captain Drake?" Mark asks Samantha directly, hoping she is not so vague. "He is on Listeria, City of Plants, in the Bombing galaxy. We are looking to harvest raw materials to power the black hole gun you obtained for us. We can be there shortly." Samantha explains, activating the thruster, launching the ship to warp speed.

The Lineage ship remains only partially repaired from the damage of the rough landing on the Alphanauts planet. The small halls provide a breeze as the crew travel through space at warp speed. Mark and Samantha are in control of the ship, feeling every movement and distortion.

"Did you find anything out about the rotating eyes?" Mark asks Samantha. "They belong to a special class of beings. We are doing research into the origin of the rotating eye you gave us. Its technology is beyond our knowledge." Samantha explains, piloting the ship while getting comfortable in her seat.

"Do you know where I can find more? The rotating eyes may connect me to where my shoes came from." Mark asks Samantha, scratching his head. "It depends on the universe you are in." Samantha replies.

"That could take forever. How many universes are around us?" Mark asks. "There are seven separate universes that we know of." Samantha replies.

"Wow, only seven? Gives me hope with tracking the rotating eyes." Mark replies in amazement. "You have no idea what you are in for. Is it worth the risk?" Samantha asks in a worried tone. "Risk is the only choice I've got." Mark replies under his breath.

"There are regions we have yet to explore, but with the black hole gun you've obtained, we can pinch time, and travel further, faster. Our crew is testing quantum theories and mechanics through trial and data." Samantha explains to the Space Jumper. "Let's find Captain Drake." Mark says to Samantha, eager to move forward. "A few more minutes in this wormhole and we will be near his location." Samantha says in her foreign, alien accent.

"Get ready, we are almost here. The city of plants is immensely treacherous." Samantha says to Mark as she decelerates the ship. The dark blue wormhole subsides from spinning, as the ship enters a region surrounded by several small planets with branches protruding from them. All of the planets are fire red, with brown and green trees sticking out to space. The ship slows to nearly a pause, where gravity controls the speed.

"Listeria, City of Plants, is the one over there." Samantha says to Mark, pointing to a small planet behind six other planets ahead.

The city of plants is red and green, combined with a fiery surface, and healthy trees. The planet is less than a lightyear away. Samantha pushes buttons on the computer system in the ship's dashboard, maneuvering levers towards the planet, staying centered away from the neighboring planets. The first planet in the region approaches quickly. Upon catching a scent of the atmosphere, the planet extends several of its long trees that reach out, and attempt to grab the Lineage ship in space like a flytrap.

"Here we go." Samantha says, vigorously controlling the ship left and right. The first planet towards Listeria extends over fifty trees with teeth as leaves, reaching out to feed off the stray anomalies that float by in space. Samantha controls the speed of the ship, moving away from the end of the branches as they float through. The Space Jumper controls the main steering from the other side of the pilots seat.

Together, Mark and Samantha slowly veer the ship away and around the volatile and lively trees extruding from the planets with deadly plants. The Lineage ship moves up, down, left, right, and forward past the large, dangerous trees as their branches follow.

Listeria, City of Plants sits behind five more similar, dangerous planets. As they move forward past the first planet, the second planet already has its teeth showing, ready to feast on the debris that is Lineage's ship. The plants on the second planet are able to reach out to the first planet, initiating contact between the hazardous trees. Samantha controls a steady pace, where Mark veers away from danger. The ship floats up and down in space, evading the grasp of the long necked trees trying to pull them down to the planet.

The planets vary in color, with most being a fiery red, and some being dark purple. The approach to Listeria is challenging, as the ship must move away from the constantly growing trees. As they move further away from the tree, they are actually moving closer towards the grasp of another tree on the neighboring planet. Together, Mark and Samantha take careful control of the speed and direction at which they move, avoiding the hostile planets of plants.

The ship veers through space, avoiding the brown wooden bark of the vicious palm trees. Mark and Samantha control the direction of the beat up Lineage ship through the valley of planets towards Listeria, where Captain Drake requires extraction. Moving towards the second planet, Mark notices more plants protruding lengthy and hungry canopies towards the ship. The trees are alive, opening their branches to show off their teeth.

"We need to pick up speed." Mark says to Samantha. She increases the ships speed to avoid the violent plants better. Mark has room to play, maneuvering away from the trees with the increase in speed. Approaching the third and fourth planets near Listeria, the trees begin to throw projectiles at the ship. As the projectiles fly across the view at the windshield, Mark and Samantha watch a circular ball made of a green material float through space. The ball explodes into fiery, molten liquids, spreading drops across the space. The Lineage ship must now avoid lengthy, aggressive trees, and the toxic fireballs they expel.

The speed at which they travel enables Mark and Samantha to watch the direction of the trees, and avoid their attacks. The trees are slow in zero gravity, requiring time to intercept Lineage. Mark and Samantha remain vigilant, and stay ahead of the attacks like a receiver avoiding a running back.

The trees find themselves behind Lineage, unable to destroy the ship. Samantha and Mark move across the fifth and sixth planet in the Bombing galaxy region towards Listeria, City of Plants. The number of projectiles thrown at Mark and Samantha double the closer they get to Listeria.

The lives of Lineage remain in their hands as they control the ship towards Captain Drake's location. The trees from the previous planets begin to throw their explosive projectiles from behind, forcing Mark and Samantha to have eyes in the back of their heads. Relying on luck, and swift movement, Mark and Samantha use their smarts to move the ship away from danger. The ship is light in the zero gravity, allowing the pilots to maneuver swiftly through space.

"That's Listeria over there." Samantha says, pointing to the furthest planet in the cluster. Listeria is mostly red, with small plots of green and brown scattered around. She rolls the ship towards the target planet, avoiding the tingly tentacle trees from the prior plants.

Samantha and Mark maneuver over Listeria, where Samantha hops on the radio to contact Drake. The ship moves forward at a steady pace as Mark moves the controls to avoid a large set of trees. Listeria, City of Plants has a fitting name with the largest trees in the area. All of the trees take offense to Lineage's presence, and throw exploding plants at them.

Samantha controls dials on the scanner on the dashboard in the ship. "I have his location, we must keep moving forward." She says to Mark with excitement, knowing they may all die at the precise swoop of a tree. The ship flies through the atmosphere of the planet, where the trees around the area begin to sway more dramatically. They attempt to disrupt the path of the ship, moving back and forth through the sky.

The ship reduces height, moving closer and closer to the ground, breaking through layers of smoky clouds, unveiling fiery mountains below. Trees reduce in numbers as they approach the surface. The trees are so tall, they struggle finding targets closer to the ground. Trees of normal height sit on the ground, and prey upon visitors, throwing plant based projectiles as a welcoming gift. Mark still has his hands full, maneuvering the ship around the volatile environment of Listeria.

The ship flies over the surface at fifteen thousand feet. Mountains are on fire, trickling down towards the ground, creating lava on the surface. The Lineage ship continues to prepare for a landing near Drake's location. Red lava flows fresh over the ground at a fiery temperature, yet plants continue to grow over the surface. The ground contains plots of green grass, surrounding lakes of lava. Listeria, City of Plants has a strange ecosystem, utilizing heat to create strange and aggressive life.

A thousand miles away from the captain, Mark and Samantha look at each other with relief. "Let's park here, up ahead." Samantha says, pointing to a spot on her map on the dashboard. Drake's location is not far from her parking area. The number of projectiles thrown has decreased from the depths of space, as the trees reduce in number. Her landing spot is located before one of the largest mountains on the planet near Captain Drake's last known location.

"Captain, we are here." Samantha says over the radio. "I see the ship." Captain Drake says back from the radio.

Mark and Samantha quickly park the ship to the fiery surface, and open the rear hatch. As the door to the ship opens, they look outside into a hellish world of fire and heat. They look up a large hill to the mountains over a mile away. "Look, I see them." Samantha exclaims, pointing at the cave to three small figures running outside.

As they look ahead, a large explosion erupts from the base of the mountains. "That must be Drake." Samantha exclaims. "You should stay here with the ship, Sam. Let me go after them. I can clear a path, and radio you when I make contact." Mark says, standing at the edge of the door to the Lineage ship. "No, he needs my help, I must go as well." Samantha replies. "No, I can't risk losing you." Mark says, holding her arm tight. The two look into each other's eyes for a few seconds, seeing who wants it more. "Find him, and radio me when you do." Samantha says to Mark, holding his body dramatically.

Mark jumps outside, and lands on the hot ground below. The surface is extremely rigid with dense dunes of a hot rock material. Small hills block the way to Drake, as Mark runs forward with his hatchet in hand. At the peak of the first hill, the Space Jumper looks ahead over the terrain. Smaller versions of the plants that throw projectiles in space flood the fiery surface. Over ten plants stand ahead, waiting to catch flies to feast. Mark takes a deep breath, and runs forward over the surface towards Drake.

The first plant ahead notices Mark through either sound, or smell. It leans back, and begins hurling red-hot fireballs at Mark with its multiple branches. The flytrap tracks Mark's movements, aiming ahead of his location like a sniper. The wildlife on this planet is smart, and desperate for food. Mark deflects one of the fireballs with his hatchet, and runs towards the six-foot tall plant.

He blocks another fireball, and slashes through the plant at close range. The hatchet halves the plant with a smooth cut across its base. The tall plant keels over, and stops throwing fire. It quickly shrivels on the hot ground. The terrain remains open, yet rigid, with small hills leading to Captain Drake. Mark runs across the heated ground towards the next plant in the way. The tall red flower throws fireballs at Mark at the same time he throws the hatchet at its core stem. The hatchet rips through the stem, and boomerangs back towards the Space Jumper. Catching the hatchet in midair, Mark takes out his BB gun, and checks his ammo.

He continues to run across the ground up small hills, unveiling new enemies in the way. He aims his gun, walking slowly forward, and blasts one of his new crystals at the next plant. He sends a large crystal through the plant before it has the chance to throw its fireballs. The crystal spikes into the ground with the core of the plant behind it. Mark runs forward, and jumps over the downed plant off the crystal, nailing it further into the ground.

A large gap is below a wide pit of fire and lava. The Space Jumper had no idea the pit of fire was beneath him before jumping high off the plant.

Soaring through the sky, Mark aims his gun at several plants below that smell his scent. The multiple plants begin to throw fireballs at Mark in the sky, like ground to air missiles. The Space Jumper avoids the attacks, and fires several large BBs at the plants, missing two, but hitting two. The large crystals spear the hot ground, knocking out the stem of the plants. The path to the Lineage ship is almost clear as Mark moves forward towards a steep wall.

Standing at the base of a cliff, Mark locks his legs in a crouch, and jumps up into the sky. He spins in the air in a three sixty, and scans the environment. Over the cliff, a few more red plants patiently wait for an excuse to let loose. The Space Jumper descends the jump, moving forward towards the edge of the cliff. Before touching the ground, Mark fires another BB forward, and bolts another enemy plant to the ground.

Mark quickly looks up the path, and fires another shot at the next plant standing at the peak of a hill. The large crystal BB soars through the stationary plant, uprooting its red and green base. Mark continues to move forward up the hill towards a small decline. Down the hill, another large plant stands before another large gap in the ground.

Mark runs down the hill, throws his hatchet at the plant, and slices off three of its fire throwing branches. As the boomerang returns to the Space Jumper, it slices off the remaining three branches, leaving the plant as only a stalk.

At the edge of the hill, Mark utilizes his speed to jump across the gap. In the air, Mark looks down to see bright red lava bubbling on the ground. An explosion occurs between the gaps, sending a fireball up to the sky after Mark lands on the other side. He turns around to find fire and lava falling back down into the gap. He turns around to look forward, finding another tall plant ahead, already throwing fireballs at him. He dives out of the way of the baseball-sized fireball, sliding on the dirt. He aims his gun at the plant and fires three times. The first two pulls of the trigger fire large, unorthodox crystals that destroy the alien plants. Nothing happens after the third shot, indicating the gun is empty.

Taking a moment to breathe, Mark pulls more crystals from his pocket, and loads his gun. He snaps the barrel back of the revolver, and looks up the small mountain.

He walks up a small hill, and finds another plant ahead. He casually fires a large shot at the plant, knocking it over from its roots. The Space Jumper continues to walk forward towards another small hill in the open terrain. Peaking from the hill, he looks up to find a steep cliff ahead. Below the cliff is a gap, leading to more lava and fire. The cliff is at an awkward angle, making it impossible to scale up or down without a pair of climbing tools.

Mark stands before the gap, looking up at the ten-story cliff, and thinks about his plan of attack. He loads his legs, and springs off the hot ground. The moment before he jumps, the gap below him shakes the ground, causing a misstep in his jump. Mark awkwardly jumps up towards the cliff realizing he is going to be short from the top. Fire shoots up from the gap of lava, as Mark reaches for the angled wall under the cliff. He clings his hatchet into the wall, and holds his position for a moment.

The Space Jumper hangs twenty feet from the top of the angled cliff, losing traction of his hatchet from the heat of the planet's molten core. Mark kicks up off the rock wall, unhinging his blade at the same time.

The wall is at an upward angle, where Mark kicks off a second time below the base, and rises towards the edge of the cliff. He swings his arm over the angled cliff, and clings the blade to the ground. Hanging on to the edge of the cliff, Mark pulls his weight up the edge to safety.

Close ahead, Mark finds Drake and two of Lineage's crewmembers lying face down on the hot ground, wearing radioactive suits and special helmets. Mark runs to Captain Drake and kneels down next to his lifeless body. "Drake, are you still alive?" He asks calmly, turning the captain's body over.

Drake's eyes are closed, calm and peaceful. Mark looks over to the Lineage crewmembers noticing they are squirming on the ground in pain. "You guys alright?' Mark yells out to the crew. "Space Jumper, we have to go. Grab the case." The crewmember says, pointing to the metallic briefcase next to Drake.

Mark looks back to the captain, and knocks his knuckle on his helmet. He waits a moment, and knocks again. The captain wakes up in a flash, and grabs Mark's arms. He looks at the Space Jumper, trying to catch his breath. "Space Jumper, let's get out of here." Captain Drake says to Mark, collecting himself. The crew's radioactive suits have heavy damage from heat wear, and cuts from the rocks.

Mark helps Drake to his feet, where he stands with a limp. The crew are also limping towards the captain. "Samantha, I'm with the captain, we need a pickup. Follow the dead trees and crystals." Mark radios in to Samantha at the Lineage ship.

"On the way, hold on for a minute." Samantha replies to the crew. Mark assists Drake by his shoulder, lending an arm. The crew hears a noise behind them, where they look back inside the blown out cave. "They're coming." Drake says, looking back at the noise erupting from the cave.

As Mark looks back, he finds over twenty, tall plants move towards the entrance of the cave. They walk forward towards the crew with four branches unrooted from the ground. They stand over eight feet tall with many branches. The first row of plants begin to throw fireballs at the injured crew. "Move to the cliff!" Mark yells to the crew.

Captain Drake grabs the briefcase from the ground, and takes out his gun. The crew take out their weapons and aim them towards the walking fire plants. Mark lifts his BB gun, and fires first at the plant that is about to throw the first fireball. A large crystal spears through several plants before losing trajectory in the heated air. The crew fire their weapons, shooting lasers at the plants. The small lasers strike several appendages from different plants, but do not do long term damage. Lineage's guns overheat, needing time to recover. Mark throws his hatchet hard into a mob of fire plants. He aims his gun while his blade flies through the limbs and branches of the hostile plants.

Mark fires several shots away from his hatchet, and rolls sideways out of the way from several fireballs. He maintains stability in a crouch, and fires several more shots into the crowd, knocking enemy plants back from their branches. The Space Jumper's hatchet flies back through the large group of fire plants, slicing several of them in half. Mark catches the blade, and immediately throws it again towards another dense group of enemies.

As the blade flies, Drake and the Lineage crew shoot their laser weapons and throw explosives at the group of plants as they continue to push forward out of the cave. The enemy plants are relentlessly pouring out from the cave, forcing Mark, Drake, and the crew back towards the cliff with the awkward angle.

As Lineage takes pause on the battlefield, allowing their laser weapons to cool down, fireballs strike the two crewmembers. They fall backwards in pain from the heat, landing at the edge of the cliff. Mark looks back, and continues to shoot large crystals at the plants. Drake also shoots his gun at the plants, not doing much damage. His small lasers only graze the dense branches of the fire plants of Listeria.

The Space Jumper and Captain Drake face an army of fire plants, as they slowly move back towards the edge of the cliff. Outnumbered in the battle, Mark hears a vibration arise from behind him. He looks over the high cliff to find Samantha and the Lineage ship rising above the lava and fire. The rear hatch to the ship opens, and levels at the end of the cliff.

"Get in." Samantha yells into the radio from inside the ship. Captain Drake drags the two injured crewmembers inside the ship as Mark continues to provide suppressing fire, taking heat from actual fire thrown at him. The Space Jumper's gun is empty as he catches his blade, walking backwards into the ship.

"Go, go, go!" Captain Drake yells to Samantha from two levels below. The hatch slowly begins to close as Mark stands by the door, and looks back at the plants. The ship rises up from the cliff, and flies up towards space.

Captain Drake and the two crewmembers crumple onto the floor of the ship, and begin to remove their gear, starting with their helmets. Samantha gives control of the ship to a copilot, and comes running down the stairs to check in on the captain. She runs across the floor, stepping over the captain's helmet, and gives him a hug. Mark stands at the rear hatch, and watches Lineage.

"Did you get it?" Samantha asks the captain, helping him stand to his feet. "We got some, enough to take us where we need to go." Drake replies to Samantha.

"What is it?" Mark asks the captain and Samantha. Drake and Samantha look at Mark, and walk to the case on the ground. He unhinges the safety latches on the case, and opens the top. He pulls out a red colored rod from inside, and holds it up for Mark to see.

"This is a rare fire energy that powers the black hole gun." Drake says, holding the rod. The device has a red energy goo inside of a glass tube, with wires connecting to a small computer on the tube. "We can use this power on the ship, and all of our other technology." Drake explains to Mark, looking back to Samantha. Captain Drake eagerly walks to the middle of the ship towards the engine room. Mark and Samantha follow behind, catching up to the captain.

Drake stands in front of the black hole gun, and opens several compartments in the main computer. He disconnects several wires, and houses the red tube in a special anti gravity microwave. The tube floats in the housing after Drake closes the device. He seals the engine closed after re-connecting wires, and walks quickly up the stairs of the ship to the pilots cabin. The remaining crew inside the ship congratulate Drake as he moves up the circular stairs to the top floor.

Captain Drake sits in the pilots chair next to the copilot, who stands up and walks back to the common area with the rest of the crew. Samantha sits next to Drake at the pilots cabin. Mark stands behind them, holding the two chairs in between.

"Alright, let's power this thing up." Drake says calmly to Mark and Samantha. The captain flips several switches and knobs on the dashboard. The ship sits idle in zero gravity, away from the hostile plants of Listeria. Mark watches the dashboard of the ship, noticing heat fluctuations on the computer. The outside temperature is rising fast, yet the inside of the ship remains cool.

Looking outside the front window, Mark discovers a red aura gleaming off the ship. "Captain Drake, I've been meaning to ask if you know where the

Mega galaxy is." Mark calmly asks Drake. The captain continues to adjust knobs and levers on the ship. "Don't worry Space Jumper. We are on our way to Mega right now." Drake replies, looking over his shoulder to Mark. "Well alright, sounds good." Mark concludes, slowly stepping back, and away from the pilots cabin. Mark walks back to the main deck of the ship, and down the stairs with the rest of the crew to lounge and play games.

The red power works around the exterior of the ship, affecting space. Captain Drake takes the ship out of idle, and begins turning towards his new location. He moves the throttle forward, when the ship takes off into warp. The red glow from the energy rod creates a vast difference in speed inside a wormhole. To the crew, the ship barely feels like it is moving.

The Space Jumper makes himself at home, walking around the top deck of the Lineage ship. He waves to the crew, and walks into the kitchen. He opens a metallic chest to find a variety of sandwiches sitting inside. He grabs a sandwich, and devours it quickly. The meat in the sandwich is foreign, and alien. Mark tosses the garbage in a trash compactor, and uses the bathroom in the next room over. He walks out of the bathroom, and back to the lounge area of the ship. From the lounge, he makes his way back downstairs to the crew quarters.

As Mark looks downstairs, he notices everyone is having a good time in the crew quarters. People are playing pool, foosball, watching television, and listening to music. Mark joins the party and walks over to the pool table. One of the crewmembers pours him a drink as he stands next to the table. Mark drinks the strong liquid with the crew, and watches the games around him.

After a few minutes of digesting the social life of Lineage, Mark walks out of the crew quarters to the engine room. The engine room is cold as ice, to avoid overheating the strict mechanical components. Mark is the only person in the room as he checks his environment. He walks to the microwave device on the wall that houses the newly acquired red power, and watches the movement of the fluid inside. The red power rod contains some kind of thick, rubbery liquid. Mark stares at the red power rod for a minute, absorbing its presence and digesting how it may work. He takes a step back, and focuses on the engine as a whole, taking in the depth of the bigger picture.

He sees components of the black hole gun he acquired from the Melon galaxy. Mark reaches his hand out to touch the gun, but before he lays a finger on it, the loud speaker above turns on. "Space Jumper, can I have a word up top?" Drake says. Mark pulls his hand back quickly in the odd timing, and makes his way back upstairs.

Walking into the pilots cabin, the Space Jumper stands behind Samantha and Captain Drake's chairs. "What's the word?" Mark asks. "Our intel from Listeria, City of Plants, suggests a major supply of red energy is on Mega. It looks like our quests intertwine, Space Jumper. If we all work together, we can find what we are looking for." Captain Drake says bluntly to Mark. "We are almost there." Samantha says to the captain, and to Mark with a smile.

The Space Jumper watches Samantha and Drake pilot the ship in the blue, white, and partially pink wormhole. "I can control us from here Sam, why don't you grab a drink and talk to the crew." Drake says to Samantha, wanting to be alone. Samantha smiles, and slowly rises out of the co-pilots seat. She looks at Mark, and walks out of the pilot's cabin. Mark pats Captain Drake's shoulder in a friendly manner, and exits the room as well.

"So what is the Mega galaxy like?" Mark asks Samantha, walking through the main deck of the ship. "We'll see when we get there, Space Jumper." Samantha replies, and continues. "Hey, meet me downstairs." She says, walking into the kitchen of the ship. Mark smiles, and walks down the steps to the crew quarters. "What did Drake want?" One of the crewmembers asks Mark. "We are getting close to the Mega galaxy." Mark replies calmly to the crewmember, who spins the handle on the foosball table.

Samantha walks down the stairs to the crew quarters and immediately looks at Mark. She smiles at crewmembers as she walks past the games. She walks past the couches facing the televisions, and heads towards the engine room. "Space Jumper, can I speak with you?" Samantha asks Mark, as he scores a goal on the table. He looks up to Samantha, and meets her in the next room, the sleeping quarters of the ship with all of the beds.

"Hey." He says coolly to her after turning the corner. She turns around from her bed and looks at Mark. She pulls him close to her where their bodies touch. "I've been thinking about you a lot." She says to Mark, playing with the collar of his thick jacket. "Oh yeah?" He casually replies. She nods her head at Mark, and begins kissing him on the lips. She steps backwards, and falls into her bed, holding Mark on top of her. They continue to kiss romantically, exchanging warmth with one another. They begin to undress in the cool bedroom next to the cold engine room.

About twenty minutes later, Captain Drake is on the radio above. "We're here guys." Drake says to the general crew. Mark and Samantha look at each other, laying in her bed with little clothes on. They smile while frantically beginning to dress, and equip gear for the new mission ahead. Samantha walks out of the crew quarters first, as Mark follows a minute later.

Chapter 8

Mega

At the pilots deck, Samantha sits next to Drake in the chairs as Mark makes his way behind them. "Check it out." Captain Drake says with excitement. Ahead, Mark looks out the window to find a large cluster of planets, all connected together using an elaborate amount of metal, and rotating parts. The galaxy spans back several light years, all connected to each other.

"What's the plan?" Mark asks the captain. "We're going to get more of that red stuff. The question is which planet has the power?" Drake responds, flying the Lineage ship slowly towards Mega. The planets on Mega are daunting, with a connected heavy metal apparatus. Solid steel holds the structure stable like a skeleton. Captain Drake flips switches on the dashboard as Mark has his eyes on Samantha, who looks back to him and smiles.

"You guys see all that red?" Mark points out to a planet connected to Mega, off in the distance. "Looks promising, we should see what they have." Samantha says enthusiastically, sitting in the co-pilots chair. "Alright, I'm dropping us in. I'm activating the peace beacon now." Drake says, manipulating more levers on the complex dashboard. The peace beacon allows the ship to travel safely to heavily populated and contested areas without a fight.

The Lineage ship follows the elevator system towards the red colored planet in the distance. Flying close to the metallic system, Mark notices human beings travelling within the elevators, transferring people to other planets within the galaxy. People move at an incredibly fast rate of speed across the heavy, metal structure.

"Mega, this is Captain Drake of the Lineage group. Come in, over." Drake says into the radio on the dashboard. There is a delay responding, as the ship continues to fly towards the bright red planet. "Affirmative Lineage, we are monitoring your approach." A voice says behind the radio. Drake and

Samantha move the ship across the metal structures connecting the planets, and quickly drop into the atmosphere of the red planet.

The new planet is beat red, with green grass and brown roots. The water on the ground is also bright red, indicating the planet reeks of the red power they seek. Lineage moves near some mountains, and finally parks the ship outside of a base in a hotspot of red energy. They park their beat-up ship on the ground, and prepare to move out. Drake and Samantha unhinge their safety belts at the same time, and begin to move out of the cockpit towards the side exit of the ship. Mark follows behind, ready to assist, aid, and discover.

Samantha, Mark, and Captain Drake walk out from the side of the ship into a humid and dry environment. Clouds hang over the air, providing hope for the Space Jumper. The mountains to the left of the ship are mostly dirt, with some fresh trees scattered around. Trees also scatter around the red ground ahead of the special base. As Mark, Samantha, and Drake check their gear for whatever may lie ahead, a small group of human scientists walk to the ship from behind a short hill.

The humans wear high tech hazard suits with helmets, carrying weapons in hand. "What brings you to Mega?" The lead hazmat scientist asks Captain Drake. "My crew and I have stumbled upon a red power rod, and would hope to learn how it works." Drake calmly explains to the scientists. "The red energy here contains an atomic matter only available in this galaxy. It turns atoms inside out, allowing a better, smoother manipulation of time." The scientist explains. "It looks like it's our lucky day." Mark chimes in from behind Samantha and Drake.

"Hey, you're that guy, the wanted guy, Space Jumper!" The scientist says to everyone, pointing out Mark behind Drake and Samantha. The trio of scientists look at each other, and quickly take out their guns from their sides. They aim their weapons at Mark, Drake and Samantha.

Captain Drake and Mark quickly take out their guns and aim at the scientists on the blood red fire planet. "You seem to have quite a reputation, Space Jumper." Captain Drake says to Mark in an annoyed tone. "Yeah, I unfortunately do." Mark replies to Drake.

Everyone quickly begins shooting at each other, with the scientists taking the first shots. Mark and Drake veer to the side, dodging green colored lasers flying through the air. Mark takes cover behind a rock with Samantha as Drake takes cover behind a rigid dune of dirt in the ground. The scientists retreat to where they came from, radioing their colleagues for reinforcement. They continue to lay down suppressing fire on Lineage as they backpedal towards their base. Mark shoots his BB gun blindly over the rock. He looks over to Samantha and smiles.

After a pause of gunfire, the Space Jumper activates his shield, and steps boldly out from cover. He walks forward across the dirt ground up a small hill. He sees the scientist in the hazmat suits clambering slowly over a small dirt mound. He crouches down, and looks back to Samantha and Drake. He motions his hand to them, indicating they should push forward as well. They pop out of cover, and run to Mark at the hill as his shield weakens. The three walk forward towards the path of the scientists.

Mark and Lineage climb over the same hill as the scientists to find them, and three other scientists aiming their guns in their direction. Mark takes a quick look, and crouches for cover immediately after. "I think they know we're coming." The Space Jumper says sarcastically to Drake and Samantha, as lasers fly over their head.

"I got this." Captain Drake says, taking a circular device from his jacket. He presses a button, and hurls the device over the top of the small hill. The device flies towards the enemies, landing at their feet, and explodes the ground beneath them. The scientists fall into a deep hole in the ground, where fire waits beneath. The hole has a twenty-foot radius, eating through the hot red dirt. Mark, Samantha, and Drake watch the scientists fall into the hole of the depth grenade.

"All clear." Captain Drake whispers to Mark and Samantha. The trio climb over the hill and move forward towards another hill around the hole. They continue forward over the hill, noticing another pair of scientists approaching from beyond the horizon. Above the horizon in the bright red dirt is another pair of scientists scoping out the area.

With four hostile scientists in the area, Mark, Samantha, and Captain Drake move closer towards what they are looking for. "I'll get the ones in the back, and you guys get the ones close by." Mark whispers to Lineage. The Space Jumper jumps high into the air, and falls behind the enemies on the furthest hill ahead. He makes contact with Drake and Samantha watching from afar, and kicks the first guard off the small hill towards the two other guards approaching Lineage. Mark quickly elbows the second guard, unaware of his position.

Samantha and Drake pop up from behind the hill and fire their weapons at the two other distracted guards approaching from ahead. The area is clear, as Mark gives a thumb up to his allies. Samantha and Drake walk forward several hundred feet across the vacant red dirt, and climb another hill towards Mark.

Space Jumper and Lineage walk across the red dirt, up several more dunes before reaching the entrance to a cave in the mountains. "These readings are off the chart." Samantha says, checking her mobile device, reading some kind of wave counter. "Let's check out this cave. Going deeper is our best bet." Drake says to Samantha and Mark.

Standing outside of the closed cave, the heavy doors blocking the front begin to open, and unveil four scientists. The scientists walk out of the cave, and move towards Mark and Lineage, kneeling on the ground. Mark takes his gun out, and fires several small shots towards the hazmat scientists. He strikes two of the scientists with medium sized crystals from Cafe, knocking them down to disrupt their suits. The other two scientists quickly approach Samantha and Drake, who rush ahead and begin fighting.

Mark reloads his BB gun, as Samantha and Drake are in hand to hand combat with two of the remaining guards in front of the cave entrance. Drake flips a scientist over, and punches him through his helmet on the ground. Samantha sweeps a scientist to the red ground, and steps on his head to knock him unconscious. As Mark looks ahead at the large, heavy door to the cave, he notices it slowly beginning to close.

"Guy's, we have to move." He yells to Samantha and Drake. Mark and Lineage sprint towards the descending gate in the mountain cave, and slide under the bottom before it makes contact with the ground.

Sealed inside of a red-hot mountain cave, Mark, Samantha and Drake check their surroundings to find a door at the end of a room at the entrance. The entrance to the cave is bright, with boxes and room for vehicles to park. The mountain cave is a laboratory, with rooms to the left and right. Mark takes his laser sword from his bag to provide light through some of the dark spots of the cave. The crew move towards a steel door at the back of the room. Mark opens the door to a room with computers and technology everywhere. The room contains tools that scan anomalies, machines that clean, and large drills to dig.

Mark, Drake and Samantha enter the machine room inside the fire cave. Hostile scientists begin to pour out from the end of the hall. Over eight scientists in hazmat suits fill the computer room and look at Lineage, holding blunt and sharp melee weapons.

A three on eight, Mark holds his gun and the laser sword. Drake and Samantha hold their laser guns, when Drake flips over a table, and begins shooting at the guards from behind cover. Samantha runs at one of the guards and begins fighting, defending herself from punches and swift blows from heavy weapons. Mark uses his laser sword to cut one of the scientists in half.

Too violent, feeling instant remorse for killing another enemy in his way, Mark holsters the laser sword in front of the scientists who just watched their ally get sliced in half. He walks towards the guards, where the scientists move away from the Space Jumper, backing to the end of the hall in the computer room. Mark kicks the nearest guard, launching him into a desk with a drilling machine on it. The guard falls awkwardly like a ragdoll over the tool and lands on the ground.

Samantha and Drake use hand-to-hand combat, fighting the enemies in the room. The three on eight quickly turns into a three on five, and soon to a three on three. Mark uses his gun to shoot small crystals at the legs of several enemies, incapacitating their movements. With one enemy left, Mark, Samantha and Drake team up to beat the life out of the scientist. Drake punches the scientist in the head, as Samantha punches and kicks his body. Mark comes in with the finishing blow, kicking the scientist back to the wall, knocking him unconscious.

With the room clear, Mark and Lineage walk to the next room beyond the computer area. The next door is an open portion of the cave, concealed by a door to the next area. Mark and Lineage continue forward to the next door amongst the familiar, red environment of the ground. Mark opens the next heavy door to a large cave within the mountain range. Inside the cave is what Drake has been waiting to see for who knows how long.

The terrain of the cave is similar to that of the outside world, hot and red. The door closes behind Lineage as they walk towards a goldmine of the red power they desire. They walk slowly inside the deposit of red power crystals, and take in all of the sights and smells of success. "Grab as much as you can." Captain Drake says to Mark and Samantha.

Mark, Samantha and Drake spread out in the large cave, and begin excavating the red power from the grounded rocks. Mark uses his shoes and special fight moves to break off large chunks of the power. Drake uses a special hammer in his arsenal to break off special pieces of red matter. Samantha uses her hands, her knife, and raw strength to create a pile of the red energy next her. The Lineage crew roam around the cave and break off key portions of the red power for extraction. Drake takes out large, durable garbage bags made of cloth to carry all of the red power.

Mark takes a bag from Drake, and begins stuffing them with the best red matter he can find. The cave is hot and moist, surrounded by an unknown energy source. The Space Jumper uses his hatchet to chop away shards of the red power, creating a pile on the ground. Captain Drake walks towards Mark and watches him work. "You're the best, Space Jumper." Drake says to Mark from behind, as he continues to collect the valuable energy. Drake continues to look at Mark, who continues to stuff his bag with red matter.

Almost filled to the brim, Captain Drake watches Mark fill his bag with the red power. As Mark is cutting down more and more of the red energy, Captain Drake stabs Mark in the back with a dagger.

"Argghhh." The Space Jumper grumbles with immense pain. The blade travels deep, and tickles his intestines, as the captain twists the blade. Drake pulls the dagger out, and takes a few steps back. Mark's vision begins to blur, as his eyes water from the rush of emotions. Pain, betrayal, and heat overcome the Space Jumper's senses as he crumbles to the hot ground. The last thing the Space Jumper sees is Captain Drake waving at him in a taunting manner, as Samantha follows him from behind.

Captain Drake grabs Mark's full bag of red energy, and walks towards the door. The Space Jumper passes out on the red dirt next to piles of red power crystals.

Everything is dark in the Space Jumper's mind. Death is unable to find him in the depths of a different universe. His body grows cold in his mind, as his stab wound oozes blood from his body, making him feel like he is melting in his sleep. His mind remains dark, and grows darker as time passes. The darkness overtakes his eyes in his moments before death. The darkness feels as though it is expanding out of his mind, affecting the blank world around him. At the point at which the darkness feels like it is overtaking his body, a flash of light bursts out of his closed eyes. The rings on the Space Jumper's shoes glow bright with power, as does all of his gear. The light from his spirit, powered by the shoes, battles the darkness of death from his mortal wound.

In his head, he is able to transfer the power of the light through his body towards the gaping wound in his back. The Space Jumper uses the light to reduce swelling in his kidney, and seal the internal wound from Drake's blade. The external wound around his skin remains open, but the internal damage slowly heals with the light from his shoes. The Space Jumper's spirit refuses to die, and will aid his body to continue to move forward. Things in his mind begin to grow dark, as a light lingers in his eyes and body. His shoes remain lit within the bright red cave.

Not long later, Mark is asleep in the cave, when a pair of scientists enter, and stand over him. Two more scientists carrying a stretcher enter the cave, and stand next to Mark. They load the unconscious Space Jumper on the stretcher, and walk out of the red cave.

A day passes by, as Mark's body awakens from a bolt of electricity. He quickly opens his eyes to a bright white light. His vision slowly adjusts behind his special glasses. He gently moves his head around, feeling a stiff pain in his back. The Space Jumper lays in a white bed in a white hospital room. He looks down, noticing his shoes are on his feet. He wears a medical gown with his jeans on. The room is empty, with a window to the bright red planet outside. There are no wires or cables connected to the Space Jumper, meaning he is there as a resting visitor.

The stab wound on his back makes his entire body ache as he tries to lean up. He lays back in the bed and closes his eyes again for only a moment. About a minute later, a nurse enters the room after hearing sounds of life. Mark hears the door to the room open, and slowly opens his eyes from his nap. He looks at the nurse in pain.

"Where am I?" He asks slowly to the red skinned, human doctor. "Ahh, you're awake." She says looking down at the plastic clipboard in her hand. Mark tries to sit up on the bed, but feels a sharp pain in his back.

"You were bleeding to death inside a top secret cave, so we took you back here. It's our job." The nurse says calmly, as if this is not her first rodeo. "Well, thank you, I mean no harm." Mark says with pain in his voice in a limited breath. Mark moves his body up the bed, and sits upright to look at the nurse. He reaches around his body, and places his fingers on the part of his back that aches. He feels a large bandage covering the part of his back that took the blade. The wound is tender to the touch, but closed, and not bleeding. The doctors who rescued him stitched him up.

"Where is my gear?" Mark asks the nurse, studying her clipboard. "It's on the chair over there." The nurse says, pointing to a chair across the room. His jacket and bloody shirts drape over the top of a metal chair, as his backpack and space board sit beneath. Mark's eyes widen as he finds his stuff. He uses his arms to lift his body up, swinging his legs off the bed to dangle them above the ground. The pain in his back is sharp, but feels better with strenuous movement. He cringes and sighs in pain.

"Sir, you are not cleared to leave yet. The police are on their way." The nurse tells Mark, who stands up on his feet.

"Not the police." Mark whispers to himself. He slumps down, feeling fatigued from the stabbing. His abs ache in the front, where his kidneys ache from the back. He slowly lumbers across the room towards the chair with his gear, and reaches for his shirts and jacket. He removes the medical garb, and throws it on the chair. He slowly puts on his clothes, and grabs his bag from the ground. The blood on his shirt has dried from the stabbing.

Dressed up, and hunched over, Mark looks over at the nurse and smiles. "Thanks for saving me." He says to her. She looks to him and says nothing. The nurse watches Mark as she moves out of the room, and closes the door behind her. Mark does some light callisthenic stretches, reaching for the sky, and to the side, to loosen up his sore body.

Mark exits the hospital room to a long hallway of other patient treating rooms. The hallway is clean and normal, familiar to Earth's hospitals. The walls are white, with lights on the ceiling. Doctors and nurses roam the halls of the hospital, actively working towards helping sick people. Mark notices an elevator at the end of the hall, and begins to limp his way towards it.

The stab wound in his back aches with each step he takes. He needs to hold the wall in the hall due to his lack of strength and fatigue. He struggles to hold himself up, limping on the side of both walls, crossing both sides of the hall. Sweat drips from his head, and singes on his electronic scarf. His legs grow weak, with the only support he has coming from his shoes. His feet have strength, sharing power with the rest of his body.

The Space Jumper takes a deep breath, on the verge of passing out again, and stands up straight. He fights through the pain in his back, tightening his internal wound through mental focus, and pushes forward. Towards the end of the hall, doctors and nurses look at him strangely, as he rushes towards the closing elevator. Sweat drips from his head again as he rushes inside the elevator. He holds a handrail inside the clean smelling, wooden elevator, as the doors close.

Moving down, Mark takes steady, deep breaths, and thinks about his next move. With so much to do now, his focus is to leave the hospital before the cops come and confiscate his shoes again. The doors to the elevator open to another narrow and much darker hallway. He exits the elevator to the cool hallway, relieving his overheating body beneath layers of bloody and damaged clothes. He moves slowly down the hall, re-learning how to walk normally while fighting the pain in his back. His gear feels heavy, causing him to sweat more.

Doors to the left and right lead to rooms the Space Jumper has no time to explore and intrude. Doctors, nurses and repair people casually walk in and out of rooms, looking at Mark like an alien. He walks down the dark hallway towards a door at the end. He walks through the door to another dark hallway, leading to a large waiting room ahead.

Walking into the waiting room with his gear, Mark pauses for a moment and looks around at everything to figure out where he is, and what is going on. He notices the main exit behind chairs in the waiting room, noticing he is still on the bright red planet with the red power. A sigh of relief flows through the Space Jumper. He looks to his left to find a window with doctors handing out prescriptions.

Mark walks to the window with a slow limp to find a doctor closing up, and starting her break. He walks in front of the window to find a set of pill bottles with a green cross, sitting in a basket. He looks left and right, and takes a full bottle from the basket. He slowly walks away from the desk, and opens the bottle. He throws six to seven pills in his mouth, and swallows them all down. People in the waiting room give him funny looks, as if he has a huge problem. The Space Jumper has much bigger problems than the pain in his back, little do they know.

The pills dissolve quickly, as he immediately feels better. The pain in his side is numb, as Mark continues toward the exit, and walks out the front door.

Outside, the weather remains warm and fiery. He looks beyond the horizon to find mountains resembling the location of the cave he was stabbed. Mark walks towards a large fountain at the center of the open area in front of the large hospital. He sits on the ledge of the fountain, and touches the water with his finger. The liquid is hot, and provides little relief.

Mark takes his tablet out from his bag, and opens his universal map application. He connects his last known signal to figure out where he is. As Mark zooms in the map, dust and dirt begin to fly up in the air, as a heavy wind surrounds him in front of the hospital. He looks up to find multiple ships landing near his location, circling around the fountain.

The Space Jumper attempts to crouch and jump away, but finds too much pain in his body. He clutches his side, and hunches down out of breath. The smooth, large, silver spaceships land on the sand in the hospital lot, as police officers emerge. They aim weapons at Mark as he stands still on the dirt. He turns around to find over five officers emerge from over five different ships. Noticing he is outnumbered, and in too much pain, the Space Jumper puts his hands up in the air.

The police appear to be human, with normal colored black, white and tan skin. They wear specialized bomber jackets made of leather and faux leather. They point large, heavy rifles at him, as over fifty police officers circle the Space Jumper. The police slowly approach the surrendering Space Jumper, knowing his capabilities. They want him alive, if not, he would be dead already.

Despite being outnumbered, oppressed, and intimidated, Mark smiles at the familiarity of police work. Three low ranking officers whip shackles around his legs and arms, saying nothing to the Space Jumper. One of the officers nearby presses a button, and activates the locking mechanism on the shackles, sending a strange tingle through Mark's arms and legs. The electronic current from the shackles disrupts his gear, and powers off everything but his shoes. His legs and body grow weak, receiving minimal support and aid from his shoes, as he falls to the ground.

The three guards who threw on the shackles walk to Mark, stiff as a board, and pick him up from his arms and legs. They carry him into one of the several ships surrounding his location. The doors to the ships close, where all of the police enter their ships, and take off to outer space in the Mega galaxy.

Ships take off through space as the cops carry Mark, and throw him in a brig inside the ship. The police leave him alone, shackled in a cage, as they exit the red planet on Mega.

Not much time passes when the Space Jumper wakes up to a pair of police officers in fancy bomber jackets. They help him up from the ground, and carry him down a hallway within the large ship.

The sun around the galaxy shines bright through a window ahead, gleaming straight into Mark's eyes. He covers his face while being dragged by cops aboard the ship.

The officers take the Space Jumper into an interrogation room with a double-sided window. He sits in an uncomfortable chair as the police tie him to a metal desk in front, anchored to the ground. He puts his head down in exhaustion from everything that has happened to him from the past few days.

The guards exit, and leave him alone in the interrogation room. His cool shoes sputter on and off with low power due to the electronic shackles around his ankles, interrupting power to his body. The lack of power from the shoes to his body rapidly increases his exhaustion. About to pass out from fatigue, a pair of police officers barge into the interrogation room and sit across from Mark.

The police officers wear fancy leather jackets with black and brown stripes and patches. They have blue jeans and comfortable tennis shoes on their feet. The police officers look like private detectives.

"Space Jumper, how are you feeling?" The white skinned officer asks Mark while checking his phone, standing behind his chair. The officer's darker skinned partner takes a seat in the chair next to him, ready to play good cop, bad cop.

"I'm more broken than ever." Mark replies, shackled to the chair and table with his head down. "We have been following your actions since you left Earth." The officer sitting in the chair explains to Mark while looking at his phone as well.

"I had a feeling you were." Mark replies with little interest, and his head down, making minimal eye contact. "We're sorry you are so hurt, and would like to help." The officer sitting in the chair says with a smile, looking up from his phone. "I'm not in trouble?" Mark asks the two officers with his head remaining down. "Not from our perspective." The officer standing behind the chair says. "We need your help tracking the mercenaries who left you for dead." The officer sitting in the chair says, looking at his phone again. "I'm in." Mark replies quickly, looking up at the officers, establishing a fiery eye contact.

"Stay here until we arrive back on Mega." The officer standing behind the chair says, as they both begin to exit the room. Mark remains shackled and alone in the interrogation room again.

After a minute, the ship begins to fly faster. The fleet of ships swoop in through the mechanized structure of Mega. They rotate and turn through the zero gravity towards one of the largest, most central planets in the connected galaxy. The core planet of Mega glows bright with power, electricity, and life.

As the ships fly down into the planet, they land on a building. After a few minutes, the police open the door to the interrogation room, and collect Mark from his chair. They drag his fatigued body out of the room, and through the clean ship.

Everyone exits the ship, as Mark covers his eyes from the bright sun, and bright city. He opens his eyes to see he is on the roof of a large building in a heavily populated city. In space, several other planets connect to the infrastructure of Mega.

The city is advanced and clean for the short moment Mark is able to see it, before the police drag him into a building from the roof. Him and a handful of police officers move to an elevator at the end of a short maintenance hall. They move down the building to another floor with clean, marbled walls. The building is official, and very white, with strong masonry splayed everywhere. Wood benches and old art line the walls in this new, alien planet. The police continue to drag Mark over a marbled floor as political onlookers watch and observe.

The large, wide, and marbled political room transitions to an uncomfortably warm room, with connected desks, chairs, and numbered televisions everywhere. The room looks like a department of motor vehicles. The two officers escorting Mark force him to sit on an old plastic, grey bench next to the window of an office.

"Wait here." The officer says to Mark. The two officers walk down a hall in the office. Not long after, the officers reappear with a third police officer, much larger, wearing the same leather jacket. "Space Jumper, follow me." The larger officer says to Mark, as the two original escorting officers lift Mark from the bench. The Space Jumper is shackled, but able to walk on his own using baby steps. He looks funny, taking such small steps wearing his advanced shoes.

The two officers escort Mark through the police office as they follow the large officer. They walk inside an office at the end of the hall, as the large officer opens the door, unveiling a large window with a great view of the tall city behind. The officer looks back at Mark, and motions him to take a seat in the chair in front of a desk.

Mark walks in to the room with an exhausted limp, as he slumps down in the chair. He looks out the window to study his surroundings. The city is unknown to him, being a new planet, on a new galaxy, in the new universe. The exoskeleton connecting the planets is large, and constantly shifting, like a globe connected to a celestial base. The officers follow Mark into the office and close the door behind them.

"I heard what happened, Space Jumper. Are you alright?" The larger officer asks. "A bit sore, but I'll live." Mark replies upset, sitting in the chair with his head down. "We need your help finding Lineage. You seem like a perfect candidate for our group, our ace in the hole." The large officer says.

"That's what the last group told me, then they stabbed me in the back, and left me for dead on a planet I have never been to." Mark replies with an annoyed tone. "We know, and it's messed up. That's why we want to get them, and bring them to justice." The large officer says, crossing his fingers in his hands. "I don't know how much more I can take." Mark replies, and continues. "Who are you guys anyway?" He asks the officers in the room.

"We are the Mega Police Unit. A special group of peacekeepers designated to protect Mega." The large officer explains. "We are like you, Space Jumper. We are human refugees from Earth, lost in a black hole many years ago. Our ancestors woke up on this planet and have expanded ever since." The dark skinned officer explains, with the beautiful view behind him.

"I like the sound of this, all of this." Mark replies to the police's offer, spreading his hands in a peaceful manner while bound in the restraints. "We are glad you do, Space Jumper." The smaller police officer says. "I think I may know where they are headed." Mark says to the officers. "Great, we would like to check out your gear, and provide upgrades." The large officer asks. Mark's eyebrows raise at the request.

"No one touches my shoes." He demands from the police. "Relax Space Jumper. We already know how they work." The smaller, white officer replies.

"Everyone in the universe knows how they work." The large officer says confidently to Mark. "Everyone?" Mark replies with a slight giggle. "The information to your shoes were sold and purchased several times from the group that initially confiscated them. Yet, you continue to inspire good throughout this universe." The large officer says, sitting in his chair across from Mark. The two smaller officers walk behind Mark and pat his shoulders for a job well done. The Space Jumper feels uncomfortable, and unsure of their commendations.

"So how do they work?" Mark asks the officers. "Your shoes utilize memory, remembering your bodily conditions for what allows you to survive. The information for the food you eat, the drinks you drink, and the air you breathe stay within the special rings like a hard drive. The rings around your shoes connect to your DNA, and yours only, to power the shoes." The smaller, light-skinned officer explains to Mark, looking at his phone. The officer pulls up a video on his phone and shows it to Mark.

The video shows a group of scientists in a garage, with one man about to try on the cool shoes. When he powers the shoes on his feet, his entire body burns with electricity and turns to ash. The shoes remain intact on the ground and the video abruptly ends. The officer pulls the phone away from Mark, and continues to browse through it.

"Cool, but where did they come from?" Mark asks the officers, as if they know the answer to his question. "Oh, we don't know." The large officer says frankly. "Is that it? I already know how they work. I need to know who made them, and where they came from." Mark replies angrily to the officers.

"That's for you to find out Space Jumper." The light-skinned officer says. Mark rolls his eyes at the lack of solid information, feeling pained and broken, yet willing to help. "Let's get this started then." The Space Jumper says to the Mega Police Unit.

The officers stand up in the office, where the larger officer unshackles Mark with the push of a button. His shoes gain power, igniting his gloves, scarf, and glasses. His tablet makes a noise in his bag. The officers and the Space Jumper walk out of the office through the police station, down several corridors to a secure room. The large officer walks away toward another room as the two smaller officers escort Mark into the room.

"Gear up, and lets get ready. I'll call the counsel." The large officer says to the smaller officers.

The room ahead of the Space Jumper looks like a bank vault, with organized cabinets containing goods. The room is mostly empty, with only a chair and table in the center. The light-skinned detective walks to a cabinet at the side of the room, where the darker skinned officer walks to the other side of the room. They use special electronic keys that materialize into the air.

They insert the special keys into the cabinets, turning them open, and each pull out a couple of small pieces of tech. They walk to the center of the room, and place it on the table.

"Take a seat Space Jumper." The darker officer says politely to Mark, pointing to the only chair in the room. Mark hesitates for a few seconds, and sits slowly in the chair. The desk is in front of him, where the light-skinned officer, remaining unnamed, places a small box down. He slowly slides the small box on the table towards Mark.

"Alright Space Jumper, we have some things for you since you are considered an ally now." The light-skinned officer says.

Mark slides the box close to his body, opens the small latch in front, and springs it open. The box is a small silver case, with a royal blue interior made of short hair fibers. A pair of gelatinous eyes sit in the case. The fellow officer slides a similar small, dark blue box over the table.

Mark looks at the officers, concerned of their technology and methods. "These are our special contact lenses. They have electronic mapping, scanning, and targeting similar to your glasses." The officer explains.

As Mark looks closer at the fake eyes, he sees the lenses sitting on top. "Can these lenses even fit me?" Mark asks, taking the fake eye out of the blue box. "They are universal. Once they are on the wearers eyes, they can see everything." The dark skinned officer says.

Mark removes his glasses, and places them on the table in front of him next to the box of contacts. With his gloves on, he gently uses his finger to slide the lens on to his fingertip. He places the damp, slightly metallic lens in to his open eye, and blinks them snug in to place. He uses the same method with the opposite lens, and secures them into his eyes.

Without his glasses, the world is blurry, but with the new lenses on his eyes, his vision becomes perfectly enhanced. The contacts power up, and synchronize with the rest of his face and body. An electronic burst of energy strikes through his nose and sinuses. An update bar scrolls over the center of his vision, completing the connection of his technical spirit.

"Open your tablet to synchronize your mapping." One of the officers says to Mark, who looks completely different without his glasses on.

Mark takes his tablet from his bag, and powers it on. He opens his NASA application with his collection of maps and information from his universes travelled. He connects the device to a special folder where his glasses used to be, synchronizing information to the new contact lenses.

His peripheral vision expands to unveil a larger heads up display of information. Temperature, time, date, and heartrate are some of the things on the corner of his lenses. He opens the map of the current universe, connecting them to his contacts. The images of his scrolling appears in front of his eyes in three dimensions, similar to his glasses. He smiles, and places his tablet back in his bag.

He grabs his glasses from the table, and looks at the officers before placing them back over his eyes. The officers are stunned at why he would do this. Mark looks up at the officers and smiles.

"I like them." He says with his glasses on over his new contact lenses. With the glasses over the contact lenses, his vision improves drastically.

Things around him are as crisp and clear as can be, with his power of depth perception at its peak. Mark is able to see the minor details in everything around him, able to zoom in to the very fabric of the officer's jacket, able to retract his vision to a normal perspective, and zoom in at the will of a squint.

The Space Jumper turns focus to the other blue box sitting on the table, and begins opening the latches. He opens the box to find a circular device, similar to the shielding device in his possession. He takes out his shield, and brings it close to the other circular device. Pulling it out of the lush box, Mark compares the two similar circles side by side, and presses the button for the new device. The Space Jumper instantaneously disappears from view, despite him being in the chair.

He sticks his hands and arms in front of his body to see they are translucent. He looks down at his body, only to find the seat and backrest of the chair he sits on. Everything internal feels normal to him. The officers struggle to track his location, being unprepared for his sudden disappearance.

Mark quietly and slowly sneaks out of the chair, and moves away from the table. He walks to the side of the room, and stands flush against the wall in front of a group of safety deposit boxes.

The camouflage wears off, as he reappears. The officers are looking around, and finally notice Mark at the side of the room with a big smile on his face. The officers take a sigh of relief, and begin to chuckle at Mark's cheeky joke.

"Camouflage?" Mark asks rhetorically, holding the device in his hand.

"Yeah, it only works for a short amount of time. With the assistance of your shoes, you can recharge it quicker than normal." The light-skinned officer explains. Mark walks back to the chair, and places the device in his pocket opposite to his shield.

"Can I keep this stuff?" Mark asks the officers.

"Sure, we have plenty in stock." The dark skinned officer replies. "If I connect these things with my current gear, I should be good to go." Mark says to the officers. "Alright, let's get a move on." The light-skinned officer says, closing the two boxes in front of Mark.

The officers escort the Space Jumper out of the technology armory, and back through the police station. They walk out of the police office, and back into the grand hall of the large, marbled building. They walk to the left towards a small room by the sidewall, where the officers open a large, tall, pair of old doors.

Inside is a large, dark room with a large oval table in the middle. The room consists of people sitting around the table with the lights off. They are watching a conference call on the main screen ahead. When Mark enters the room, the lights automatically turn back on.

As the Space Jumper looks around the room, he sees military personal everywhere. He sees the large police officer from earlier, and waves to him with a big, goofy, friendly smile. All eyes are already on Mark, being the outcast in the room.

"You're right on time Space Jumper. We were just talking about the thieves of the red mines, and your attackers." The officer says to Mark, standing from his seat, and walking towards him.

"Everyone, this is the Space Jumper. One of the few humans left who cares about the common good, and who will help us track the pirates robbing the red mines." The officer says in a loud voice, wrapping his arm around Mark's shoulder. The military generals look at Mark, and nod in affirmation of his existence. Mark waves to the military personnel in the conference room around the oval table.

"I don't like him. How do we know he is not going to turn sides?" A military general says from the end of the table.

"They tried to kill him. He would be a fool to go back." The large officer replies, speaking on Mark's behalf.

"I'm not doing this for you guys. I'm doing this for me." Mark says to the room, knowing he is the outlier. "Don't make us regret trusting you, Space Jumper." A female officer says from the table with a fierce look on her face. Mark looks back at her, equally fierce, agitated, and pained.

"We have their most recent location on a red power mine in the Anchor galaxy." One of the officers says to Mark and the room from the table. "Space Jumper, we will give you first priority on tracking Lineage down. The location to Anchor is here on this data pad. Connect your information to acquire the location." An elderly general says from the end of the table close to the projector equipment.

Mark walks to the data pad, and places his tablet on the table. He connects his device to the machine on the table, where a download bar shows up on his screen. The Space Jumper's tablet downloads the information as he looks around the room. "We'll be right behind you until our jurisdiction wears thin. See what clues you can find on Anchor." The large officer says to Mark and his smaller officers.

The download of information is complete. Mark opens his tablet, and explores his map application. He has a message for a new location in the Anchor galaxy, five million light years away. He pinpoints the objective, making it appear over his glasses and contacts. He lifts his glasses over his eyes for a moment, testing to see if his contacts are able to locate the objective. They do, with enhanced peripheral vision.

He keeps his glasses over his forehead for when he gets to space. "Alright, let's move out." One of the generals says from behind the table, sliding his chair back. Everyone begins to stand, and move out of the large conference room.

As everyone leaves the room, Mark is with the two escorting officers, and the larger officer in charge. "You ready, Space Jumper?" The dark skinned officer asks. "Yeah, let's go." Mark says, awaiting their escort out of the building. The two officers lead the way out of the room, as the large officer waits for Mark so he can lock up the conference room.

Everyone walks through the large, marbled central room towards the elevator to the roof. They move up the elevator to meet up with more of the crew following the Space Jumper. The officers walk to their ship on the roof and stand before an open bay door.

"Radio us when you make contact Space Jumper, and don't deviate from the mission, or we will charge you with abandonment. When you make contact, we will send reinforcements." The large detective says. Mark does not reply to the officer, but lifts his hand in front of him. The officers shake Mark's hand, and enter their space ships on the roof.

Chapter 9

Anchor

Mark takes a deep breath, angling his vision towards the new galaxy ahead as the police take off from the roof. He crouches down, and jumps as high as he can into the air. Landing on a cloud, he takes another deep breath, relieving some of the pain in his back. He crouches on the cloud, and jumps higher up to reach the depths of space. After a pair of painful jumps, he begins to float in space above the core planet on Mega. He corrects his vision, strapping his glasses over his eyes for protection. His vision is clear and crisp, noticing all of the planets connected to the Mega exoskeleton ahead. Standing in space, a glare crosses his glasses from his right side.

As he turns around, a large metal beam glides directly towards him. A rotating arm supporting the planets of Mega shift quietly and quickly through the depths of space. Mark takes notice of the behemoth support rod, and maneuvers awkwardly above it. He slides his body across the flat part of the metal beam, and slips off back to space. The metal arm makes a heavy swooshing noise as it continues its course over the planet.

"I've gotta get out of here." Mark says to himself, taking another deep breath.

He rubs his back vigorously, and aims his focus toward the location on his glasses and contact lenses. He moves to a nearby gravity field, and crouches low above it. He jumps lightly into space to see how he feels. A mild pain strikes his back as he springs his torso upward. He floats to another gravity field, and crouches down again to jump off higher and further than the last. His pain begins to minimize as he pushes his body harder. The Space Jumper is used to pain, and knows how to utilize it with the power of the cool shoes.

His glasses display a map of the location received from the Mega Police Unit. His contact lenses improve his vision, and contain information for his body. He watches the numbers to the Anchor galaxy move down in astronomical units. Floating above the metal rafters of the Mega galaxy, Mark moves gingerly towards the Anchor galaxy, several million lightyears away. A thermal index on his glasses indicate whether he is hot or cold to the last location of Lineage.

The Space Jumper inserts his headphones into his ears, and plays a soundtrack to ease his mental stress.

Space jumping grows gradually easier as the distance separates him from his painful past. Mark's body loosens beneath his bloody and battered clothes as he flies fast through space. His speed is not as fast as warp speed, but he moves at a pace untraceable to the naked eye. The final planet around Mega fades behind his peripheral vision, as he continues to blast forward towards the Anchor galaxy.

Progressing forward through a blank and boring space, Mark hears a strange vibration from behind through his headphones. He takes his headphones out of his ears for a moment to listen to his surroundings. He turns around to find one of the ships from Mega warp up behind his location. He halts his jumps from the next gravity fields to focus on the ship nearly touching him. He looks inside the cockpit of the smooth, circular space ship to find the crew of the MPU looking at him.

Mark salutes the police, indicating their presence. The crew in the ship salute back, and flash the alien lights on their ship. Mark turns around to continue his pace ahead through space.

He jumps from various colored gravity fields to build more speed. Taking a quick glance behind him, he finds the Mega space ship still tracking him from a long ways back. In the area ahead, the number of gravity fields begin to decrease, making him have to choose his paths carefully to maintain speed.

The blank canvas of space with millions of stars in the background is a breath of fresh air for the Space Jumper, as he wishes to be mostly alone to work through his problems. Things from Earth still linger in the back of his mind, despite being so very far away from home. He thinks of his family, his parents, his brother, his ex girlfriend, and all of the things close to his heart. He begins to contemplate if things would be better off back at home. Betrayal on another universe adds a new depth of darkness to his already broken heart. The emptiness of space allows him time to move freely at his own volition, without worrying what anyone thinks.

Thinking of all the negative things occurring in the Space Jumper's life allows him to jump faster through space. He utilizes the spiritual aspect from his cool shoes, without thinking about distance. The Space Jumper is in warp speed, moving through a tunnel of light. Continuing to dread on his broken heart, his speed continues to increase through the warp tunnel. He snaps out of his dark trance to find he has veered from the course displayed on his glasses. He does not slow down, but corrects his path, and continues forward.

Thinking about the internal wounds to his heart makes him forget about the external wounds on his body, allowing his stab wound to heal faster. His space board moves side to side on his backpack as he blasts through his warp tunnel. His backpack is snug on his back, with his tools and ammunition jingling inside. His legs remain strong over his cool shoes as he listens to a playlist acquired from a planet called Equalia, near Planet Hollywood from his home universe. The music is unique, and matches his pace, jumping through space.

The astronomical units on his glasses reduce by the millions, as the Space Jumper follows his path to the waypoint through the white light of warp speed. A green glow begins to shine bright at the end of the tunnel. He slows his pace to study the galaxy ahead.

The Anchor galaxy begins to stand tall, surrounded by a green gas around its wider ranges. The galaxy has multiple layers of galaxies stacked on top of each other, with a heavy base at the bottom. The galaxies have various shapes and depth, giving it the appearance of an anchor. The line Mark follows to Anchor slowly vaporizes, and disappears into the green haze.

The Space Jumper continues to move towards Anchor, as the heat signatures begin to pick up the trail set by Lineage. As the numbers of distance continue to drop, a thermometer appears on Mark's heads up display. The temperature fluctuates from negative to positive as Mark looks and studies the set of stacked galaxies. The Space Jumper powers through gravity fields towards Anchor.

Standing before the new galaxy, Mark pauses in space. He studies the galaxy using his improved and multiplied vision. His glasses utilize tools from his NASA application, where his new contact lenses enhance the scope to his vision. He zooms into the planet, tracking the heat signatures from Lineage's trail. Things warm up as Mark moves closer to a portion of the galaxy near the center. He constantly studies the thermometer to help him figure out how hot or cold he is.

The heat signature on his glasses grow hotter, as Mark follows the thermal index towards the top center of Anchor. Approaching the galaxy, Mark notices several sets of planets in orbit around the many layers of the tall galaxy.

Using gravity fields to swoop in to the hot part of the galaxy, the Space Jumper breaks through the green fog surrounding Anchor, and swirls into the depths of its space. The heat signature continues to rise, indicating he is approaching Lineage's location. Standing at the edge of the galaxy, Mark takes a minute to look around, finding several planets located less than a few hundred thousand miles away from each other. He zooms in to the planets to scan their heat signatures for Lineage. The first few closest planets are cold.

Mark finds a gravity field, and pushes through the Anchor galaxy. Space remains relatively vacant, with the exception of weird gusts of wind. He rides the breeze to the next set of planets not far away. He scans the remaining few planets within the upper portion of the Anchor galaxy. The heat sensor blasts off the chart, as Mark focuses on a small planet in the distance.

The planet is brown, and appears mostly vacant. Within the Space Jumper's mapping applications, the planet marks green on his glasses based on intelligent life. Lineage's last known location is close.

As Mark approaches the planet in question, he sees it is heavy with trees and forests, with pockets of water scattered around. The remainder of the planet contains dry dirt beneath a few scattered mountains and cliffs. The planet is not only hot on the thermal index, but also hot in thermal temperature.

The Space Jumper spikes through a layer of clouds, landing hard on a vast and open grass area. Sliding on dirt, Mark stops on grass, and takes a deep breath. The air he breathes is warm, indicating he is hot on Lineage's tracks.

Mark's glasses outline a vapor of heat, highlighting the last known remnants of Lineage. He follows the heat signature up a dirt hill, and looks down into a canyon at the top.

He finds a bubbling pool of red lava, and jumps over the gap, treading the world carefully.

Mark jumps over the gap with red lava below, and slides down a small, dirt hill leading to grass. The platform of grass ends with another gap of lava. The Space Jumper continues to hop gracefully over the gaps, continuing forward towards the heat signature.

For anyone without special shoes, the gaps in the ground would lead to dead ends. Mark jumps twenty feet in the air over another large gap of lava.

The landing spot is steep, at an intense upward angle. The Space Jumper holds his ground, and continues to trek up the small hill towards more gaps in the ground. The air remains dry and warm.

The next landing hill is as steep and awkward as the first. Mark jumps high enough over the gap to land safely on the other side. He maintains momentum forward as he lands on the ground. The hills of the broken mountain are a mix of dirt and grass. The grass is slippery, and the dirt is loose. The angle of the mountain is steep, as the Space Jumper moves forward.

Reaching a plateau after a steep hike, Mark looks around the world to study the heat sensor on his glasses. The location of Lineage is across another large gap with gaseous lava below. The decline from the mountain contains more gaps in the ground. The Space Jumper hops over the first gap down the mountain, and lands on a flat area of grass. He slides on the grass, where his board and bag remain intact. He carries momentum to jump over the next large gap in the ground ahead.

He lands on the grass of the hot planet, and slides down a small hill. He quickly notices another gap directly below the small hill. He uses his instincts to jump over the large canyon in the ground towards a lower section of the mountain.

Time slows during the jump as he looks down to see a pool of red lava. He lands on more grass at the base of the mountain, and slides his shoes over the dew. He catches his feet, continuing to jog across the hot grass, following the heat signature to Lineage.

After jogging a few hundred feet of open grass, Mark discovers a large divot of dirt in the ground. He looks closer in the divot, and finds a strange anomaly at the center. He takes his tablet out of his bag, and checks the map of the planet. The heat signature is flashing at a hundred percent, meaning the anomaly in the field is part of Lineage. Mark moves closer, discovering the anomaly is a pile of bones scattered around the ground.

A small pool of blood sits in the dirt in the middle of the bones, appearing human. Mark walks close to the bones, noticing some stray clothing scattered around. The clothes resemble a member from Lineage.

"Someone was hungry." Mark says rhetorically while scanning the remains of the Lineage member with his tablet.

The person was a crewmember from Lineage, one of the mechanical engineers on the ship. Mark notices a few sets of footprints leading away from the body. As he reads the details from his scanner, he feels vibrations in the ground.

The Space Jumper plants his feet on the ground to feel the vibrations deeper. He turns around to find a fifteen-foot tall dinosaur charging him from behind. Mark's eyes widen at the sight of the beast. The dinosaur looks hungry the way it charges the Space Jumper with an angry look on its large face. Shocked, Mark stands in the dirt circle next to the dead member of Lineage.

The Space Jumper takes his BB gun from his hip, and focuses his aim at the dinosaurs head, in front of its long neck. The dinosaur looks like a brontosaur, but to identify species in a new universe is nearly impossible. Mark takes a deep breath, and fires a large crystal BB from his gun. The crystalized bullet travels large and wide through the air, striking the dinosaur in the body below its neck. The dinosaur slightly slows speed for a second, but powers through the shot as the crystal deflects off its thick skin.

Mark gasps, and quickly holsters his gun. He looks behind the dinosaur, noticing a fleet of over ten more dinosaurs following the first one.

Mark's feet almost give out beneath him at the sight of the apex predators. He turns around from the stampede of dinosaurs behind him to find a lone dinosaur waiting for his next move ahead.

Surrounded by dinosaurs on another hot planet in a new galaxy, Mark uses what he knows, and quickly jumps over the single, menacing dinosaur ahead.

He continues forward, following the tracks of Lineage up another large hill, running on dirt as fast as he can, fighting his back injury. He climbs up the base of the mountain towards a flat surface, and continues up by jumping to the next peak, high in the mountains.

He lands on dirt and rubble, looking down at the dinosaurs behind him. He watches most of the large dinosaurs run into the mountain, and struggle to climb. The smaller dinosaurs behind the large ones take the lead, and begin climbing up to follow the Space Jumper's scent.

Mark realizes he has no time to rest, and continues up the mountain. He jumps to the next peak to find another smaller dinosaur looking and smiling at him, as if its lunch delivery just arrived. A bead of sweat drops from Mark's head as he stands still, face to face with another unpredictable dinosaur. The small dino opens its mouth and screams loud, brandishing its sharp teeth. The Space Jumper crouches low, and punches the dinosaur in the jaw with his power gloves. The punch utilizes fire, electricity, and crystal shards, critically affecting the enemy dinosaur.

As the dinosaur stumbles back from the punch, Mark moves around and continues up the mountain to the top. The footsteps from Lineage continue to move forward, where another large gap down, lies ahead.

Mark checks behind to find several dinosaurs reaching the peak of the mountain. The Space Jumper looks down into the gap, and jumps with moderate power to reach the other side. He rolls on the dirt on the opposite side of the canyon, standing on his feet after the roll.

He turns around, and looks up the cliff to find a quiet delay in hostility. He continues to move forward, and looks back again. As he checks behind, he sees one of the dinosaurs from the top of the mountain jumping across the gap, flying in the air towards him.

The Space Jumper quickly turns around to find another dinosaur ahead of his path. He continues to run forward, putting a juke on the dinosaur ahead. He moves quickly left and right, shifting the feet of the dinosaur. Mark grazes his back past the dinosaur, and continues forward across a flat portion of green grass. As he runs forward, a steep downhill causes him to slide into another divot. He loses footing, and rolls down a hill.

He stops rolling at the center of the divot, checking his backpack and gear as he dusts himself off. The divot is hot and foggy with steam in the air. Mark covers his mouth as he looks around. Strange animal noises echo across the dusty divot as he looks around. Footprints from fellow humans linger ahead. Mark circles around, trying to get a clue of what is going on. He looks forward, and slowly begins walking across the dirt. As he treks his cool shoes across the soft ground, a large bird swoops in from the sky and tries to grab the hair off his head.

"Buzz off." Mark says, brushing his hair and the air with his hand. He takes out his BB gun and hatchet, continuing to walk forward across the dirt. The dirt divot ends ahead, leading to a cliff towards the surface. As he walks towards the cliff, another dinosaur approaches up ahead. It jumps down into the divot, ready to fight the Space Jumper.

Mark takes a few steps back to gain a central position in the divot, turning around to find another set of dinosaurs approaching from behind. He looks up to find a fleet of flying pterodactyl dinosaurs, shading his position above.

Looking around his body, the dinosaurs of the planet surround the Space Jumper again, ready to eat him and his shoes. Mark sweats bullets on the ground, where they sizzle on the hot dirt below. He runs quickly towards the single dinosaur ahead, and aims his gun up while moving forward. He shoots a couple of quick, large shots at its feet.

The crystals strike the dinosaur's legs, causing it to kneel its body and head down with its long neck. Mark continues to run forward, and steps on the dinosaurs head, spiking it further into the dirt. He climbs up its large body, and jumps towards the top of the divot from the dinosaurs tail.

The pterodactyls swoop down into the divot, and try to grab the Space Jumper in mid-air as he makes his escape. A flying dinosaur soars close, but as it gets dangerously close, Mark backhands its beak with a strong, fiery fist. The flying bird falls back into the divot, and crashes hard on the dirt. Mark lands at the edge of the cliff near the hole, and continues forward to follow the footsteps of Lineage.

Another steep hill stands ahead, with a couple more dinosaurs hanging out on the cliffs. Behind, Mark hears the pitter patter of dinosaur feet moving across the divot towards the edge of the hill. Mark moves forward, and begins jumping and climbing up the mountain. He avoids the first dinosaur on the dirt cliff, continuing to jump upward. He soars above the next cliff up the mountain, and elbow drops the second dinosaur down as it gives him a funny look. Mark stands back on the ground, and quickly jumps towards the top of the mountain.

Landing at the top of the mountain, Mark finds the area to be vacant of dinosaurs for the mean time. The Space Jumper walks forward over hot dirt towards another gap in the ground.

The footsteps of Lineage disappear from view, with the indication of a large ship that previously landed and took off. The gap ahead is much more than a gap, and the mountain he stands on is much more than just a mountain. A large bowl of liquid, hot lava sits inside the wide and long peak of the mountaintop.

The mountain is a volcano, explaining the heated dirt below. Mark leans his head over the cliff, and looks down at the volcano, over a hundred feet wide.

The Space Jumper shakes his head side to side, sarcastically accepting everything going on, and turns around. He back walks towards the edge of the mountain, and looks down the cliff to find the dinosaurs he ran into earlier climbing up to see him.

The flying pterodactyls circle upward in the sky to stalk the Space Jumper. Mark wastes no time, and moves towards the opening in the volcano. He runs full speed, and springs off the dirt at the edge of the volcano opening. He soars into the air over the scorching hot lava sitting inside. As he jumps over the scolding canyon, the dinosaurs make it to the top of the mountain.

The Space Jumper clears the volcano, and lands with a slide on a steep downhill on the other side. He slides down the mountain, holding on to the dirt with his crystal hands for support and deceleration. He slides down to a flat area beneath a canopy of trees, hiding his presence from the flying predators above. He lands hard and uncoordinated on the ground after falling from a steep height. Dirt and dust kick up as he struggles to stand.

The drive for exploration keeps the Space Jumper moving forward. He turns around, out of breath on the hot, dry ground to find a small cave behind him. The cave leads inside the volcano he jumped across, beneath the depth of the liquid, hot magma.

Mark brushes off dust from his gear, and walks with an injured limp into the cave. The cave grows dark, as the temperature rises inside. The walls are tall, providing room to move comfortably. Mark progresses forward, where the walls narrow down around him. Molten hot rocks heat the walls to his sides, providing a dim glow of light.

Mark slowly walks forward through the narrowing cave with red-hot stalactites jutting from the ceiling. Ahead, an opening in the cave leads to a bright source of energy. He walks through the opening in the cave to discover a deposit of the red matter Lineage is dying to find.

He walks forward into the open space, and moves around the small amount of red matter. He follows the path through the cave ahead, moving completely around the glow of the red power. Mark continues down the path, leaving the red matter behind, hoping to find traces of Lineage.

The cave narrows after walking away from the red matter. He walks forward over the soft, hot dirt to another opening, leading to another cave filled with red power. His nostrils flare at the sight of the power ahead of him.

Using his brain, he takes out his tablet, and messages the Mega Police Unit, tracking his movement. He sends a message, including the coordinates to his location, directly below the active volcano above. He walks forward with his tablet in hand, when the ground beneath his feet begins to crumble like cracking into a crème brulee. He hits his head forward on the ground as his body falls into a hole, dropping deeper into the volcano.

Weak from his previous falls and runs, Mark drops mercilessly down the hole, crashing his body back and forth into every side of the cave. After some time of unforgiving falling, Mark crashes through another thin portion of ground, and falls another several stories through a wide cave towards the ground. He lands hard on the side of his body on a soft, yet unforgiving dirt. His tablet lands on his calf as he lays on the ground in pain.

Mark lays on the ground for a few extra seconds, embracing the physical pain that flows through his body. He takes his time standing up, as his arms and legs shake with exhaustion. He crumbles back down to the dirt, and flips his body over to his back to look up at the hole in the ceiling he dropped in. He coughs up dirt and dust inhaled from the fall.

Lying down on the soft, warm dirt in the cave is therapeutic to the worn out Space Jumper. He smiles and laughs at his own misfortune, appreciating the thrill of exploration.

Dust and rocks shift to his right, raising his attention, and end his nap. He forces his body up to look at the noise at the side of the dark cave.

He slowly rises, checks the integrity of his bag, and takes out his laser sword, activating only the flashlight. He shines his light around the dark cave to check his warm surroundings. He discovers a path leading up to a narrow entrance in the cave. Mark sighs with exhausted pain, and rises from the dirt. He stands up, and clambers over a small hill ahead of him.

The cave is pitch black, and smells like dust and ash. Mark shines his light around the area to illuminate the cave with his beam. The cave is very tall, but not wide. He shines his light forward to find another small hill on the ground. Mark walks with a limp to the hill, and shines the light around the cave, opening up more of the darkness.

Rocks shift around him, echoing in his ears. He frantically shines the light towards the noises, not finding anything relevant. He continues forward across the path of the cave, moving up towards a small hole in the wall.

As he moves slowly forward, small rocks fall from the ceiling, and land on his head and arm. He shakes off the dust, and looks up to the top of the cave. His light reflects off a rectangular red creature, hanging from the dirt above.

As Mark looks closer at the anomaly, he finds it has a set of eyes looking down at him. He shines the light further around the cave to find several more of the rectangular, red creatures, hanging around.

The first red rectangle drops down from the ceiling, lands on the ground, and looks menacingly at Mark. Several more rectangles fall from the ceiling, and lodge into the ground in front of the Space Jumper's path.

Mark shines his light at the red rectangles, ready to fight if they try to attack. The first rectangle hops out of the ground using a bolt of red power, and lunges towards Mark, who punches the creature away.

The rectangle is heavy and blunt, as Mark swipes it away from his body. It falls to the ground, and picks itself up to stand straight. It continues to look at Mark with a set of beady eyes, and slanted, angry brows. Mark jogs forward, and kicks the next red rectangle on the ground, punting it like a football to launch it high into the cave. The third rectangle jumps at Mark, who punches it quick with an angry fist, shattering it to pieces.

Mark moves up and down hills within the dark cave, rising and falling to escape the jumping rectangles approaching behind. The enemies are difficult to see in the darkness. Mark's flashlight can only light up so much of the area around him. The rectangular creatures jump towards Mark, startling him like bricks thrown at his face. He flinches away left and right while moving forward through the dark cave.

Shining the light ahead of the cave, Mark finds a small opening up a longer hill. He equips his hatchet, activating the boomerang blade attachment. He quickly bats away a rectangular creature falling close around him. The blade clings off the red enemies dense body, shattering the rectangle to pieces. Mark shines the light ahead, using his hatchet to defend himself, moving across the soft dirt.

After a climb up a large set of cliffs, Mark continues forward towards the small opening in the cave, somewhat high up. He slowly climbs up rocks towards a transition of red light beyond the opening.

The Space Jumper crawls prone through the narrow opening in the cave towards the dim, red light on the other side. He leaves behind the red rectangles as the cave begins to widen.

He crouches down at the opening of the new cave high above the ground. He looks down at the center of the cave to find a giant, bright red rectangular creature. The monstrous rectangle stands over twenty feet tall and is over ten feet wide on each side. It has the same large, beady eyes as the smaller rectangles, and the same menacing eyebrows as well.

The Space Jumper looks around the large cave, the home of the mother of all rectangular creatures, to find hundreds of baby red rectangles dangling from the ceiling. The walls of the cave circle up from the ground to the ceiling. The dirt on the ground of the new cave is flat, being the landing nest to the strange creatures. Mark stands at the top of the cave, and looks down at the large enemy in the middle. It turns its large body around, sensing the Space Jumper's presence in the area. It looks at Mark with its large eyes, and lowers its brows in anger. The large creature jumps up a few feet in the cave to its left to block something behind.

Mark slides down into the cave, and stands on the same ground as the towering red monster. The creature stands four times taller than the Space Jumper, as it looks down at the puny human. Mark equips his laser crystal attachment to his flashlight, turning it into the laser sword.

Wielding the laser sword and boomerang hatchet, Mark stands in front of the creature in the cave. As the two stare each other down, Mark looks up using his instincts to find several small red rectangles drop down from the ceiling. Mark slides to his left over the dirt.

The small red creatures land on the dirt with a thud. They turn their bodies to look at the Space Jumper with their beady eyes. As Mark looks up, he finds several more of the rectangles dropping down towards him. He checks back to the large rectangle to find it jumping towards him. Mark jumps away towards the side of the cave to avoid the cluster of enemies. He hangs on to a stalactite where the wall meets the ceiling, and throws his blade at the large rectangle.

His hatchet spins slowly in the dark, with light provided by the glowing attachment opposite the blade. Mark has his feet pressed against the wall of the cave while holding on to the dark red stalactite on the ceiling. The spinning blade slashes a cut across the hard surface of the large rectangle. The hatchet flings off the enemy and flies back to Mark, who catches it out of the air while holding on to the wall. The red brick begins jumping around the cave, gaining position over the Space Jumper.

Mark jumps from the wall directly towards the rectangle and throws a punch at its eye. The rectangle looks unfazed, as Mark's hand hurts from punching the solid enemy. Mark falls below the big brick after losing his momentum. The rectangle jumps up in the cave, and drops back down over Mark. The Space Jumper rolls back and out of the way from the square-based rectangle. The red enemy thunders down to the ground, sending an aftershock around the cave.

The vibration rattles the entire interior of the cave, shaking everything around. Mark feels the heavy shockwave, sitting on the ground in front of the large, red rectangle. The Space Jumper rises to his feet, and looks up to find smaller red rectangles raining down from the ceiling. The rectangles surround Mark, landing dangerously close to his position.

As the rectangles jump around the cave, Mark kicks and punches anything near him. The Space Jumper continues to focus on the large enemy in front, who continues to jump around the cave, blocking an exit at the back. The large rectangle lands firmly on the ground, and charges power inside of its dense shell. It glows bright red, and sends shockwaves around the cave to all of the smaller rectangles. Mark stands back and watches what is going on. He studies all of the hostile creatures around him, while smashing smaller rectangles near him.

The large rectangle reduces power after charging up its little ones. All of the smaller rectangles glow bright red, and shoot shots of the same red power at Mark, who has his hand in his pocket. The Space Jumper activates his shield as the beams of power fly towards him like bullets. The red electricity strikes Mark's body, sending a strange taste coursing through his shield. The shield connects to his shoes, transmitting the red power through his body. The red tastes like blood and granite, as Mark absorbs the attacks. He flexes the red energy away from his body, and looks at the large rectangle behind the smaller ones. His shield minimizes as he puts his hand in his other pocket to activate his new cloaking device.

Invisible in the cave, Mark quickly sneaks around the smaller rectangles towards the large one. He moves with a quick finesse through the crowded cave floor, and kicks the large rectangle in the lower front of its body. His shoes send a shock of power through the large rectangle, creating a crack at its base. The sneak attack deals critical damage to the rectangle as Mark's cloak runs out. He stands in front of the large enemy, punches the rectangle with two fists, further expanding the previous crack.

The large rectangle jumps away, and plants firmly back down on the ground. Another shockwave sends several more small rectangles down to the ground. They surround the Space Jumper, and shoot small shots of red power at him. When not encased in a shield, the small red powered electric blasts sting through Mark's clothes.

Feeling some pain, Mark jumps back to the side of the cave, and hangs on to another stalactite on the ceiling. He uses his free hand to equip his BB gun. He checks the ammo, noticing it is a full mix of BB's and crystal bullets from King Rox on Crystal.

The Space Jumper tinkers with the particle accelerator to shoot large sized bullets. He aims his gun at the large red enemy, blocking the same exit from before. Mark pulls the trigger, and sends a shot through the cave, creating a loud pop within the confined space. A BB the size of a bowling ball flies through the cave and hits the rectangle directly in its eye.

The large, red enemy flinches back in pain, as Mark looks away from the sights of his gun to watch the aftermath for a moment. He quickly looks back down the sights, and fires another series of shots at the large enemy.

A set of crystals hit the large rectangle in different spots of its square face. Larger cracks begin to develop around the enemy as the bullets strike all sides of its body. One of the last bullets in the set chips away a huge chunk of the dense, red rectangle. Mark hangs on to the side of the cave, when the small rectangles begin to draw near, and shoot red electric shots at him. Stray electricity kicks up dust and rocks from the side of the cave, dropping sharp stalactites from the ceiling. Mark evades away from the electric shots, and jumps towards the large, injured rectangle.

The Space Jumper utilizes his momentum to strike a swift overhead attack on a large crack in the rectangle. Using his hatchet, he slices away another huge chunk off the side of the large, red rectangle. Mark flips past the enemy and slides his feet on the ground.

He turns around, and runs towards the base of the rectangle. He finds another large crack in the rectangles body and begins punching and kicking it in a combo of fight moves. Thrust kicks lead to double fist punches, switching to backhand punches, Mark chips away at the enemy before knocking another large piece from its body.

Mark quickly dives back to the center of the cave and faces the large, injured rectangle. The smaller rectangles struggle to keep up with the Space Jumper, as he takes out one of his only remaining explosive devices.

He ignites the explosive, and throws it at the center of the large, red rectangle. The bomb explodes upon impact, blowing an immense hole in the center of the creature, exposing its red power core.

The Space Jumper covers his face to block debris from the explosion. He takes out his BB gun during the dismay of the enemy. He loads half of the chamber with crystal ammo, and snaps back the barrel. He aims the gun at the center core of the monster, and pulls the trigger.

A large crystal BB flies fast through the cave, and strikes the glowing red matter within the red monster. The sharp crystal pierces through the heart of the monster, and blows a hole out of its back. The light inside of the red creature begins to fade, as its body begins to crack further, until completely breaking apart to smaller pieces. The large, red rectangle cracks under pressure, evaporating into dust, and falls to the floor of the cave.

Mark stands up straight, and checks his surroundings. The small, red rectangles lose their glow of power and stand lost in the cave. One of the small creatures jumps high into the air, and sticks itself back into the ceiling of the cave.

One by one, all of the small rectangles begin to follow suit, jumping up, and sticking to the top of the large cave. Out of breath, the Space Jumper watches the enemies surrender, as the exit emerges behind the dust of the boss.

Mark walks through the cave towards the exit behind the large pile of dark red dust from the large rectangle enemy. The Space Jumper kicks up dust from the crumbled corpse, walking over bits of the rectangle. The exit to the cave is narrow, and leads up a long, steep hill. Mark climbs up the hill narrowing down around him the further he goes.

The Space Jumper uses his hands to detect the space of the walls around him. He jumps up a steep cliff to reach a higher elevation in the cave. Without special shoes or proper gear, a regular man would be lost in the cave.

Walking through the cave, the walls around him begin to grow red, starting from a darker hue. The further he goes, the wider the cave spreads, and the brighter red the walls turn. The narrow cave opens up to a larger cave, unveiling a goldmine of the red power that Lineage seeks.

Mark walks into the cave towards a large deposit of red power sitting on the floor. The size of the red power is incredible, appearing to weigh multiple tons. The Space Jumper walks around the back of the deposit towards a good spot, and uses a backfist attack to punch a chunk of the power free.

Red power crystals fly in the air, and rain down over the Space Jumper. Mark kneels down to the ground, and begins scooping up select pieces of red power. He stores several pounds of the red power in his bag, while holding sizeable pieces in his pocket. He continues to walk around the red power source, and rises up a hill towards a light at the end of the tunnel.

He catches his breath, and begins to jog up the cave towards the light at the end. The light expands, unveiling the hot, outside world. The exit to the cave is small, on the other side of the base of the volcano. As he walks forward and looks down, dirt transitions to grass, where walls of red power transition to tall trees. He continues out of the cave, and walks down the grass.

Bushes and trees stand over the ground, allowing the Space Jumper to breathe a little easier. The trees and brush grow more and more dense the further down the small hill he walks. Everything is quiet around him, besides a slight rumbling in the ground beneath his feet.

As Mark walks forward through the tall trees in the warm temperature, he discovers a small segment of wide-open land, circled within the grass. He stops for a moment, and looks at the circular shape of a small ridge, strung together using dried up kindling from the surrounding trees. The plot of land appears to be a nest, as Mark crouches low. He climbs up the dense ridge of brush, and creeps towards the outer lip of the nest. He climbs the lip, and looks inside of the circular plot of land.

At the center of the circle, nestles a small dinosaur, only slightly larger than the Space Jumper. The dinosaur has light blue and white skin swirling around its body like a zebra. Its long tail swirls behind its back, starting wide, and narrowing towards the end. Its legs tuck in to its body, sleeping tight. Mark stands at the edge of the nest, and studies the sleeping dinosaur, contemplating if he should approach it.

Being similar in size to the dinosaur, Mark climbs in the large, nested area, remaining low. He slowly walks towards the dinosaur when he steps on a crunchy stick beneath him. The sound of the breaking stick awakens the dinosaur. It lifts its head from the ground, and lazily takes interest in the noise. It awakens from a deep sleep, and begins to stand up completely. As the dinosaur begins to stand, Mark takes a step back, realizing the actual size of the creature. With long legs and arms, and a long neck, the dinosaur stands upright at around ten feet tall. It turns its head, and looks back at Mark. It studies the Space Jumper for a moment with white and blue eyes.

The blue and white dinosaur's mouth slowly moves, chewing something after its nap. It notices Mark, and slowly walks in his direction, who grows slightly petrified standing still in the nest. The dinosaur calmly swings its sharp tail behind its body as it approaches the Space Jumper. The large lizard has a friendly smile beneath large, derpy eyes. It walks slowly towards Mark, and carefully moves its head towards his jacket pocket. Mark stands still, allowing the large dinosaur to sniff around his ensemble. It sticks its nose inside Mark's pocket, and pulls out a chunk of the red power he collected from the cave.

The dinosaur pulls the red power out with its teeth, lifting its neck away from Mark. It leans back and crunches the red power crystal like biting an ice cube. It breaks the small crystal down to bits like an afternoon snack.

Mark smiles and laughs as the dinosaur enjoys the red power, and at how non-aggressive it is. When the dinosaur finishes the piece of red power, it looks back to Mark, and slowly moves its head towards his same pocket. Mark slides his body back and away from the dinosaurs head, and smiles.

The Space Jumper grabs another piece of red power from his pocket, and holds it out in his hand in front of the dinosaur. The blue and white dinosaur moves its head around the power crystal, and sniffs it out. The dinosaur waits for Mark to either give him the piece, or take it back. Mark begins to walk around the large, circular nest, as the dinosaur watches the red crystal. Mark plays with the red power piece, throwing it between his two hands, hiding it behind his back. The dinosaur grows disappointed, and moves its head away from Mark. It walks back to its original spot, and lays back down in the nest.

"Aww, I'm just kidding buddy. You really like these things, huh?" Mark asks the dinosaur, not expecting an answer. The blue and white striped dinosaur purrs a tone under its breath. The Space Jumper walks next to the resting dinosaur, and places the red power crystal next to its head. He slowly moves his hand to the side of the long neck of the dinosaur, and pets its rough, armored skin.

Electricity from Mark's gloves sends friction through the dinosaur's neck. It perks its head up, and enjoys the comfort of the electric feel. The dinosaur remains resting in the nest, as Mark pets its scaly neck. It moves its head from the ground, and munches on the crystal placed next to it. As the dinosaur chews the red power crystal with its head on the ground, Mark continues to rub its neck, when a vibration shakes the ground beneath the nest.

The Space Jumper and the dinosaur exchange looks of worry. They turn around to find the volcano is erupting. The ground shakes as the volcano begins to shoot large chunks of red power like an umbrella from the top of the mountain. The surrounding trees shake and vibrate from earthquakes on the ground. Mark stands next to the dinosaur and rubs the back of its head. The Space Jumper takes the opportunity to mount the dinosaur, where it stands up.

"Let's get out of here!" He yells out to the dinosaur, smacking its right hindquarter. The dinosaur crouches down, and begins to walk to the lip of the nest. It looks back at Mark and to the volcano erupting behind. Mark holds out another small chunk of red power in the form of a sugar cube to the dinosaur, where it eats it off his glove. Mark looks back, finding bright orange and red lava roaring over the ground in the distance. Mark wraps his arm around the dinosaurs neck, as it jumps high off its nest.

Soaring above the tops of the trees, Mark holds on to the dinosaur by the neck, as they fall to the ground together. Mark sits tight on the dinosaur, clenching his legs hard on its torso, providing power with his shoes. The mix of the Space Jumper's tech and the red power create some sort of unity within the dinosaur, as they land back on the ground.

Mark maintains hold of the dinosaur as it stabilizes its landing to a run. As earthquakes continue to shake the planet, a gap separates the land ahead. The vibrations move the ground away from each other, creating large and wide holes.

"Jump ahead, buddy." Mark says calmly to the dinosaur as it continues to dissolve the red power with a smile. The connection of power from Mark's gear allows the dinosaur to jump higher and run faster, away from the lava on the ground, and from above.

"Man, you really crush those diamonds. I think I may have found your name, Diamond Crusher." Mark says to the dinosaur, as they run down a hill before the expanding gap.

Sprinting at a good speed, the dinosaur jumps high over the expanding gap in the ground. Lava flows behind Mark and the dinosaur, and falls into the hole in the ground. Excess lava seeps out of the gap, and continues to follow them down the hill.

"Keep moving, DC." Mark says to Diamond Crusher, the dinosaur. They move up a small hill towards another gap in the ground. DC jumps over the hole, landing on the other side, down several feet. The dinosaur slides its thick paws over the loose dirt, and continues to move forward.

A large mountain approaches ahead as Mark and the dinosaur run across the trembling ground. The surface continues to split apart, as Diamond Crusher runs up the base of another steep hill. DC has to jump high up the hill to continue moving forward as the lava approaches quickly behind. The gaps in the ground grow taller and more dangerous as they continue forward. At the peak of the mountain, Mark looks back to find an ocean of hot lava making its way up to their level.

At the top of the mountain, Diamond Crusher begins to run out of energy, and plops down in the dirt. Mark reaches into his pocket, and pulls out another small chunk of red power. He holds the red diamond in front of DC's nose, where it smells the power. DC lifts his head, and takes a bite of the red power from the Space Jumper's fingertips. Diamond Crusher perks up and checks its surroundings.

At the top of the mountain, another large gap separates them from safety. "Jump across, DC." Mark says to the dinosaur, pointing to the opposite side of the wide hole.

Diamond Crusher begins to run across the dirt, and springs a jump before the end of the hole. Together, they fly through the air over another treacherous gap. As Mark looks below, he notices a pool of red power lava glowing inside the hole. They land on the ground on an elevated island at the top of the mountain.

"Another volcano?" Mark asks rhetorically, standing on the island. He looks back to find the lava that is chasing them, fall into the large hole. The ground begins to tremble more ferociously than before with the displacement of red power.

Standing next to the mountain, Mark and DC watch the scolding hot lava fill the new volcano. Moments later, another explosion erupts dangerously close to them. The loud noise startles DC, as he spins in circles.

"DC lets go." Mark yells, rubbing the side of his neck. Diamond Crusher wastes no time, and builds speed for the next jump off the elevated island to another narrow split of land. He jumps off the island, and drops down to the new island below. As Mark looks behind, he finds the new volcano begin to spew and shoot lava from its main hole. The old lava from the first volcano overflows out the top, and follows them down the gaps at a quicker pace than before.

The air and atmosphere turn bright red due to the heat and smoke from the red powered volcanos. Diamond Crusher runs down a hill from the volcano as Mark hangs on to his neck. The lava is heavy, but moves fast, quickly matching DC's speed. Some of the lava touches DC's feet, making him whelp in pain. Diamond Crusher picks up speed, and jumps across another gap in the ground. He lands on dirt as the hill begins to level out ahead. Chunks of red power land on the ground nearby as they continue forward. The hill from the volcano transfers back to a flat, forested area. As they move forward, Mark watches the surrounding trees melt and erupt in flames around him.

Diamond Crusher moves fast, jumping over several more gaps in the ground. Dirt transitions to grass, as they continue to pick up speed. The tremors in the ground begin to subside as they further themselves from the volcanoes. The surrounding trees fade away, leaving an open plot of grass around them. Lava continues to follow behind the Space Jumper, nipping at DC's hooves.

Ahead, an incredibly steep cliff leads to another forest below. The fall would kill Diamond Crusher, and heavily injure the Space Jumper, who wants to save his new friend. The lava would eventually catch up to them if they were injured.

Mark's tablet begins to vibrate, catching DC's attention as well as his. Diamond Crusher slightly slows down before an uphill near the cliff. Mark presses some buttons on his tablet, and opens his radio application.

"Space Jumper, look up." A voice says from the other end of the tablet. Mark looks up and behind him to find the familiar ship from his new allies, the Mega Police Unit.

The MPU ship flies ahead of Mark, and positions at the end of the cliff. It begins to open its rear hatch as Mark rides DC across the open plot of grass. A heavy wave of lava quickly approaches from behind, practically touching the dinosaurs feet. DC runs fast to the edge of the cliff, and launches towards the open hatch of the ship.

Mark holds on for dear life, and looks down at the height of the tall cliff. Time slows down in mid-air, as DC slides into the rear hatch of the ship. The lava from the volcanos spew over the cliff, creating a bright red and orange waterfall of fire.

Diamond Crusher and Mark slide over the metal surface of the large ship, and crash into a stack of boxes towards the cockpit.

"He's in, let's move out." One of the MPU officers yells to the pilot. The bay doors to the ship close, as they accelerate up towards space. The pilot maneuvers through smoke and red fireballs in the sky. The sleek ship is nimble, and moves through the debris with ease. The outside of the planet melts into black ash, as the ship flies out of the atmosphere.

The Space Jumper and Diamond Crusher recover from the jump, where the allies have their guns aimed at the dinosaur. "Relax guys, he seems friendly." Mark says to the intimidating officers. Mark reaches into his pocket, and crunches a red power crystal into smaller pieces. He hands the good-sized pieces to some of the crew, so they may put their weapons down.

DC sits on the metal floor, resting from the running and jumping. He does not watch the people around him, until Mark hands off chunks of the red power. DC stands up as Mark walks to him, and feeds him another red crystal. He pets DC as it crunches down the red power. The dinosaur stands docile on the ship flying to space. The police lower their weapons, and look at each other as they realize Diamond Crusher is an ally.

DC walks curiously towards one of the MPU agents in the back, asking for another piece of the red crystal treat. The lead Mega Police agent walks to Mark, and reaches for a handshake.

"What happened down there?" He asks Mark, helping him stand up straight. "Lineage was there, looking for the red power crystals, but dinosaurs made it difficult for them." Mark replies. "Who's your friend?" The officer asks, motioning to the dinosaur, eating red crystal pieces from the crews hands. "I call him Diamond Crusher, DC for short, because of the way he devours the red power crystals." Mark explains.

Everyone looks at the dinosaur, as one of the soldiers feeds it another red crystal. "The red crystals power him up with jumps and speed." The Space Jumper explains to the officer in the room.

Diamond Crusher walks slowly to the center of the open room. As Mark looks back to DC, he watches the dinosaur warp itself into a singular black hole in the blink of an eye, and escape the ship. A breath of confused air escapes the wormhole, as everyone stands stunned at the disappearing act from the dinosaur.

"I'll see you later Diamond Crusher." Mark says to the receding vapor trails of the wormhole. The crew look upset at the departure of the dinosaur, when the pilots door slides open.

"I see you found some red power crystals." A high-ranking agent of the MPU says to Mark, as he walks towards his crew. The officer wears a brown leather jacket, and has a black moustache. "Volcanoes blew most of it sky high." Mark replies, presenting the small chunk from his back pocket. He shows the MPU agent, as he places it back in his pocket.

"Now you understand the rarity of its power, as volcano eruptions occur often." The MPU agent says to Mark. "What's the condition of the planet?" Mark asks the officer, who stands next to his other officer, and lower ranking crewmembers. "Most of the region looks glassed." The officer replies.

"At least my buddy made it out." Mark says, looking at the crew. "Who's your buddy?" The high-ranking officer with the mustache asks the Space Jumper. "You just missed it sir, it was a dinosaur." One of the lower ranking recruits who fed Diamond Crusher says to the officer. The high-ranking officer motions to Mark to follow him, as they begin to walk towards the pilots cabin.

"Any leads to Lineage?" The officer whispers to Mark, as they walk into the pilots area. "They didn't appear to stay long. I found the bodies of some of their crew." Mark replies, watching the officer sit in the main pilot chair. He presses some buttons, changing the layout of the map screen displayed at the center of the console. "They're close Space Jumper, good work." The officer says, continuing to manipulate the computer screen.

"Look here Space Jumper." The officer says back to Mark, who stands behind the chairs. The officer points to the screen, as Mark looks closer, noticing a color scheme of the red power used from Lineage.

"It appears they are heading to Rogue at their current flight path." The officer says, looking at Mark. "How far is Rogue?" Mark asks obliviously. "The Rogue galaxy is a few million light years away. You have to be careful out there. That is Alter Zone distance." The officer explains to Mark. "We can take you close, but not all the way." The officer says, sitting back in his chair. "I understand." Mark replies with firm affirmation.

"I'll send the map of Rogue to your tablet. It shouldn't take too much time for someone such as yourself." The officer says to Mark, who looks out of the main window to space, studying the symbols of the stars. "Are we allowed in?" Mark asks the captain of the ship, continuing to make its way to a preferable launch point. "Not exactly, we need special permission from The Man Who Runs Uphill." The officer says looking up to Mark.

"Who's he?" Mark asks the officer. "He is the Director of Rogue." The officer replies. "Directors don't seem to like me very much where I come from." Mark says to the officer. "It could be trouble Space Jumper." The officer says, taking a deep breath. "That's probably what Lineage wants us to think." Mark responds to the officer. "You make a good point." The officer replies.

The Space Jumper's tablet vibrates with an unknown message from the universe. He does not read the message in front of the officer. "Alright then, let's get closer to Rogue." Mark says to the officer, who manipulates electronic switches on the dashboard. "Let's roll out." The officer says over the intercom to the crew.

Chapter 10

Rogue

The MPU ship slides through space. Mark is with the crew, standing in a circle, as one of the soldiers tells an old war story involving flying ships and space weapons.

The Space Jumper holds on to a red power crystal in his pocket, and mentally fades away, thinking about Diamond Crusher, the friendly dinosaur. A red light begins to flash in his head, striking lightning through his eyes. He feels the rumble of the bay door opening to the west of his view.

"We're as close as we can get before whatever is through that fog. Radio check Space Jumper?" The pilot of the ship says to Mark and the crew.

"Check." Mark replies, slipping his glasses over his eyes. The technology from his tablet synchronizes his gear to his glasses. The connecting views appear three dimensional within the switch. His tablet battery is on overload, connected with the power of his cool shoes.

The crew around the room salute Mark as he rises to a stand. His body is shaky from the immensely critical, and life threatening amount of damage he sustained to get to where he is, mentally and physically lost in a cosmic twist of damage to ones heart, mind and soul.

The Space Jumper turns around, and begins running towards the end of the bay, where he jumps nearly horizontal into the cold, open space. Fragments of the Rogue galaxy lay within, and behind a thick green haze, transitioning from a purple glow of light from the open space. Mark aims his jump away from the parked ship, and looks back at the pilot. He points to his own head, marking the signs of communication are a go. The pilot parks in the space, and slowly floats around. Mark carries momentum away from the ship, and matches the waypoint on his map to view.

A thick green fog circles around the new galaxy. Between all of the space ahead, Mark focuses close, in search of heat and light signatures to jump further. He flexes his phantom feet muscles inside his shoes, creating a signature flow of power in the glowing rings. He continues to hold on to the red crystal in his pocket, as gravity fields approach his feet. He forms a crouch on the field, and sprints fast towards the crossing of purple light, into the muddy, green fog. His air withheld from the tastes of space provide little support for his health. Breathing within the special barrier from his shoes tastes of a dirty and mossy atmosphere as he glides forward.

He drinks an old water pill from his bag, providing hydration for his body. He collects his feet over another gravity field, and glides forward.

His gear glows as he goes through space at a moderate speed. The purple outlines of light begin to fade as Mark approaches the heavy, gassy fog. After jumping from several more gravity fields, his visual perception significantly decreases to the point where all he sees is green fog, and subtle lighting from behind the distance. His cool shoes begin to sputter, going through all of the thick fog. His momentum alters as he enters the galaxy.

He figures out a way to make his shoes return to normal in the fog, and finds jumping through space is easy as a breeze. He pushes forward thousands of miles through thick green fog to emerge quickly into the open space of the new galaxy.

His speed increases as the thickness of the mysterious fog powers his shoes. The dark green fog slowly changes to a lighter shade of green. Before the Space Jumper knows it, he is inside the bright orbit of the Rogue galaxy.

He pauses in space for a moment, carrying tremendous momentum with him. He spins his body to look behind, discovering the fog from which he emerged.

From the same green fog, almost a hundred and eighty degrees behind him, groups of large space ships slowly creep out of the green. The square ships are the size of mountain faces, and move in to position behind him.

Mark prays for a gravity field in front of his location, finding one behind him. He flips around in the zero gravity space, and allows the power of his shoes to absorb the gravity field. He crouches down, and quickly springs from the field. He alters his position, utilizing momentum to steer his body. From the perspective of the large barge space ships, Mark moves away while flowing up and down.

Behind the Space Jumper, the large barges begin to unload fleets of smaller ships from its lower front corner. The ships fly fast towards Mark's last known location, and follow the airflow from his exerted gravity fields. Mark collects speed and begins to maneuver past asteroid fields in space. Stars surround the black backdrop, as planets grow more obvious. His glasses direct the location to the Mega Police Unit's last known location of Lineage, several lightyears away.

Heaps of space ships begin to shoot lasers ahead of the Space Jumper's gravity fields. Small groups of three silver attack ships are in front, with another three groups of three larger attack ships behind. The large, barge sized space ships begin to turn at the border of the mossy, green fog. Their trail is hot for the suspicious intruder of the galaxy.

The Space Jumper is several lightyears ahead of the battalion of cruisers behind him. He moves sporadically left and right, collecting momentum to increase speed at each gravity field. Everything on him is intact, from his board to his bag, when a sliver of purple light shines off his reflective lenses. He turns his head around for a split second to find a red laser beam about to melt his face.

He quickly turns away, and begins angling his body to carry a significant amount of forward momentum away from the path of the laser beam. His speed carries him only a handful of miles away from the depth of the beam.

Hoping he is miles away from the light, Mark turns around and looks below his body to find where the beam comes from. The trail leads to his east, where his direction is north. The beam follows his initial trail according to the map on his glasses. He follows the tracks of the heat signature back through lightyears of space. He squints his eyes, focusing in to a large and wide group of ships circling in towards him.

Mark looks to his side, and scrambles his momentum towards a small gravity field below. From a green and yellow gravity field, he builds an unnerving amount of strength, and powers down a jump that shocks his heart as he escapes the space. The shoes beneath his feet absorb a part of Mark's soul as he nearly disappears from the field. He warps with one jump toward the location on his glasses.

With no immediate threat of planets or other obstructions, Mark cruises through space towards the destination, only half a million lightyears away. Another set of lasers pass the Space Jumper as he moves towards the approaching planet. The ships eventually catch up to speed with him, and begin to shoot lasers close to his position. They follow Mark's trail, as he controls his movements on gravity fields in the space.

The fleet of ships size up the Space Jumper as they give chase within Rogue. Planets are scattered and spread across many lightyears, as Mark tracks the location planet of his old, backstabbing crew, Lineage.

A stray laser beam pings off the space board on Mark's back. The force pushes him off track as he slows momentum, descending into the colorful planet. His glasses gather heat signatures connected to the red matter he has been collecting. The trail grows cold and hot with significant signatures.

In space, above the clouds of the planet, are another pair of large, barged ships, patrolling the atmosphere. Mark's heat signatures fine-tune his direction to a camp, directly below the heavy ships. The Space Jumper swings his momentum down and continues to descend, moving through the clouds with a fleet of ships behind him. His trail remains hot, as the shots on him remain cold, where everyone approaches the surface of the planet at risk.

Mark redirects his momentum to swim horizontally through the healthy clouds above the suspected location. The approaching ships lose track of the Space Jumper, as he flows through a breath of fresh air. His momentum reduces to hold up inside the cloud with his gear and shoes. His scarf holds his head, with the assist of his electronic gloves, allowing him time to rest for a moment, as his shoes collect power from the clouds. He collects himself and his gear, and waits inside one of the largest clouds in the atmosphere.

The elements of the land appear native, and mostly tribal. Indications of power are scarce, connected to the main village. As he scans the landscape of the camp, his heat signature indicates a hint on the ground, not far from his position. Mark checks his tablet, ready to send a message on the radio. "I've found the clowns, check the indicator." He whispers to the microphone on his tablet.

The ships from space pour into the planet and spread across the sky. The barges begin to drop in, as Mark notices one falling over his head. He pushes off the cloud to the side, giving himself enough space to hitch a ride into the atmosphere. As the barge drops down through his cloud, Mark jumps down towards the surface to match its speed. He finds a small hinge on one of the lowest parts of the landing gear, and hangs on to it with his hand. He holds onto a metal bar below with his shoe.

Reluctantly for Mark, the ship is heading in a similar direction to his waypoint. As he hangs on, he checks his surroundings, finding a similar barge sized ship, moving down towards the surface. All of the barges appear to be heading towards the central landing port at one of the most populated cities on the planet. Only miles away from the heat signature on his glasses, Mark jumps off the side of the barge towards the location of a small, dark camp.

Detaching from the barge, Mark skydives through the air, utilizing the low hanging clouds to control his pace. Over an empty and rather cool part of the desert, Mark dive-bombs into the planet, and lands with a roll on a soft plot of sand.

The village of interest houses tall buildings made of clay, tarps, and bricks, amongst many other points of interest. Collecting himself over the sand, Mark looks around to find no indications of space ships. The Space Jumper cracks a smile at his classic evasion tactic, and takes a step forward towards the city. Upon taking that casual first step, space ships pull up over his location.

Three of the small, silver, patrol ships from space spin circled lights above his position. Mark looks up into the light, and takes out his gun at the same time. As the lights hone in on his position, he begins to move across the sand towards the lights of the city. Small dispatch crews from two of the three ships drop to the ground, and try to track the Space Jumper's location.

Mark moves quickly on the sand, hiding, sliding and gliding over the dunes and bumps. Ground troops begin to stomp over the sand, and take fire at Mark as he utilizes cover within the dunes.

Dodging fire from the alien enforcers, Mark dives into a lake of water amongst the sand. The water in the lake is dirty and unhealthy, as Mark's cool shoes absorb the raw elements through the rings. He swims to the other side of the shallow pool, and stands when he gets a safe chance.

He crouches low, and jumps out of the lake, pulling a large pocket of sand and water with him. He lands on top of a sand hill, where lasers from the security fly overhead, and kick up dust on the ground.

The Space Jumper runs across the arid desert, finding a pair of enemies on top of a hill of sand. He aims the gun from his hip, and spins the particle accelerator to its widest depth setting. He pulls the trigger, shooting a cannon ball at the feet of the hill. Sand blasts up into the sky, along with a pair of heavily armored space enforcers. They hunch down when they fly in the air. Mark continues forward towards the growing city lights.

Rising up a small hill, the Space Jumper fights two more armored thugs in the sand. He kicks and punches them in crucial knockout spots. He kicks one of the space security into a different pool of water. The space enforcer floats in the water, where Mark jumps off his unconscious body to the other side. The dunes of sand reduce, as the lasers from his enemies increase. The number of ships following him has reduced to only one, with a shaky light following his movements.

Mark jumps horizontally over the sand, quickly gaining entrance to the oasis city. The city is tall with high buildings made of clay and brick. Business runs through the city through shops and stalls on the ground. Mark runs in between a pair of tall buildings, successfully sneaking into the city. Standing next to the pair of buildings, Mark looks around the area for a trace of red power leading to Lineage.

Space ships fly over the city, with spotlights pointed at the ground, looking for the intruder. Mark stands next to a light post, blending in with the crowd of mixed species. A gust of wind from one of the hovering ships above sends a blanket skirting into the street. The spotlight quickly turns away from the area.

The Space Jumper springs for the blanket, and rolls his body over it on the dirt. He wraps the blanket around his face and body, and runs down the street towards a faint flicker of a heat signature. Aliens of many various species hang around the shops of the dimly lit city in the sand.

As Mark runs down the sandy street, a spotlight takes notice of his sporadic movement. As the blanket hides his identity well, Mark moves fast in between the small shops. Another ship pulls up ahead of Mark's desired route.

A group of armored alien enforcers slide down a rope from their ship into the street next to the shops. The group splits up, and spreads out across the block of markets and medium sized buildings. Mark crouches on the sand next to a shop carrying metal and gold trinkets. He sits on the sand, and listens to the steps of the armored aliens as they approach. As a guard approaches, the Space Jumper turns the corner of a shop, stands up, and kicks the guard across the market.

The other guards in the area hear the wreck of one of their comrades crashing into a merchant's stall. They struggle to follow where the kick originated from, as Mark moves forward, following his faint heat signature.

Crossing the street near merchant stalls, Mark moves forward through the city streets as tall buildings tower overhead. Another armored security officer takes notice of the running Space Jumper. Before he has time to call for reinforcements, Mark has already hit him with a backfist. The armored alien soars through the air above the ground, and falls backwards to a shop down the street.

Mark turns left down a small corridor in the dark and tight village. He makes his way further into the thick of the city. The carpet he snagged from the dirt in the dark covers his head, face, and glowing parts of his gear. His board remains attached to his bag, providing a firm sense of stability behind him.

He crouches low around the corner of another shop, when an explosion of red light from his glasses pops up in front of his eyes. The core of the heat signature stands in front of his eyes in the form of Lineage's ship.

Mark checks his tablet for information from the scans of the ship. Refueling at a port on the planet, the ship is the very same one belonging to Lineage. Mark presses the radio button on his tablet.

"They're here. Check my location." Mark says briefly into his tablet's microphone array. He clings his tablet back to his side, and looks up at the ship to find a pair of alien spaceships hovering overhead. Mark moves left within the security of the market stalls.

He stands across a large, vacant parking lot, open for another large ship. The hovering spaceships above the plot of sand circle around and rotate their lights. Mark waits for an opportune time of darkness to sneak across the sand unseen. The ships circle around towards the main street, as Mark stays low and moves into darkness. He slows pace to feel the outside of Lineage's ship.

He holds the side of the ship as he walks towards the front bay door around the other side. Walking around Lineage's ship, Mark feels the cold sensation of betrayal from the crew, and the cold blade of the backstabbing by Captain Drake. Strong energy shocks the Space Jumper's feet through the powerful rings of his shoes. He walks forward towards the door at the side of the ship.

Standing next to the door, Mark takes cover while taking a breath, as he browses the inside of the ship from the outside. Everything appears normal and quiet from the angle he saw. He keeps angling his perspective down the corridor towards the front of the ship. Behind the door, towards the back of the ship, a crewmember of Lineage is asleep in a chair by the wall.

Mark steps inside the ship, and sneaks quietly inside using the power of his shoes. He controls the vibrations of the impact using the rings on the cool shoes. The Space Jumper stays low, and wraps around the wall towards the downward stairs.

The ship is cold and quiet, as the Space Jumper searches for quiet retribution. Mark crouches down the steps, careful of his volume. Everything is quiet in the recreation area, meaning the crew must be out on a mission, or asleep in their quarters. Mark takes a chance, and continues down the ship towards the engine room and garage. He walks slowly past the crew quarters, listening for creaks in the air. He continues past the vacant crew quarters, and makes his way to the engine room. He checks the corners for situations, only to find another empty room.

With a bright idea, the Space Jumper walks slowly and quietly towards the special compartment in the engine, which houses a bright, glowing chunk of red power, along with his black hole gun obtained a strange amount of time ago. He powers down the engine, similar to how Captain Drake rebooted it.

The Space Jumper utilizes the tools in his arsenal of weapons and gadgets to open the chamber housing the stable, red power. He scoops out the hot, red power core, and places it in his pocket. He begins to close the metal chambers, stuffing wires inside the housing. Before he closes it all down, he notices the black hole gun in another compartment to the side of the engine. He opens the other housing square, and yanks out his black hole gun from several metallic, wiring harnesses. The gun appears to be intact, as Mark pulls it out of the mechanism, similar to how Captain Drake put it in.

The ship continues to have power, despite the removal of the red core and black hole gun. Mark looks around the ship for activity, and begins to sneak out of the engine room, not knowing if people are officially there. He breezes past the crew quarters, feeling familiar findings from fast times. He jumps up the spinning staircase to the second floor, and crouches low at the top. He remains low, and peeks from the corridor towards the exit door.

The Space Jumper stops for a moment, and really listens for any noise from the engine room. He stays still for about five seconds, honing in to the silence. No noise erupts from the ship, besides the guard snoring at the door. Mark stands up straight, holding the black hole gun in his hand. He takes out his main BB gun, and aims both weapons at the sleeping guard at the entrance. The particle accelerator is set to shoot large diameter ammo. He begins to walk to the door when he smells a seductive scent in the air.

The scent of a familiar woman scurries around the ceiling of the ship, as Mark feels a rush of emotions to someone close to his heart. He follows the scent trail, leading out of the ship. He continues to aim his weapons at the sleeping guard, and quietly sneaks out of Lineage's spaceship.

Back outside in the dark city, lowering his guns, Mark dawns his native blanket found in the street, and continues to track the smell of Samantha's scent. He looks in the sand, where his glasses begin to follow multiple sets of footprints down the street. He begins to crouch walk over the sand, following the direction of the footprints from the Lineage ship. He stays low, blending in with the foreign alien community past several more shops and markets. He moves quick, knowing he is a wanted man on the planet, and the galaxy, and probably the universe.

The buildings in the city begin to grow in scale, rising higher and higher from the ground. Mark checks his corners, and sneaks across the sand, following the footprints. His glasses lead the way down the street towards the taller part of the city.

Standing on the corner of a street, Mark looks up to notice everything going on. A vendor pulls a large cart full of rugs and linens down the sandy street. Most of the species on the planet vary, and are mobile, as they walk down the roads.

As the Space Jumper looks up to smell the roses, he follows the tracks down the street to a building on the corner. He begins to walk down the side of the street, when a space ship flies over his head, and shines its lights near him. Mark quickly takes cover beneath the entrance awning of a building to the side. He makes sure his face is completely covered. His shoes continue to glow bright, as his persona hides his identity well.

The spaceship hovers around the area for a moment, before flying away up the street towards the Lineage ship. The Space Jumper begins to run down the remainder of the street towards the illuminated building. He approaches the wide building, discovering a bank inside. He peers through the wide window in the front of the building to find Samantha and Captain Drake holding hands inside, surrounding themselves with bags full of red power crystals. Mark thinks about his vulnerability out in the open, and jumps high into the air. Samantha looks outside, finding a carpet falling from the sky, as the Space Jumper clears the plane of view from the bank.

Mark lands on the roof of the bank with a heavy heart, and walks towards the center to hide from view. His glasses pick up a red-hot vapor trail rising from a vent in the corner of the roof. Through a brief moment of heartache, Mark looks up at the red and orange highlighted smoke. He takes a deep breath as he walks to the vent.

Investigating the smoke, the Space Jumper detects that the heat signature is the same red power marked at the bank's location. The vapor reeks of the same material he has in his pocket. He reaches in to his pocket, and holds his stash of red power. When Mark touches the piece in his pocket, the vapor trail in front of his eyes highlights green.

The city is booming with noise and chatter from the markets. Mark reaches his hand inside the square vent, and clutches a fist. The spikes he obtained from the lakes of the Café galaxy grow out of his hand. The tough, crystalized spikes spread within the metalwork of the grate, and lock to his arm. He crouches down on the roof, and uses his shoes to lift his arm in the vent. He waits until power emits from the base and rings of his shoes. As a vibration sparks his phantom feet, he gently lifts his legs and arm in a twisting angle, removing the vent from the roof.

Releasing the clutch in his fist, the spikes in his hand snap away from the squares in the vent. He places the vent on the roof, and looks inside the open hole. Smells and sounds from within the bank erupt from the hole. As Mark listens closely, he is able to hear Captain Drake in a dialogue with the bank manager. Samantha walks next to them, as the remaining crew behind carry all of the loot. The commotion between the gang indicates they are about to make their final deposit into the vault. The hot trail of smoke is also an indication the vault is somewhere close beneath the vent.

Mark continues to listen to the dialogue between the crew, obtaining a better understanding of their position. As they walk down to the lower depths of the bank, Mark hears the red power crystals make noise around the Lineage crewmembers backs.

The Space Jumper takes a step away from the spewing smoke vent, and jumps slightly above the hole. He uses the red power vapor from the vent to jump high into the sky through the clouds, and almost to outer space in a heartbeat. He peaks in the sky, and begins to drop back down to the planet. He pauses momentum of the drop using the clouds to aim his jump back to the bank.

Maneuvering his way down a series of cloud formations, Mark relocates the bank to his main view. The hint of a successful, green light indicates the open hole in the roof. Approaching the final layer of thin clouds above the surface, the Space Jumper gently hops off the cloud, and drops through the open air. Building plenty of speed, he makes sure to aim for the open, green vent on the roof of the bank.

Approaching the roof, Mark forces an anti jump within the green vapor exuding from the vent. The red power vapor reverses momentum and forces back into the vent as Mark drops into the open hole. A combustion of energy explodes directly downwards, breaking through pipes, metal safeguards, and clay support structures. Mark slices into the bank like a hot knife through butter, where he finally falls into a large, brightly lit room.

Landing over a dense and unforgiving marble floor, Mark stands around a cloud of dust and debris, as the large door ahead begins to open slowly. Debris continues to scatter around the room, as the door opens enough to unveil the Space Jumper, standing at the corner of the vault. He looks at Captain Drake, who looks at Samantha, who is looking at him. Everybody looks at everyone in a triangle of lies in the vault of the bank.

"Space Jumper, nice of you to drop back in." Captain Drake says to Mark, as he drops a rugged bag full of red power crystals at the entrance of the vault.

"It appears I have arrived at an unfortunate time, for you." Mark responds with his hands in his pockets. Captain Drake looks furious from his face down to his legs. He takes his gun from his side, and quickly points it at Mark. Immediately taking notice of the draw, Mark kicks over a table in front of his position for cover. He falls backwards, and crouches to a seat as the table drops flush to the ground.

Drake fires a shot above the table, and continues pouring rounds towards the Space Jumper. Mark presses the camouflage button in his pocket, and disappears from sight behind cover. He rolls away from the table, and stands in front of the back wall. Utilizing momentum and speed, the Space Jumper hops up a little, and runs on the organized vault boxes on the wall. He corners the room while invisible, and gains momentum away from Drake's gunfire. Mark corners the vault again, and jumps towards Drake, standing next to the open door. The Space Jumper throws a heavy punch on Captain Drakes face, catching him in a blind spot. As Mark lands on the marble ground of the vault, his invisibility wears off.

Captain Drake slides on the floor with a huge welt on the side of his face. He sits on the ground, and holds his gun up. He aims at Mark, who kicks over another desk for cover. Captain Drake stands up and approaches the desk. Mark hears his footsteps over the marble floor within the quiet bank. At the right moment, the Space Jumper uses both of his legs to kick the desk forward. His cool shoes propel the heavy table across the floor at Drake and a couple of Lineage crewmembers. The table sends Drake face forward to the floor, as his midsection is muscled by the heavy table.

The Space Jumper takes a few steps back, and rises from a crouch to a stand. He looks at Samantha, standing back over the wide plated staircase, separating herself from the hostility. Inside the vault, Mark notices Captain Drake and the crew hit by the table begin to move back towards the staircase. Covered by his team, Drake aims his gun at the Space Jumper in the vault.

Mark looks to Samantha, and activates the shield button in his other pocket. The shield creates a powerful barrier of energy around Mark, utilizing the power of the shoes. He begins to walk out of the vault, transitioning momentum to a jump. He springs into the table that struck Drake and his crew, lifts it off the ground, and uses it to ram them further up the stairs.

Lost in a panic, the bank teller runs up the stairs, away from all the chaos to warn the security to intervene. Mark stands at the base of the stairs, ready to slash the table in half, and cut Drake down to pieces. He uses his crisp blade to slice a large corner off the table, exposing Captain Drake's face as he struggles to move back up the stairs.

The crewmembers try to kick the table back down the stairs, but find little avail. The Space Jumper swings the blade, hammering energy into the table for control. Mark continues his momentum to cut the destroyed table in half, sending it back down the steps towards the vault door.

Samantha stands frightened in the corner of the vault, as she studies the bags full of red power crystals. The vault is cold from the hole the Space Jumper created on the roof. The sound of commotion arises from the bank. Mark's shield is about to fade away, leaving him vulnerable to gunshots and blunt combat. He thinks of what the right thing to do would be, his only answer at that moment is to keep fighting.

The Space Jumper switches his blade to his opposite hand as he watches Captain Drake and the two Lineage members scramble up the short, but long steps. He takes a small breath, and activates the camouflage button in his pocket. He fades away from view, as the crew begin to shoot their weapons down the staircase. Mark leaps to the side of the large room with the flat steps, and stands directly next to Lineage, looking down to where they are shooting at.

The Space Jumper keeps his back flush with the wall, as he shuffles quickly up the stairs. About to reach the top of the cold staircase room, Mark sneaks quickly under the radar into a bright, open door. Hoping he is still invisible, the Space Jumper stays flush with the wall of the bank as he feels the device in his jacket pocket begin to overheat. He takes a breath, and presses the shield button in his other pocket.

The room is a security holding area, with bags full of red power crystals scattered everywhere. In the middle of a deposit, Captain Drake and the Lineage crew run up the stairs, and into the same holding room as Mark. It takes a couple seconds for them to notice the Space Jumper, thinking he would be long gone.

Instead, Mark stands calm with his shield on. Drake and his crew realize they are travelling too fast to slow down and fight the Space Jumper alone. They run out of the room to the entrance of the bank. After a couple of seconds, Mark begins to follow them out of the rich, deposit room.

Approaching a much smaller and singular door, the lovely lights of the bright bank entrance strike Mark in the face. With his shield at half use, Mark looks around the room to find the bank security, pointing their guns at him. Everyone is standing and moving around the main, open area of the bank, as Mark is behind strong, brass security bars attached to a desk.

With the amount of red power crystals in the deposit room, and in the vault, the Space Jumper knows Lineage paid the bank. Everyone who looks like a security guard, or Captain Drake, is a dead man to Mark.

The guards around the room begin hunting the Space Jumper, firing bullets out of advanced technological guns. The two Lineage members also shoot their laser weapons at the clerk's counter with shiny brass bars. As his shield runs dry, the Space Jumper activates the camouflage button in his pocket. With the dense noise of bullets striking his cover, and lasers zipping overhead, Mark cloaks to the room, and springs out from behind the desk.

Sliding on the shiny and clean, marble floor, Mark takes out his gun, and spins the particle accelerator to fire small rounds. While sliding on the floor, and holding on to the particle accelerator, the Space Jumper aims the gun at the nearest bank security guard's leg. He fires a single shot, striking the thigh of the loosely armored guard. He cringes in pain, as the Space Jumper takes cover behind a desk at the side of the entrance.

The bank guard falls down, and stays down. The other bank guards hear the gunshot and commotion, and look to their downed friend. Mark stays low, and utilizes the silence of sliding on the floor. He kicks away from the corner of the wall towards the main entrance of the bank. The closest guard runs over to his colleague, as Mark moves away from the trouble. He slides across the floor like a penguin on ice, holding his gun up to observe the room.

Two more bank guards stand by the entrance, cautiously watching the scenario. Mark continues to slide towards Captain Drake, where he shoots a pair of hard shots at the shorter Lineage crewmember's leg and glute. The guard flinches and crumbles to the floor, as Drake and his other crewmember struggle to open the glass door at the main entrance. Mark slows his slide, and crouch walks towards the two bank security guards at the side of the room.

Invisible, the Space Jumper crouches towards the nearest bank guard and uppercuts his arms holding the weapon. He throws the gun in the air, where Mark kicks him in the chest, sending him flying towards the other guard nearby. Together, the two guards crash into another desk, creating a mess around the bank. The guard's gun drops to the ground. Mark stands up straight, as his camouflage runs out, returning him to view. He looks at Captain Drake and the crewmember open the front door to the bank.

Outside, Mark notices a few more members of Lineage run towards the bank to assist the captain. Drake takes cover behind his allies with a breath of fresh air in the street. Mark watches Lineage pour into the bank, and look at Mark, standing in the middle of the room. Most of the Lineage crew stand around the entrance, look at Mark, and tease the weapons on their sides.

The Space Jumper begins to move backwards to the next room in the bank. As he slowly moves back, three members from Lineage run towards him, and begin fighting. They punch and kick the Space Jumper, where one of the Lineage members uses a pipe to attack. They bash Mark down as he tries to defend himself. His only resort is to retreat to the deposit room. He blocks the blunt attacks from Lineage as he moves slowly behind the brass bars.

Moving while fighting back into the deposit room, the Space Jumper utilizes his focus to block the onslaught of punches and kicks from Lineage. In the middle of the deposit room, in the middle of blocking a flurry of attacks, the Space Jumper vanishes away from view.

Activating his cloaking device, he takes advantage of the non-hostile window by punching the members of Lineage. Circling quickly around the deposit room, the Space Jumper punches the closest member of Lineage in the face, knocking him to the floor. He sneaks under a stray punch from the second member of Lineage, and punches him in the mouth, knocking him down to the ground. His head hits a large sack of red power crystals, spilling some to the floor.

For the last guard in the room, Mark crouches low, and sweeps his leg from under him. The guard falls to the stiff floor, where Mark spins forward, and punches him in the head.

With all the Lineage guards in the room taken down, Mark crouches on the ground as his camouflage runs dry. His image restores, as he begins to move back towards the vault. As he moves back to the steps, another set of guards burst into the deposit room, with Captain Drake standing behind them, looking angry. Two of the three guards point guns at the Space Jumper, as does Captain Drake. Mark takes cover at the side of the stairs, as Lineage loses sight of him. They run across the deposit room towards the door to the stairs.

Standing next to the door with his back flush to the wall, the Space Jumper activates the shield in his pocket, and listens to the enemy's movement. As the Lineage members approach the open door, Mark waits patiently.

Crossing into the room with the stairs, the first guard utilizes military tactics, looking left and right. As he focuses his weapon to the left, Mark delivers a devastating thrust kick to the Lineage member. The gun soars to the back wall of the opposite side of the stairs. The Lineage member's hand breaks from the kick, incapacitating him. Mark begins to move down the steps, as he takes out his BB gun. He crouches low while moving down the steps, when the next two guards enter the room. One of the guards dawn a gun, as the other wields a knife.

Moving down the steps, Mark fires his weapon up at Captain Drake and his crew as they force their way down. The Space Jumper shoots a mix of small crystals and BB pellets at the guards, striking one in the leg. Captain Drake and the Lineage members shoot back at Mark, who deflects four to five bullets.

Nearing the bottom of the steps towards the vault, Mark points his gun up the steps at Lineage and Drake. He pulls the trigger to his gun, but no bullets fly out. His gun is empty as his shield lowers, as does his guard. "Wait, wait." Drake whispers to the Lineage members.

Captain Drake and the two remaining members of Lineage approach the Space Jumper at the bottom of the steps with their guns drawn. Mark flips his gun around, and holsters it back to his side. He puts his hand in the air, indicating mercy. He continues to move backwards, slowly entering the vault. He looks behind to find Samantha standing behind the last upright table in the vault. Continuing to move backwards, Mark has his hands up as Drake and Lineage enter the vault.

"It's nice to see you again, Space Jumper. No hard feelings?" Captain Drake asks Mark, slowly pushing aside his two bodyguards. The Space Jumper continues to move backwards towards the opposite side of Samantha at the end of the vault. Mark stops moving, as Drake continues to press forward. He sticks his hand out to Mark, looking for a shake.

Standing at nearly an arms length away, Mark looks down in exhaustion. During the middle of a breath, Captain Drake swings his opposite arm forward, and punches Mark in the chest. A circle of red power erupts from the punch, sending the Space Jumper flying back across the room.

Smashing into a wall, Mark crashes through a set of lockboxes to unveil a dark passageway down a slight hill. Rolling down a small dark path, the Space Jumper falls headfirst into an open sewer hole. Falling down the hole, Mark grabs onto a connected ladder to slow his descent. He flips around, and falls down the ladder to a wet, dirt ground below.

Up above, dust and debris from the powerful punch scatter across the vault, as Captain Drake takes his time approaching the open hole in the wall.

As paper and stocks fall to the floor of the vault, Drake and his crew begin to move into the hole to finish the Space Jumper. Mark is slow to stand up in an ankle high pool of water, feeling a twisting movement in his stomach. He takes a moment to reload a few bullets to his gun.

Struggling to stand, Mark utilizes what little power he has left to take out his flashlight. Activating his laser sword attachment, Mark is able to see around the room to find a door to another room. The Space Jumper hears footsteps and rolling rocks from above the sewer.

He walks to the old, wooden door in the small sewer room, and lowers a wooden lever. Unlocking the door, he finds a medieval themed room, housing ancient artifacts, relics of various colors, books and notes.

He looks around the dark room, using his flame fist attachment on his power glove to light a stray candle on the wall. Scattered high and low, the lighting of the first candle ignites the other candles around the room. He walks inside of the ancient room, and moves towards the center.

The vault is a mausoleum hosting a vast array of artifacts with astronomical worth. Mark walks towards the back of the increasingly glimmering bank room, as the small pool of water at the bottom of the sewer splashes.

The secret vault in the sewer lights up with old treasures and old candles. Mark crouches in the corner of the room, and stalks the members of Lineage as they approach. He holds his laser sword and hatchet with the special boomerang blade tip.

Wielding his most deadly combo, the Space Jumper's colors send odd gleams of light across the abundance of ancient treasures. His laser sword uses a crystal that separates a wide spectrum of colors through an aura of light, creating the deadly hot laser. The special tip of the hatchet has a pulsating blue light that catches clear colored crystals in the room.

The first Lineage thug enters the vault with an assault rifle, and a flashlight. Mark stays low in the corner of the vault, and waits to hear the movement of the first Lineage member. He moves to the opposite corner of the vault, and checks his angles.

The second Lineage agent enters the room, and moves to the opposite side of the first agent. As the two Lineage guards marvel at all of the treasures in the room, a third set of feet splash down in the small pool at the base of the ladder in the sewer.

As the two Lineage members search the ancient vault, the Space Jumper counters their moves by cornering to fresh cover. Mark stays low, and crouches towards one of the guards moving to his original position at the back of the room. The guard holds his assault rifle and flashlight close to his body as he looks around the corner of a treasure on a waist high pedestal, checking angles. Mark turns the corner from his cover and thrust kicks the Lineage guard.

The Lineage crewmember leaves the ground, and crashes through a bookcase in the vault, creating a huge hole to another secret room in the sewer. The Lineage guard splashes down into another dark hall with ankle high water. He lifts his head from the ground to look at Mark, and falls back down unconscious. The last Lineage guard in the room hears the crash, and looks to Mark, who looks through the open hole in the wall.

The vault is dusty from the crumbled walls and artifacts. The Space Jumper looks back at the familiar, unarmed guard, and runs through the open hole in the vault. The Lineage guard gives chase, as Captain Drake slowly emerges into the vault.

Mark runs past the downed guard, splashing his cool shoes across the wet floor. The room is dark, but has a glow that escapes from the medieval vault. Ancient torches ignite the wall as the Space Jumper runs across the water towards the end of the line.

The Lineage member in the room hears the splashes of the Space Jumper as he moves near his downed brethren. He runs through the hole in the wall, and lands on the watery ground. The first thing he sees is the Lineage guard laying in the shallow water, and Mark standing before a rough rock wall in the cold cave. The Space Jumper hears the Lineage crewmember hit the shallow water, catching his attention.

Mark crouches low, and checks behind the noise. The Lineage guard only has a combat knife in his arsenal, as he looks at his crewmember, laying in pain on the ground. His eyes utilize light from Mark's gear across the water to locate the gun of the Lineage member.

Mark watches his ex-crewmember locate the assault rifle, and thinks defensively. Remaining low in a crouch, the Space Jumper uses a large boulder behind him at the dead end to kick momentum towards the Lineage member.

Rolling over the water towards the downed Lineage member, the Space Jumper focuses on the gun at the same pace of the Lineage member. They both bolt towards the alien assault rifle, ready to destroy or deter. As the Lineage member reaches down to grab the gun off the downed guards hand, Mark kicks the gun towards the corner of the open hole in the wall.

The gun flies through the air, where the Lineage guard backs away from the painful kick to his hand. The Space Jumper takes out his hatchet, and spins it around in his hand, as the Lineage member equips his short, shanking blade.

Water splashes as the two former crewmembers move defensively in the tunnel. The Space Jumper stays low, as the Lineage guard stands straight, and watches with the blade in his hand. As Mark stays low, he notices how lousy the Lineage member's guard is.

Staying low, the Space Jumper utilizes his environment, and cups his gloved hand open over the ground. He scoops some water into the small cupping of his glove, and flings it at the face of the Lineage member.

Reacting to the water, the Lineage member blocks his eyes for a moment, where the Space Jumper uses his blade to sweep his leg from beneath him. The Lineage member falls slowly to the watery ground within the ancient tunnel of the bank. Mark uses the flat part of his special blade attachment to slap the face of the downed Lineage member.

The mix of the electronically attached blade, and water on the ground, burns the face of the Lineage member, sending a shock to his brain. As the blade quickly detaches from the enemies face, markings of burnt veins from the electricity root deep beneath his skin.

The Space Jumper stands above the two downed Lineage guards, wielding his hatchet. His gear glows bright silver over the dark water in the cave. The space board latched around his back glistens as the electronic attachment from his blade sends shimmers of light around the depths. As Mark lifts his head, he slowly focuses his blurry vision to the dark hole in the vault. He stops moving, and listens to everything around him. Footsteps walk slowly towards the open hole in the wall. A dark silhouette of a person stands with a limp in the doorway.

"End of the line, Space Jumper." Captain Drake says with an echo in the tunnel, holding his gun at his hurt hip while walking down to the watery ground. Mark stands in the middle of the open tunnel, with nowhere to go in the water, and nowhere to hide in the shining light. He looks at Captain Drake with an angry frown on his scrunched face.

With obvious frustration, Mark begins to walk slowly backwards towards the dead end of the vault. He hides his hatchet behind his back.

Captain Drake continues to point his gun at Mark, pressing him back towards the end of the tunnel. As the Space Jumper moves backwards over the uneven ground, he clips his heel over a rock, and begins to fall backwards. Everything slows down for Mark, clutching his hatchet tight. As his momentum carries him down to the water, he sidearm throws his glowing hatchet towards Captain Drake's gun on his hip. The hatchet soars through the tunnel, skipping over the water at a slight, upward angle. Mark falls on his back, almost fully submerging his head in the dark, shallow water.

Drake is slow to react to the toss of the blade, as it whacks the tip of his gun, sending off an accidental discharge upon impact. The blade cuts Drake in his abdomen, releasing blood into the water. An intense, red ring shoots from the large barrel of Captain Drake's gun, sending a lasso of a laser at the rock wall behind Mark. Lying under the shallow water, the Space Jumper watches the red laser zip above his face. The smooth rocks that form the end of the tunnel explode as the laser pierces through with heat.

The Space Jumper sits up, and looks at Drake to watch his gun fling away from his wrist, and fall into the water with a kerplunk. Rock and debris fall into the water behind Mark on to his wet lap.

Pushing himself off the ground, Mark stands up, and watches his hatchet fly back in his direction. He catches the blade in the air, as Captain Drake sits back on the water. Mark turns around and looks in to the super secret room behind the obliterated rocks. As Mark looks into the super secret vault, Captain Drake stands up and begins to run through the watery tunnel towards him.

Mark fails to hear Drake's loud, popping, footsteps across the water, blocking everything else out at the sight of a bright gold relic in the vault. Captain Drake exclaims anger while tackling Mark forward, carrying and throwing him into the powered vault.

As Captain Drake slams the Space Jumper on the ground, he stands up and begins to kick his body. Mark has the wind knocked out of him from the tackle, and lays on a thin red carpet for a moment. Drake kicks Mark hard a few more times with his military boots.

He stops, and steps back for a moment to take his knife, and slash the Space Jumper's leg as he is about to stand up. Mark yells in pain, rolling forward towards a metal table at the center of the super secret medieval vault. Drake throws his blade at Mark as he spins into the cover. The blade sticks hard into the dense metal desk.

Captain Drake takes cover behind a large, fragile display with an ultra rare artifact inside of a glass case. The Space Jumper rolls around the floor, staying low in a crouch to avoid the view of Drake. Mark moves to the right side of the room, opposite of Drake. He moves closer towards Drake as he looks in the opposite direction. Mark rolls quietly on the red ground towards Drake, and slashes his thigh with his hatchet. Drake crumbles to the ground for a moment, and stands up quickly to recover. Mark rolls behind another display case of artifacts, losing sight of the Lineage Captain.

Drake begins to move around the vault again, as Mark stays far and low. Drake approaches the Space Jumper, crouching behind a corner of the room. The captain has no idea Mark is behind the cover. Drake continues forward through the aisle, when Mark swings the pointed tip of his blade into his calf. Captain Drake yells in pain, and falls low again as the Space Jumper rolls away in the opposite direction.

The Captain hears the Space Jumper roll towards the center of the vault. He rises to a stand, and follows the noise. Drake uses the same cover maneuver Mark is using to bat away his hatchet. The Space Jumper's blade flies towards the corner of the vault, breaking a small glass sculpture.

Standing face to face, both injured from fighting, Mark and Captain Drake put their fists up, and begin trading blows at the most open spot of the super secret vault. Drake moves left and right, while throwing a jab at Mark, and another jab with his other hand. Mark moves away from some of the punches, and throws a thrust kick at Drake's chest. Captain Drake catches the kick, and turns Mark's leg sideways. The Space Jumper jumps from his free foot, and kicks Drake in the head, spinning his body around.

The two create distance, and return by throwing more unique punches. Mark uses his two-fist punch on Drake's head, sending him back a few feet. Drake comes back with chops from the side of his hand, striking Mark in his neck.

Back and forth, the Space Jumper and Captain Drake exchange attacks inside the vault. At one point during a break, Mark takes out his BB gun, and aims it at Drake. He checks the dial of the particle scope, and pulls the trigger. A small, sharp crystal travels fast, and strikes Drake in his leg. The pink crystal passes through his leg, dropping Drake to the floor. The Space Jumper crouches low, aiming the gun forward. Mark stands upright, and walks slowly to Captain Drake in the middle of the vault.

The Space Jumper uses the side of his gun to smack Drake in the face as he kneels with an injured leg in. He falls back, using his hand to lean up for stability. Captain Drake moves back on his hands and legs, looking up at Mark with a worried and sorry face. Drake stops moving, where Mark begins to walk on top of him. He moves his BB gun close to Drake's face, nearly forcing the barrel into his mouth.

With his finger massaging the trigger, the Space Jumper leans his head in close to Drake. "Take it easy, Space Jumper. It was only business." Drake says with the gun pointed at his face. "It was more than just business." Mark replies, using his thumb to lock the hammer back. "I have my own agenda." The Space Jumper says close to Drake in a normal tone. He leans his head back, but keeps the gun close to Drake's face.

Ready to fire, Mark's finger is on the trigger, when a hand calmly touches his shoulder. The hand massages his arm, slowly pulling the loaded gun away from Captain Drake's head. Mark checks behind to find Samantha, looking up to him for a moment, and back down to the ground in shame. The Space Jumper's cold, dark heart opens for moment, as the grip on his gun loosens. She rubs his back, asking to spare Captain Drake.

Thankful to be alive and with the shoes, Mark holds the gun as tight as he can for a moment, and releases his grip, allowing the gun to dangle from his hand. He turns around to look at the treasures in the vault, quickly turning back around to punch Captain Drake in the chin as hard as he can. Drake falls back to the red carpet, bleeding and unconscious. Mark moves his fist back to his body, and looks back to Samantha.

"Leave me alone." The Space Jumper says to Samantha. He begins to walk out of the vault, bloodied and bruised, as Samantha stands still, looking at Mark, and her downed Captain.

The Space Jumper walks out of the dark, medieval vault into the dark, watery path. He climbs back into the hole from the next vault, and walks through the destroyed treasures. He emerges out of the vault to the ladder back up to the main floor. He slowly climbs the ladder up to the surface, and walks up the path to the original vault. He dusts debris from the sewer off himself.

Walking out of the vault, the Space Jumper takes out his tablet, and stands on the staircase leading up to the lobby. He contacts the MPU, pressing and sliding things on his touch screen.

"I've got Drake and most of his crew down here in a bank on Rogue. I had to cancel their transaction." Mark says towards the tablet. A few seconds of dead air goes by, as Mark lowers his tablet. "We'll send a team there immediately. Great job Space Jumper, meet us back on the ship so you can continue your service." An officer says back from the tablet.

"Service?" Mark questions back over the call.

"You owe us a lot of time for saving your life, and for the damage you've done." The voice behind the microphone says, cutting off at some parts of the transmission.

"The service is done, what more do I owe?" Mark replies to the tablet. "Report back to us, or we will take you down Space Jumper." The voice says strictly over the choppy radio. The waves are silent in the air, and in the bank.

As Mark continues to walk out of the deposit room, he scoops a handful of the red power crystals from one of the bags. He exits the holding area, organizing the gear in his pockets, to discover the local police about to storm in through the front door.

Mark's eyes widen at the sight, where he turns around, and runs towards where he came from. Moving low, he backtracks into the security holding room, and back down the steps. He stumbles to a run through the door to the steps, where he moves quickly. Through every thing he has done, the power of his shoes push him through the pain. Open cuts on his body and in his gear glow bright white from the power of the rings on his shoes. He runs back into the vault towards the open hole in the roof. He positions himself beneath the narrow hole to space.

As the local police enter the destroyed vault room, they discover the secret hole to the sewer system. Several well-armed guards storm the vault. Mark crouches next to a table, and springs up into the air through metallic debris and a burst of cool air conditioning. Several guards from the assault team point there guns at Mark as he darts quickly away from the scene.

The jump is moderately high, with enough power to land on the roof. He drops down to the roof in a roll towards the front of the bank. He walks quickly while staying low, moving towards the head of the action.

At the edge of the roof, the Space Jumper glances over the waist high ledge to observe the scene at the front of the bank. Local police, along with several crews of MPU members, with affiliates of unions, park around the front of the bank.

Mark slowly looks away from everything, lucky not to draw attention to himself, and rolls away from the edge. He moves softly to a secure spot on the roof to go unnoticed. His glasses are clear of objectives, as the Space Jumper crouches next to another vent on the opposite side of the building. He sneaks a peak over the edge of the roof to find a better way to leave the scene.

The street to the side of the bank is full of mobile police officers, separating crowds of civilians from the area. Mark looks back to the roof, and takes a breath. His heart races with adrenaline, beaten and bruised, internally and externally.

The Space Jumper walks forward around a large ventilation unit towards the back of the bank. He scrambles around for a moment in the open area on the roof. He checks his gear, and crouches down with his shoes glowing bright with power. His gear sends out shocks and sparks, from his scarf to his gloves. He jumps into the air, soaring high, past layers of purple clouds.

As he lifts up, he hears a hard thud from the ground in front of the bank. With all of the initial momentum from the jump, Mark turns around at the point of the impact to find a person crash landing on the dirt in front of the bank. Mark continues to accelerate up through the thin layer of clouds, watching the scene unfold below his glowing shoes.

The man who lands at the bank wears a rubbery, yellow tracksuit with red stripes, dawning a shiny silver jacket, while sporting a pair of shoes similar to Mark's. His shoes have a pair of rings around the top, colored red and white.

"The Space Jumper was here. He just left to space." One of the leading military officials in charge says to the yellow suited human. All of the guards point to the sky to a set of clouds with a donut shaped hole through it. "I've been waiting for you, Space Jumper." The yellow suited person says to the sky.

Chapter 11

Alter Zone II

Catching gravity fields to space, Mark flees the scene from his revenge against Lineage. Casualties or not, everyone involved had a choice, where survival of the fittest is the name of the game. Mark jumps off gravity fields to reach deeper parts of space, away from the bank on Rogue.

He continues to carry momentum upwards until the weight of his movement decreases. He drifts above the planet, losing sight of the bank after some jumps from gravity fields.

The Space Jumper does not want to look back, but struggles to look ahead, as he continues to jump away from the oncoming planets and moons to his left and right. His gear is light and abused from all of the fights. In the depths of space near a separate planet several thousand lightyears away from the bank, Mark ceases to sprint across gravity fields to check his tablet.

He pierces his body through space as he opens his map application. At the edge of the Rogue galaxy, an Alter Zone stands close to his location. The police warned him about the Alter Zone.

Soaring through space, Mark digs around his bag, finding a pair of food and drink pills from his cache. He pops the food pill first, letting the liquidized flavors sink in. The ingredients of a burrito dissolve on his tongue, and begin to fill his stomach. Overwhelmed with flavor, he pops the drink pill in his mouth, and rests it on his tongue. Coffee fills his flavorful palette with caffeine and energy. The saturations of food and drink flow through his body, connecting to his shoes. His scars begin to heal noticeably quicker after the refuel. The number of bright white extrusions on his body minimize to only his shoes, as the Space Jumper takes a deep breath of blank, space air.

At the outskirts within the Rogue galaxy, the Space Jumper gradually moves upward, hanging out in the low gravity. He checks his tablet, searching through notes, messages, and alerts. He has a lot to look at from the places of his past. His goal remains the same, moving forward past Earth to the next best thing. A different galaxy sits several million lightyears away from Rogue, back around the direction he came from. The Alter Zone to this universe is less than fifty thousand lightyears away. It takes another five lightyears to exit Rogue.

As the Space Jumper contemplates his route, a roaring whooshing noise screams past his ear.

"Hey." A voice says calmly behind the Space Jumper.

Mark looks around the space ahead, locating a small anomaly many miles away. His glasses highlight a target, and track the distance.

The mysterious figure stands still in space, and looks back at Mark, who looks ahead.

"Who are you?" The Space Jumper asks the small figure far away. As Mark stands calmly in his spot, the flying person moves across the space towards him. The person has tan skin, wears a bright silver jacket over a yellow and red tracksuit, with similar red and white cool shoes on. Mark notices the shoes, and draws immediate concern.

"My associates call me The Man Who Sprints Uphill, sometimes. My real name is Mark." The yellow suited man says, swooping towards the Space Jumper and his gravity field. He looks at Mark as if trying to look through him. The two advanced beings float in the space, and stand face to face. "You think you're good, Space Jumper?" Sprints Uphill asks Mark, breaking apart his name slowly. "Yeah, I think I'm actually pretty good." Mark replies. "Yeah, we'll see about that. Follow me, Space Jumper." Sprints Uphill says to Mark, jumping away in front.

The Man Who Sprints Uphill jogs across the open space, catching inclines in zero gravity like climbing a steep faced mountain. The Man Who Sprints Uphill picks up his pace, propelling farther with each step in the cold space. His jumpsuit is bright and easily visible within the dark space. The contrasting colors make it easy for the beings in the universes to notice. Sprints Uphill begins to sprint through space as the Space Jumper lacks behind.

Unsure what to expect, Mark follows Sprints Uphill at a casual pace through space. Sprints Uphill begins to move fast at the speed of lightyears, casually leaping and galloping through the universe, as Mark continues to track him from behind off gravity fields. The Space Jumper does not want to lose sight of Sprints Uphill, catching gravity fields within the designated circumference around his location.

After some time of jumping through space in the new universe, Sprints Uphill begins to reduce his speed, approaching a belt of dark red asteroids, circling around in a field. "Keep up, Space Jumper." The Man Who Sprints Uphill yells over his shoulder to Mark.

Sprints Uphill moves in-between a pair of asteroids that circle the belt. He turns around to locate Mark, rolling up slowly to the scene. The Space Jumper enters the ring, guiding himself through the rotating red asteroids.

"Enter Space Jumper." He embellishes to Mark, who gradually enters the space. Mark slowly confronts Sprints Uphill at the center of the red asteroid belt.

"You really think you're good, but what about all of this, Space Jumper?" Sprints Uphill asks Mark loudly.

He flings a disk into the open space in front of Mark, where it rotates around until slowing momentum a few turns later. The disk begins to play a hologram projection of a video that shows the Space Jumper fighting a group of enemies at one of the military bases with Samantha. The perspective from the footage of Mark is intrusive, as if shot behind a veil.

The Space Jumper indulges in the old footage of himself, fighting the oppressive enemies in his path. The video disk ends, when Sprints Uphill throws another similar disk next to it in the circled space.

The new disk plays a scene of Mark and Samantha breaking into the police headquarter and incapacitating the officers. The cut and clipped footage is a montage of criminal actions by the Space Jumper and Samantha.

Sprints Uphill casually flings disk after disk into the space within the asteroid belt, displaying harsh actions by the Space Jumper. Clips of Mark shooting his gun, fighting, throwing his blade, and hurting many creatures, light up the space inside the asteroid belt.

"Do you still think you're good, Space Jumper?" Sprints Uphill asks again, in a more hostile tone, as the videos continue to play and expire. "What makes you think you are so good? What do you even know about the space beyond your Earth?" The Man Who Sprints Uphill demands aggressively to Mark.

He throws the rest of his incriminating disks into the forward space, overwhelming Mark as he begins to lower his head.

"I just want to live, away from Earth." Mark says in a calm and low voice.

"Was your Earth really that bad?" Sprints Uphill asks while moving around the set of decaying videos to get a better perspective.

"At this point, I don't even know anymore." The Space Jumper replies.

"Why are you here, then?" Sprints Uphill asks calmly and curiously with his arms crossed.

"Circumstance." Mark replies with haste and assurance. "Great answer, so why am I here? If you are here by circumstance, then that means I am as well." The Man Who Sprints Uphill asks with sarcasm in his tone.

"Why are you following me?" Mark asks Sprints Uphill. "I'm here to send you a message of unfortunate circumstance, for all of the crimes and chaos you have committed." Sprints Uphill explains. The final video disk in front of Mark and Sprints Uphill stops playing. The light of the footage retreats in to the metallic floppy disk. Space grows eerily quiet between the two, where the only noise is the hum of their gear. They float inside the circle of asteroids in a tense stare down, waiting to see who is going to attack first.

A dense, body tingling vibration erupts inside of the circular belt of asteroids. The dim red lights within the rocky belt begin to glow, forming into electricity, connecting the asteroids together like links in a chain. Circling with power, the asteroids glow with electricity. The connection of the red powered asteroids begin to form a fence over the top and bottom of the belt. After a few seconds, the fence is complete, locking the Space Jumper in the belt with The Man Who Sprints Uphill. The space inside the fence is approximately five hundred miles apart in circumference.

Standing within the limited, red glowing asteroid circle, Sprints Uphill slowly moves away from Mark, and creates space. The Space Jumper takes notice of the subtle movement, and studies the space between them. Sprints Uphill wastes no time, and equips a bulbous pistol with a wide, metal barrel. The gun looks capable of shooting medicine balls with the size of the barrel.

Sprints Uphill equips the gun with one hand, and quickly aims at Mark. He takes a moment too long to calm his hand before firing a large missile at Mark, who notices the draw, and jumps to the side.

The missile quickly floats through the space within the belt, and collides with a surrounding asteroid. The explosion is enormous, sending a fiery cloud of debris into space. The Space Jumper slides to the edge of the red electric fence, slightly touching it with his electric gloves. The fence sends a painful shock through his veins, absorbing a portion of energy from his shoes.

He looks across the space within the rotating belt at Sprints Uphill, who aims his gun back at Mark.

The Space Jumper takes out his BB gun, and fires a pair of quick, reactionary shots at Sprints Uphill. The bullets are small, travelling fast through space. Sprints Uphill appears undamaged by the shots as he aims at Mark. He fires another whopper of a projectile into the space towards Mark, who flips backwards, plants his feet on the red powered fence, and springs across the circle. The heat from the nuclear blast quickly catches the Space Jumper, warming his body and face.

Landing on a gravity field, Mark realizes this may be his toughest battle faced in space. He takes a breath, and checks the ammo in his gun. Six shots sit in the chamber, as he snaps the chamber back, and alters the particle accelerator. The fight begins.

The Space Jumper lifts his gun and fires three large caliber crystals at Sprints Uphill. Two of the three large crystals strike the asteroids behind Sprints Uphill, disrupting the flow of red power everywhere. The fence sputters for a moment, but returns to full strength. The opening of the asteroids send a strange fluctuation of power through Sprints Uphill's special shoes. He twitches away the distortion of power, and cringes his face with annoyance.

Mark stands in the space at the opposite end of the belt, looking up at Sprints Uphill, who slowly moves to the side. Obtaining a better perspective of the Space Jumper, Sprints Uphill floats within the large circular fence around the asteroids. Moving high and low, Sprints Uphill tracks and chases down the Space Jumper, who mirrors his moves from across the belt. Moving clockwise in the low gravity, Mark reaches his hand into his pocket, and activates his camouflage. He presses the magic button on the device to disappear from view.

"You think I can't hear you, smell you, or feel you?" Sprints Uphill says, aiming his gun at Mark's last known position. He takes a minute to track where he thinks the Space Jumper is located. Mark quickly moves away from the location he turned invisible, as Sprints Uphill aims his gun slowly to his right, and sends a rocket in that direction. Mark is away from the line of sight, physically calling out Sprints Uphill's bluff. The barbaric missile sinks down into space, and explodes upon impact with the red powered fence.

The fiery explosion destroys a couple more asteroids in the belt, slightly altering the energy from the red fence. With his cloaking device running out of juice, Mark jumps towards Sprints Uphill, and performs a double-fisted punch on his face. Sprints Uphill spins around from the knock, dazed for a moment.

Exposing his camouflage the moment he strikes Sprints Uphill's large and jagged head, the Space Jumper circles around the wide fence of the belt. He returns to Sprints Uphill, and places his foot on his back to perform a powerful, anti gravity thrust kick.

Space Jumper circles around to the opposite side of Sprints Uphill, aims his gun, and shoots the remainder of his shots through the space. The large caliber crystals strike Sprints Uphill, deflecting at least two of the rounds into the red power asteroids. The bullets melt the asteroids into dust, sending another shockwave through everything connected. The belt continues to spin, as Sprints Uphill looks to be getting damaged, and physically weaker.

Mark snags the gun back to his hip, and equips his special hatchet from his bag, glowing bright in his hand. He places his opposite hand in his pocket, and clicks the special button, activating his shield, spawning power from his shoes. Covered in the digital shield, Mark tucks his legs back, and springs fast forward towards Sprints Uphill.

Recovering from gunfire and explosions, Sprints Uphill turns around to find the Space Jumper flying fast in his direction. He aims his bulbous nuke launcher to sight, and tracks Mark's movement ahead. He pulls the trigger, launching a large grenade in the flightpath of the Space Jumper.

Mark tracks the nuke as it floats through the low gravity towards him. He swaps the blade to his lower left hand, clenches a mighty power fist with his open right hand, and punches the space forward in the path of the explosive. The Space Jumper connects his punch to the nose of the nuke, detonating the bomb in front of his face. The nuke explodes, sending a fiery blaze into the space within the red powered belt. Mark disappears from view behind a fireball of red and orange for a moment, before finally emerging out ahead, complete and intact.

The shield around Mark remains strong and true, protecting his battered body with the power of his shoes. Blasting through a nuke, the Space Jumper's fist glows a bright ember of crystal, fire, and electricity, as he flies fast towards Sprints Uphill. He swaps his blade to his power fist, sailing and steering his momentum towards his foe. He swoops down towards Sprints Uphill's legs, and cuts a slice of his hamstring. Mark rises up from beneath, and quickly stabs Sprints Uphill's back in a smooth combination.

The Man Who Sprints Uphill roars in pain, as Mark digs the blade through his special suit around his spine. Mark rips the blade out of Sprints Uphill's back, and jumps down in the space away from the agitated enemy. Mark circles around the base of the red fence towards the red asteroids circling the belt. Standing a fair distance away from Sprints Uphill, the Space Jumper awaits a response from his foe.

In tremendous pain, The Man Who Sprints Uphill hunches forward, and tucks his body down. The electricity within the red asteroids begin to shift towards him, as his gear slowly harnesses the power. His legs begin to pump up in size, and grow longer in length. His arms do the same, as does his torso.

Sprints Uphill remains in a hunched over position, but has more than doubled his size. The fence surrounding the remaining asteroids in the belt grow stronger, collecting fragments of power from beyond the space.

The Man Who Sprints Uphill has achieved his true form, sending a cold chill down the Space Jumper's much smaller spine. He stands at over ten feet tall with bulging, muscular legs from sprinting up so many hills. His torso is in great shape from all of the cardio he constantly does in space, where his arms are massive from shooting nukes at his enemies. Space Jumper sits in a shadow cast from a glare glowing off Sprints Uphill's stretchy clothes.

Standing in shock at his newly reborn foe, the Space Jumper looks up at Sprints Uphill, as he loads a fresh round of crystals to his gun. He equips his space board from the straps of his bag, miraculously still attached to his back. He throws the board to his feet, creating power, and a strong anti gravitational energy. He moves down the cold space within the narrowing red fence of Sprints Uphill's red power.

The silver board catches energy from the red powered asteroids, distorting the space between the bottom of the board, and the strength of the fence. Building speed around the red asteroid fence, Mark rides closer to Sprints Uphill.

Mark's cool shoes glow bright white, with a dense vibration exerting from the rings to the special rubber base. Connected to the board, Mark angles his acceleration to loop and spin around the shrinking red fence. Flying above the taller Sprints Uphill, Mark takes his hatchet back out from his belt, and wields it alongside his BB gun. He maintains speed on the board, upside down over Sprints Uphill on the red powered force field. He throws his blade down through space, with the special glowing attachment spinning around in zero gravity, carrying momentum. The blade utilizes Mark's vision from his glasses, which targets Sprints Uphill, glowing red.

With all eyes on Sprints Uphill, the blade carries momentum through space, connecting the special tip to the side of his thick neck.

The blade cuts its slice, and turns like a boomerang to return to Mark, who continues to ride the fence on his board. Space Jumper catches the blade with his open hand, and aims his gun down with the other. As Sprints Uphill looks up to the stars at what hit him, Mark aims his gun, and pulls the trigger, rapidly firing a trio of large sized crystals at him. The large projectiles move and spin through space towards the weary Sprints Uphill. A large crystal cuts through the side of his abdomen, as the other two large crystals strike a set of asteroids behind. The red power asteroids explode, sending power through Sprints Uphill's special suit and shoes.

The remaining asteroids close in, tightening the belt, as the red fence brings Space Jumper and Sprints Uphill closer together. Sprints Uphill shakes off his cuts and scrapes, and tracks Space Jumper as he races around the red force field on his board. Using lightning fast movement, Sprints Uphill nearly teleports to the side of Mark, and kicks him hard, as he rounds the red force field. The Space Jumper and the space board fly upward to open space.

Damaging his knee, Mark flies backwards in space as his board follows. Sprints Uphill quickly approaches Mark as he loses momentum, and begins punching his body and face. The Space Jumper begins to block the heavy punches, using his shoes to evade the melee.

Creating angles, Mark defends himself by moving around the attacks. He counters Sprints Uphill's combos with a few punches of his own. Mark strikes Sprints Uphill in his large head, slightly powering his special gloves. He ducks down to evade another punch, where he hits Sprints Uphill in the stomach.

As Sprints Uphill belches in pain from the punch, Space Jumper falls down the empty space. He drifts beneath Sprints Uphill, utilizing a mix of small gravity fields, and red powered energy from the asteroids and fence.

Mark quickly checks his bag in search of applicable gear. His hand scrounges around the base of his Earth based material in his worn backpack. He feels a familiar, yet ancient device from his arsenal.

The Space Jumper grabs his last emergency explosive from his home universe, and places it in his pocket. He continues to dig around, finding only food and water pills, some tools, and rotating eyes.

He closes his bag, and veers towards his space board, floating away in the distance. He reaches out in the space, and grabs the board. He secures it to his backpack, and quickly jumps away from the spot. He toys with the bomb in his pocket, rubbing some friction onto the wick with his fingertips.

Circling around Sprints Uphill, Mark hovers above his position within the fence, and quietly uses his shoes to light the explosive in his hand. He sparks the wick, and drops the bomb over Sprints Uphill's head. The bomb falls slowly though the zero gravity space, as Mark grows worried the drop will miss. Sprints Uphill continues to look around the area for the Space Jumper, who stands in the space above him.

The bomb continues to drop towards Sprints Uphill, landing next to his shoulder. The explosive touches Sprints Uphill's shoulder, forcing his attention upwards. Before he is able to look at the Space Jumper standing above him, the bomb explodes, sending a blast of elements across the space. The bomb infused with the EMP chip from the Andromeda galaxy on Mark's home universe, sends a disruption through Sprints Uphill's uniform. The bomb explodes in the space directly after the EMP, sending fire and destruction into Sprints Uphill's face.

Affected by the explosive impact of the bomb, Mark turns his momentum another direction, and evades the destruction. The damage from the bomb lays a heavy impact on Sprints Uphill, as his face bathes in a controlled heap of fire. Sound grows irrelevant to Sprints Uphill, as his eardrums fight off the massive vibrations from the explosion. He struggles to breathe safe air from space, as Mark sneaks low in front of Sprints Uphill.

Space Jumper takes out his gun, and aims at Sprints Uphill's large, vulnerable legs. He tinkers his particle accelerator, twisting the dial to its absolute maximum setting. He takes a nice, cold, deep breath in space, and pulls the trigger with his other hand on the hammer. Timing the shots, he fires three rapid rounds like a gunslinger at Sprints Uphill, who struggles to realize what is going on.

The silver and black crystals expand to the largest size out of the barrel, spinning and rotating through the bright red space within the fence. They soar and roar towards Sprints Uphill's lower body, striking his shins and shoes. His feet and body flip around from the impact of the shots.

One of the three large crystals deflect off Sprints Uphill's space tracksuit, and knock into an asteroid, creating a sputter throughout the red barrier. Mark takes a moment to smile and laugh, standing in the crumbling space.

The Man Who Sprints Uphill looks like a beaten wreck, as he flips around a couple of times. He collects the little strength he has left to stand up straight, only to find the Space Jumper soaring towards him. Mark swoops in on Sprints Uphill, kicking him hard in the side of the head again, knocking his eyeball from its socket. The eye flies back and away from the force of the kick, as Mark carries Sprints Uphill's head and body with his foot.

The Space Jumper recognizes the eye by its color and shape. The whites around Sprints Uphill's eyes are fake, and uses a screen to hide how they rotate behind.

Mark kicks off Sprints Uphill's lifeless chest and head towards the eye ball floating away to space. Sprints Uphill's body continues to fall back and away towards an oncoming set of asteroids rotating around the belt.

With his shoes damaged by the shots, and his eyeball missing, Sprints Uphill is running out of power. He falls lifelessly into a set of asteroids, stopping them in their tracks. The disruption of the circular motion of the belt crowds several of the asteroids together. The connection and crumpling of the volatile asteroids create a red powered explosion, engulfing Sprints Uphill on fire, sending his body flying through the space.

The red barrier circling the belt follows a singular bolt of energy into the core group of asteroids that caused the explosion. Mark moves away from the explosion, catching the eye in his hand. The aftershock from the blast rolls through his body, sending him and Sprints Uphill tumbling into space beyond the destroyed and spread asteroid belt.

The Space Jumper holds on to Sprints Uphill's eye, as they drift towards each other in the open space. Mark recovers quickly from the large blast, and checks the area with haste. He finds Sprints Uphill laying lifeless in space with stars in the background. Mark corrects his path and slowly jumps towards him. As he moves towards Sprints Uphill, he places his rotating eye in his jacket pocket.

The space around Mark narrows as he approaches the unconscious Sprints Uphill. Everything around the space returns to normal, as the blown up asteroids separate, and fade away in the distance. Space is quiet, as Sprints Uphill looks dead.

The Space Jumper hovers over Sprints Uphill's body for a moment to check his vital condition. His shoes appear to be off due to damage. His clothes sputter a painfully dim light connected to his broken shoes, and up to his torso.

As Mark checks Sprints Uphill's head, he notices no signs of breathing. The explosion and fight killed The Man Who Sprints Uphill.

"You should've left me alone." Mark says quietly and calm to Sprints Uphill, as he places his two fingers on his dead neck, checking for a pulse.

The moment the Space Jumper's skin touches Sprints Uphill's neck, a small shock transfers upon contact. Sprints Uphill's one remaining eye flicks open, and looks at the space around Mark before finally noticing him directly in front. Sprints Uphill's first reflex is to grab the Space Jumper by his neck, and squeeze tight. Sprints Uphill's hands and arms remain huge like logs, as he holds Mark in place, and begins to punch him in the head.

Eating fists like food pills, Mark can only accept the rounds of punches from Sprints Uphill, who mixes in several different kinds of attacks. Throwing hooks and jabs of medium to heavy power, Sprints Uphill uses Mark as a punching bag, dead set on murdering him. After around twenty punches from the furious Man Who Sprints Uphill, Mark drifts out of consciousness as his shoes begin to sputter off and on.

Seeing the Space Jumper's shoes sputter shows Sprints Uphill he is almost dead. He lays one final punch on Mark, gripping his throat as hard as he can.

"Now I've got you." The Man Who Sprints Uphill says to the Space Jumper's lifeless body, carrying him upward in a chokehold through space with one arm. Sprints Uphill begins to jog across the space, catching speed while pushing Mark along with the carried force and momentum of his re-booted powers. He carries the Space Jumper like a bag of groceries as he leaps forward through space. The white-hot stars begin to mesh to create the white-hot wall of the Alter Zone.

Using his shoes to stop his fast momentum, Sprints Uphill stands in front of the Alter Zone, holding the Space Jumper's unconscious body by his neck. "You almost had me, Space Jumper. You could have had me, but now I have you." Sprints Uphill says.

Space Jumper has a dim pulse in his neck, beating slowly from his hibernating heart. A small spark of life remains in the gradually fading rings around his shoes. He drifts away in his mind from the darkness of space, to the light within his shoes.

In a dreamlike state, Mark sits in a gentle lake of shallow, blue water over a sandy beach. A gentle wave sneaks behind him and flows endlessly ahead. As he gains control of his vision, he begins to look around, noticing his expanding surroundings.

"I've been here before. Is this heaven?" He says to himself, noticing a tall, jagged mountain formation around the wide, shallow lake. He uses his powerless gloves to push himself up to a stand. His body is healthy, and cured of his scars. His feet connect to his legs, securely planted back in his powerless cool shoes. The air he breathes within the mountainous region is sweet, almost like finely grounded sugar.

The tall mountains are white at the peaks, transitioning to a rocky grey and brown. The mountains transition to low cut grass towards the base, leading to the sandy beach and water he slowly walks forward through. His shoes take in water, soaking the same socks he has been travelling space with since Earth. He lugs his backpack with him, with the dense space board attached behind. The water appears endless, as do the mountains behind the far away beach.

"This feels very familiar." He says aloud to himself. His voice carries across the water, echoing into the mountains. The word familiar echoes back to him from the soundwaves over the lake. Startled by his own voice, Mark stops for a moment, and checks his outer space.

As he looks across the lake for sanctuary, he only finds more water leading to an impossible to climb mountain. Mark uses his well-being in the oddly particular time and space to run across the shallow water. He looks up at the white peaks of the jagged mountains, and focuses over the terrain of the peaks. He looks up to the deeper parts of space, craving the desire to be out there, and away from whatever is going on in the current planet. He delves deeper and deeper into the stars before noticing a pair of the same rotating eyes he has, or had in his possession.

Mark pulls his vision back, noticing the first set of eyes peering over one of the dirt colored mountain peaks. He slows his motion from a jog, to stand still in the shallow lake of the mysterious, reflective liquid. He looks at the rotating eyes over the mountain, discovering it is a larger version of the enemy from his home universe, The Man with the Rotating Eyes.

The villain behind the mountain stands monstrously larger than the original he had once fought. Behind Rotating Eyes, the Alphanaut agent with the spiky blonde hair emerges with the same set of rotating eyes Mark has in his possession.

Two of his defeated villains stand tall and healthy behind some of the further mountains in the distance. Mark stands still in the water and looks up in terror. He quickly glances down, continuing to remember he has no power in his shoes. He looks back up to the endless set of mountains.

His most recent foe, The Man Who Sprints Uphill, emerges behind, larger than normal. He appears to be maintaining well, despite just having a severe beat down from the Space Jumper. All three of the foes harness rotating eyes, when another mysterious blue suited person appears behind Sprints Uphill in the row of Rotating Eyes.

The new person with similar rotating eyes cracks his silver plated knuckles behind Sprints Uphill, standing behind the Alphanaut agent, standing behind the Man with the Rotating Eyes. All of the eyes bare down at Mark the Space Jumper, standing in the center of a shallow lake between the tall, jagged mountains. As he continues to look around for salvation, more people with Rotating Eyes begin to unveil their positions, standing behind the mountains. They circle around the lake Mark stands in, all wearing unique costumes while harnessing special tools, powers, and abilities. The masters of time and space look down at Mark, the obstructer, the intruder to the large game of life.

"Do you think you can just, master the universe wearing these? Nice try, there are rules to space, Space Jumper." The voice of the blonde haired Alphanaut agent says to the area around the lake, and to the fellow members of Rotating Eyes. "You think you're good, Space Jumper?" The Man Who Sprints Uphill says into the shallow lake, and to the group of Rotating Eyes. Mark looks up to the mountains, and listens to the Rotating Eyes.

Meanwhile, away from his dream, the lifeless Space Jumper floats unconscious within the power breaking grasp of The Man Who Sprints Uphill, who holds him in front of the Alter Zone.

"You won't need this anymore." Sprints Uphill says to the Space Jumper, taking his gun away from his side. Sprints Uphill holds the puny sized weapon in his grandiose hand, making a face of wonder as he flings it away into the Alter Zone. Marks BB gun floats quickly through space, merging completely into the vast overwhelming white of the Alter Zone.

Sprints Uphill continues to run through the Space Jumper's pockets, taking his rotating eye back. He blows on the metallic eye, and pops it back into his head. He continues to route around the Space Jumper's pockets, seizing the gear close to his chest. Mark has his tablet in a special pocket on the back of his damaged jacket. Sprints Uphill spins the Space Jumper's body, and yanks the tablet and headphones from his gear. He takes the tablet from his pocket, and brings it close to his face. He cringes as the power lights up in his large, red face. He moves the tablet away from his face, and throws it across the empty space towards the Alter Zone. It quickly pierces through the white wall, when a trail of blue begins to blend with the white. Sprints Uphill is intrigued by his own throw, as he continues to scrounge through the Space Jumper.

Sprints Uphill unhinges the space board from Mark's bag, and brings it closer to himself. He lets go of Mark's space board, and floats it in front of his own face. The board slowly gravitates towards the Alter Zone, when Sprints Uphill grabs it out of the space. He holds it between two of his fingers and spins it into a separate area of the Alter Zone. The board drifts away through the wall of white.

He opens his backpack and digs through his things from Earth. He pulls out some ammo, and holds it in his hand as it drips into space like dust. Sprints Uphill grabs the laser sword from Mark's bag, and quickly flings it away like trash into the Alter Zone.

Meanwhile, back in the depths of the Space Jumper's subconscious, the water he stands on begins to dissipate and recede into the sand below. The sand quickly dries, leaving him standing on the bed of small crushed rocks. The people with Rotating Eyes begin to surround the mountains, spreading to a number close to a dozen. They focus down on Mark, berating him with questions of his moral code. Forcing him to dig deep to what he is really doing in space. He closes his eyes, listening to everyone speak at once in a mumbled catastrophe of pulverizing dialogue.

The mountains in his dream begin to vibrate at a heavy rate. Rocks and snow shuffle from the peak, sending debris and dust down towards the base. As the members of the Rotating Eyes complete the enclosure of the Space Jumper at the center of the dried lake, they look menacingly down at him like a gang of spiritual thugs. Mark, being fully aware of his situation and surroundings, slowly circles around the sand with his eyes closed, feeling the world and state he is enduring. All of the voices fade away through the vibrations of the falling mountains, sending rocks crumbling down closer and closer to his location.

"Is this not what you wanted, Space Jumper?" A deep and familiar voice says from his own head amidst the dead silence. The world remains mute, despite all of the people with Rotating Eyes standing over him, yelling down with the crumbling mountains.

"I just want to be a good person, and live, so I can find where my shoes came from." Mark replies emotionally with tears dripping from his eyes from the deep pains of his past.

"It appears you are beginning to understand." The voice says within his head. Mark opens his eyes, and looks around at everything going on, as his world crumbles around with everyone hammering strong words down at him.

"I hope so." Mark says aloud into the crumbling terrain. The rocks fall closer towards him, where his vision begins to darken. The group of Rotating Eyes disappear one by one into the depths of space behind them. The mountains are almost all crumbled down, where the rocks begin to overtake Mark's view. The Space Jumper closes his eyes, and fades away to a deep and dark sleep.

Back in reality, Sprints Uphill has stripped the Space Jumper of his gear and gadgets, and tossed it all into the Alter Zone. Mark stands unconscious in his white t-shirt, jeans, and cool shoes. The grasp of Sprints Uphill's large arm continues to press against the Space Jumper's throat, holding him inside the universe.

A dim pulse on Mark's neck slowly begins to stop beating. The Man Who Sprints Uphill focuses on what to do with Mark, rather than focus on the condition of his heart.

Sprints Uphill releases his grip on Mark's neck, standing him in the close space.

"Good luck without your gear, Space Jumper." Sprints Uphill says sarcastically, watching him slowly veer towards the Alter Zone. The Man Who Sprints Uphill rises up slightly in the open space, and quickly turns his body sideways.

Kicking Mark in his unconscious face, Sprints Uphill roars upon contact. Mark lies backwards, quickly flipping over the open space towards the Alter Zone.

Mark's body remains limp, as he transitions through the white walled Alter Zone. Sprints Uphill watches the Space Jumper fade away through the white Alter Zone, dusting off his hands together. He waits another few seconds before jumping away from the Alter Zone.

Flipping out through a sea of white, the Space Jumper looks dead, and unaware of his transition through the Alter Zone. In his head, everything is dark, yet he sees space, drifting away at a fast pace. His lifeless body continues to flip and spin amidst the emptiness of the Alter Zone. No sound, no sight, only an empty state of nothing. The momentum of Sprints Uphill's kick amplifies Mark's speed within the white space. His dead body moves through the Alter Zone.

The Space Jumper's lifeless body emerges through the other side of the Alter Zone, and floats in an empty plot of zero gravity. Stars surround his still body, floating unconscious in space. As moments of peaceful serenity go by, Mark's heart sends a shock to his shoes, igniting light back into the rings.

Lightning Source UK Ltd.
Milton Keynes UK
UKHW011010080320
359928UK00002B/42/J